You Can Come Out Now

Erotic Lesbian Stories, Vol. 1

S. R. Cooper

You Can Come Out Now, Erotic Lesbian Stories, Vol. 1

Library of Congress Cataloging – in-Publication Data has been applied for.

Paperback ISBN: 978-1-7373494-6-4
E-book ISBN: 978-1-7373494-5-7

PRINTED IN THE UNITED STATES OF AMERICA.

Editing & Typesetting: U Can Mark My Word Editing Services
Publisher: Pen Legacy Publishing
Book Cover Design: Christian Cuan

FIRST EDITION

Dear Readers,

First and foremost, I want to express my sincere gratitude for your purchase. It's been quite a challenging journey for me in the search of good art—either written or on film—related to black lesbian love. Therefore, I decided it was vital that I write it myself.

It was extremely important for me to write these short stories to describe some of the lives and loves that my fellow black lesbians and I share, as we are not imaginary beings. I'm hoping to change the narrative with these stories and hopefully invoke some much-needed entertainment and arousal either emotionally or physiological or both. In addition, I want to give the readers a glimpse into our normal lives, which will show how similar our relationships are to others. I want to try and erase some of the negative stereotypical views placed on most of these relationships, especially within the black community itself, as there are many.

I often remember how excited my then-girlfriend and I were with the *L Word* series that premiered on HBO back in 2004. Although I enjoyed the series very much, there were no depictions of black-on-black love for us to relate to. We both verbalized wanting to be represented, as our love for and commitment to each other was just as important and needed to be seen, as well. However, we both ultimately became aware that the series was written from a writer's point of view that wasn't ours. Now, it's my turn. I WILL be the writer of the Black L Word!

I want you to sit back, relax, and escape into the lives of the characters in the stories I've written for EVERYONE'S reading pleasure.

This is only the beginning!

Table of Contents

Prelude

No, I don't hate men. No, I don't have daddy issues. No, a man has never cheated on me or lied to me. (Well, not as far as I know.) No, a man has never disrespected me. No, a man has never put his hands on me in an abusive manner. To the contrary, when I've dated men, they treated me like royalty! I love men. It's just that I prefer not to be intimate with any of them anymore. I was once married to a wonderful man, who is a wonderful father to our two beautiful children. But I knew I couldn't make him happy after my second child was born because I wasn't happy. I would best describe my love for women as wearing my favorite color every day. Why? Because it looks good on me and makes me happy. I prefer women—nothing more, nothing less. You may be thinking, *Why was she with a man if she didn't want to be with a man?* My answer to that would be...Good question!

My immediate family didn't buy into the idea of traditional relationships, e.g., a man must be with a woman, a woman must get married to a man and have kids, etc. You get where I'm going, right? I'm part of the typical Black American culture where homosexuality is still viewed as a sin in most cases. However, that wasn't the case in my mother's house. My mother was a "live and let live" type of woman who had all kinds of friends. Some stayed in our home, and others she partied with outside our home. She surrounded herself with sex workers, transgender, homosexual men and women, playboy bunnies, hustlers, substance abusers—you name it! It didn't matter to her who they were or what they did because they were people, too.

I don't like labels, but for the sake of commentary, I'm considered a "Lipstick Lesbian." I don't care to be referred to as a "fem" or an aggressor, aka stud / dyke. Depending on what the mood calls for, the mood I'm in at the time, or what the woman who I'm with desires, I can be both. However, I'm not the one who criticizes those who wish to be labeled. Live and let live. Yup, just like my momma taught me!

Love is Love,

You Can Come Out Now

You Can Come Out Now

Erotic Lesbian Stories, Vol. 1

In the Beginning

Rolling over, I looked at the clock.

Wow! I slept a long time. It's seven o'clock in the morning! I'm usually up before now. Hmmm, maybe it had something to do with that glass of wine I drank last night. Yeah, that's got to be it, I thought, scratching my head.

After a good stretch, I got up to use the bathroom, brush my teeth, and brewed myself a cup of Bustello—with a splash of carnation milk and three sugars—to have with a warmed buttered roll from the toaster oven. I like the way the edges of my roll get a little burnt with the butter melted and pooling in the middle.

Yassss!

I dunked a piece of my buttered roll in my coffee and took a bite.

Mmm-mmm-mmm, this tastes so damn good! Reminds me of being back in the city when I lived with my parents.

I'm originally from Spanish Harlem, New York—specifically 116th Street between Madison and Park Avenues. When I was growing up, the first thing you smelled in the morning in my neighborhood was the strong scent of Bustello in the air. It was either emanating from the hallways of our apartment building or at the bodega on the corner. And it wouldn't be right without a buttered roll; one without the other just won't do! Ir de la mano veras—they go hand in hand, you see—as my mother would say. Oh, let me not forget about the Telenovela that would be playing on the TV behind the counter in the bodega while the Latin music blared on the radio in the background.

"What'chu got, Mami?" the owner would shout out at us.

I miss that; I miss that a lot.

With my eyes closed, I took another sip of my coffee, inhaled a deep breath, and exhaled. This moment was taking me back to my childhood; I smiled 'cause those were the good ole days. One would think I, being Puerto Rican, would speak Spanish fluently, right? Well, I don't, and neither does my best friend, Leslie. Both of our parents left Puerto Rico and came to America in search of a better life, and they got it! They hated that we didn't speak their native language growing up. Shit, they still do! We understand just enough Spanish to get us by. I'm supposed to be bilingual, damn it!

Last spring, I bought a condo in Westchester with Eddie, my childhood sweetheart, because I thought we would be together forever. Well, that is until I found out he cheated on me with some random chick and got her ass pregnant! He didn't even have enough respect for me to wear a fucking condom! Damn! We were supposed to get married that upcoming November. We had a date set and everything—November 26th, the day after Thanksgiving. To say I was devastated would be an understatement. I thought I was going to die. I never imagined Eddie would do something so fucked up to me after all we had been through. That shit was whack on so many levels. I threw my engagement ring down the sewer in front of the building with him standing right there and dared his ass to say something about it. Sure, he gave me half the money for the down payment on the condo, but his ass wasn't getting shit back!

"Go live with your fucking baby mama," I shouted at him while throwing his clothes down the incinerator and bawling my eyes out.

I cried so much over this man that the eye doctor prescribed me artificial tears. Well, that was a little over two years ago, and I am over him now. I'm just mad he wasted my fucking time, that's all. His betrayal fucked it up for everybody else, that's for damn sure. I don't trust a living soul anymore. But, hey, at least I can think straight, and most importantly, not cry over his sorry ass anymore. I'll NEVER forgive him for doing that to me. We can never be friends. I don't care how many years go by. Fuck him!

I'm making it ALL about me from here on out! I won't be putting myself last in any type of relationship ever again, and you can bet your last dollar on that shit, baby. I'm not even thinking about a relationship. I'm going to focus on myself and go back to school.

I enrolled myself into the College of Westchester part-time to finish my master's degree. I don't wanna take a chance and sign up full-time for fear of getting overwhelmed with trying to juggle coursework and my job. Plus, I still need to have a social life, don't I?

I'm currently working as a real estate agent for Coldwell Banker; the office is within a two-mile radius of my home and the college. So, I don't foresee any major roadblocks hindering me from getting to my classes on time.

It's Tuesday, and I don't have to be in the office until ten o'clock today. So, I'm gonna take the extra time to straighten up my place a bit. I might as well throw a load of clothes in the washer while I'm at it. I usually get to work half an hour early no matter what, and today won't be any different. When I arrive at the office, I like to settle in and drink some coffee or something before I start conducting business, especially when I have to do walkthroughs with clients. Once walkthroughs start, it takes up most of my day. With my first class being tonight, I better get my ass moving.

Narrator, take it from here…

Lynn opened her work laptop to check and answer her emails. It totally slipped her mind that she had two clients scheduled to look at properties this afternoon at two o'clock.

Thank God the properties are not too far from the office, she thought.

The owner had just hired a new mortgage broker, and he was a stickler for the rules when it came to the agents taking their lunch break. They had to take them as scheduled; if they didn't, they forfeited it—unless out in the field.

Hey, I just work here, which is precisely why I'm going back to school. I don't plan on spending the rest of my life taking orders from other people or making other folks rich! But, in the meantime, I'll be taking my ass to lunch when I'm scheduled, Lynn thought. *Hell, I'm starting to get hungry now.*

She glanced down at her luxury brand watch.

Good! It's only a quarter to one. I have some time before the showings.

Lynn took the leftovers she brought from home into the break room to heat up in the microwave. When her food was ready, she started to sit down at one of the tables but decided to eat outside since it was such a nice day. So, she left the building and walked to the park across the street, where she sat down at one of the picnic tables under a big oak tree near the duck pond.

Yay! There's nobody here. Thank goodness. Now I can eat my food and read my book in peace, Lynn thought to herself as she opened the cover to her new best-selling romance book—*Spencer's Secrets*.

Twenty minutes later, the sound of a woman's voice made Lynn look up from the pages.

"Hey, Ms. Lady,"

A strange woman stood there waving her hand frantically, trying to get her attention.

"You mind sharing your table?" she asked. "There doesn't seem to be any more shareable ones available."

The woman smiled as she looked around, double-checking for any empty tables. Lynn couldn't stop staring at her. This woman was stunning with her pecan-tanned complexion, honey brown eyes, and perfectly coiffed natural hair. She made Lynn nervous for some reason, and when Lynn was nervous, she tended to play with her hair.

"Sure!" Lynn responded, shaking her head to snap herself out of the trance.

Lynn cleared her throat and moved her things closer to her side of the table. Then, while touching her hair, she gestured with her free hand to the available seat.

"I'm almost done anyway, so you'll have the whole table to yourself in a few minutes," Lynn told her with a friendly smile.

"Thanks so much! By the way, my name is Bailey. Nice to meet you," Bailey said, extending her hand before she sat down.

"Hi, Bailey," Lynn said, almost chuckling for some reason as she shook Bailey's hand lightly. "My name is Lynn. Nice to meet you, as well."

"I couldn't help but notice you're reading *Spencer's Secrets,*" Bailey said, sitting down.

Bailey removed her sandwich from a brown paper bag and popped the tab on her can of ginger ale.

"It's a good read. Oh, let me shut up," Bailey said, playfully waving her hand. "Finish reading your book, Lynn. I apologize. Just act like I'm not even here."

Bailey took a bite out of her sandwich while she stared into Lynn's eyes without so much as blinking. Lynn felt this woman was trying to put her under a spell by looking at her so intensely. Her eyes were seductively hypnotic and a little creepy all at the same time.

Damn, she's gorgeous, Lynn thought before pretending to cough, giving her a reason to look away to avoid any further eye contact.

"Well, my break is over now," Lynn said as she placed the lid on her container. "Time to head back to work now. Have a nice day."

"Okay. Have yourself a nice day, as well," Bailey said, covering her mouth that was full of food. "Do you work over there at the hospital?"

"No, I don't. I work at Coldwell Banker next door to it."

"That's nice. Are you a broker?" she asked, taking a sip of her ginger ale.

"No, I'm working as a real estate agent right now."

"Oh, okay. I work as a paralegal at the law offices of Bailey, Lance, and Franco," she said, pointing to the building in front of her.

Lynn nodded her head and smiled.

"Maybe I'll see you around sometime, and we can talk about the book when you're done reading it," Bailey said, still maintaining her intense gaze.

"That sounds like a plan. I've never met anyone else who likes to read these kinds of books before," Lynn said, holding up the book and glancing at it while chuckling softly. "I'll see you around."

Lynn waved goodbye and quickly walked off.

I hope so, Bailey thought with a seductive grin as she continued to watch Lynn.

Once Lynn was back in the office, she couldn't stop thinking about how beautiful Bailey was, but she had to shake it off and get some work done.

The following hour, Lynn was out in the field showing two scheduled properties to the prospective homebuyers. She began to panic after noticing the time.

Oh my God! It's four-thirty! I gotta finish up and get out of here.

Lynn finished showing the property to the clients within the next half hour. After giving them paperwork to complete, she locked up the home and left the property. Her co-worker, Travis, was at the house next door and had just finished his showing, as well.

"Are you headed back to the office?" Travis asked her.

"Yes! I gotta get my stuff. I have a class tonight," she said, walking quickly across the lawn.

"Alright, come on. I'll give you a lift back," Travis said.

"Thank you so much, Trav."

Once at the office, Lynn gathered her belongings.

"Let me change out of these heels and put my sneakers on," she mumbled to herself. "Shoot! I can't remember if I put my syllabus and textbook in my bag... Okay, here's my syllabus, and here's my textbook. Alright, I'm good to go."

Lynn tied her sneaker strings, used the restroom, said her goodbyes, and hustled out the door to the bus stop. She forgot her car's inspection was scheduled for that day. So, before leaving for work that morning, she called her best friend, Leslie, who she had given her spare set of keys, and asked her if she would take the car in for her.

"Your ass betta be glad I'm off today, woman!" Leslie teased.

"You're a lifesaver! That's why you're my bestie! Love you...mean it! I gotta run," Lynn said before abruptly hanging up the phone, grabbing her briefcase, and heading out the door.

"I hate when she does that! Urrrgh," Leslie said from the other end, choking the phone's receiver while holding it in the air.

Lynn also forgot to obtain a permit to park on the campus lot before class started, so she would have to get one before leaving the building tonight. She hated taking public transportation because people were rude as hell, but she also didn't like having to look for a parking spot when running late.

Why does tonight have to be an economics class? Why couldn't it be something fun, like art history or something? Lynn thought while sitting in class. *This professor is long-winded as fuck, too, which makes the lecture hella boring. He has one of those lullaby voices—a voice that rocks your ass right to sleep! This shit is ridiculous! Somebody, please…make it stop!* she screamed in her head. *Maybe I should go to the restroom and splash some water on my face,* she considered. *Nah, I'm at the end of the row and will have to say excuse me to everybody as I pass them. Plus, I don't feel like getting up.*

Lynn didn't realize she had fallen asleep until the sound of something hitting the floor startled her awake.

"Well, damn!" Lynn said out loud and started laughing.

"Did something I said amuse you, Ms. Lopez?" the professor asked.

"No, professor," Lynn replied, clearing her throat. "Nothing funny at all. Excuse me."

Lynn sat up straighter in her chair.

"So, I have your permission to continue with this lecture then, right?" he continued, raising his arms in the air, being extra.

"You sure do!" Lynn sarcastically said. "Please… continue."

Lynn opened her book, pretending to follow along.

Okay…he's really playing himself, for real. It's not that serious, Lynn thought, shaking her head.

"Right. Okay, where was I?" the professor said, tapping his temple. "Oh, yes! The biggest and most common mistakes mortgage brokers make fresh out of school."

Some of the students were low-key laughing at the professor and Lynn's exchange. She rolled her eyes at one of them and tried once again to pay attention. Suddenly, a female came tip-toeing in the classroom.

"Excuse me for being late," she said, slowly closing the classroom door. "I couldn't find the class. I'm sorry."

"Just find a seat, young lady," the professor responded in an annoyed tone while gesturing with his hands for her to hurry up.

It's her! It's Bailey! The woman I met today at the park.

Lynn knew it was her even though she didn't have on the same business attire she wore earlier. Her beauty could not be easily forgotten. Bailey had changed into a pair of dark denim, low-rise, hip-hugger Levi jeans, a beige long-sleeve waffle Henley top, a wide brown leather belt, and some brown leather Durango cowboy boots.

That's probably why her ass was late.

Lynn didn't realize her mouth was hanging open until the girl next to her started tapping her pen on the desk, snapping Lynn out of her trance.

Why was I looking at her like that anyway? Lynn thought to herself. *I like girls now? Really?*

She was most definitely wide awake at this point—wide awake indeed! After the lecture was over, Lynn felt compelled to go down to where Bailey was sitting and say hello. When the crowd cleared out, she walked down to the row where Bailey was still seated.

"Hey, Bailey."

"Hey, Lynn!" Bailey said, smiling as she looked up at her. "We couldn't make this shit up, could we?"

Not only did she have the most beautiful eyes Lynn had ever seen, but her smile was gorgeous, too!

And here she goes looking at me all intense again. I'ma stop reading into it, 'cause most likely, that's just the way she looks at people. Her voice sounds sexier, raspier now, though. She didn't sound like that earlier. I'm just gonna ask her about it. Maybe she's getting sick.

"Funny you should ask me that," Bailey answered jokingly while rubbing her throat. "For some reason, the last couple of years during nightfall, my voice drops. It's the strangest thing."

Bailey shook her head in bewilderment while putting her book in her backpack.

I kinda like it, Lynn thought to myself.

"Do you have another class tonight?" Bailey asked her.

"No. Do you?"

"Nah, I'm only going to school part-time."

"Me, too!" Lynn said, sounding excited, although she didn't know why.

"Did you drive here?" Bailey asked.

"No, not tonight. But thanks for reminding me that I need to get a permit before I leave."

"You can't. The office is closed now," Bailey informed her, throwing her backpack over her shoulder. "Where do you live? I can give you a ride home after I use the bathroom if you wanna wait for me."

"Oh wow! Thanks!" Lynn said, blinking her eyes

rapidly and not knowing what else to say.

"No problem," Bailey said, flexing her wrist. "I don't live too far from this area."

They continued walking side by side down the vast hallway, looking for the women's restroom.

"I live here in Westchester County—about fifteen minutes by car," remarked Lynn.

"Oh! That's cool. I live in Yonkers, so I have to pass through your neck of the woods on my way home anyway," Bailey said, smiling at her.

"I think I better use the bathroom, too. Oh, look! It's right over there," Lynn said, pointing to the left.

Bailey excused herself and did a light jog ahead of Lynn, indicating she really had to go.

Lynn finished first and decided to wait for Bailey outside. Bailey exited the bathroom wearing a neutral-colored lip gloss that was extra shiny and smelling like that cotton candy body spray by Body Fantasies.

"Damn, she's fine and smells good, too? Ummm," Lynn mumbled to herself. *Why do I want to kiss that lip gloss off her lips right now?* she thought while unconsciously looking at Bailey's lips. *I am NOT about to tell her how good that lip gloss looks on her lips either, because I don't wanna play myself if I'm wrong about her. But my gut is telling me she's flirting with me. She certainly wasn't wearing no damn lip gloss earlier or smelling all sweet before. I'ma just keep smiling and pretending like I don't notice any of it.*

"Okay, I'm ready," Bailey said, adjusting the belt on her jeans.

Her hips are looking good in them jeans, too. Damn, girl, Lynn thought.

"Are you cold, Lynn?" she asked.

"Cold?" Lynn responded with a puzzled look on her face. "No, I'm not cold. Why you ask me that?"

"Oh...because your nipples are standing at attention, that's why," she said, smiling and staring at Lynn.

"Oh shit!" Lynn laughed and tried to cover them up by crossing her arms over her breasts.

Nobody knows this except that stupid-ass Eddie, but my nipples get hard when I get excited. Thank God I don't have a dick 'cause she would know what I was thinking for sure! Lynn thought, chuckling to herself.

As they walked towards Bailey's car on the campus lot, Lynn decided to go ahead and tell her how much she liked her "nightfall" raspy voice. When Lynn told her, Bailey stopped walking, removed her car keys from her backpack, and turned to look Lynn square in the eyes.

"Oh yeah? Tell me, what do you like about it, Lynn?"

Well, damn, Lynn thought, caught off guard by her question. She looked back at Bailey with the same intensity. *I think this woman is trying to hypnotize me for real. What's up with the intense eye contact?* Lynn thought, her eyes moving from left to right with Bailey's.

Lynn figured Bailey would look away if she stared back at her with the same intensity, but she didn't. Instead, Bailey smiled alluringly at her. So, ultimately, Lynn had to blink and look away to break the stare.

"Well, to answer your question," Lynn said, walking away slow and aimlessly, "I like how raspy voices sound, and I always wished I had one."

"Really?" was the only response Bailey mustered up as she pressed the remote button to unlock the car door.

Lynn tried hard not to look in Bailey's direction to avoid the intensity of her stare. Bailey was making her nervous, a little fuzzy inside, and even borderline shy—and Lynn wasn't the shy type. AT. ALL.

"I like something about you, too," Bailey said.

"Oh yeah? What's that?" Lynn answered curiously.

Bailey chuckled, almost sinister-like.

"I like your hair. It's beautiful. Can I touch it?"

"Oh! Okay. Thank you," Lynn said, her response almost sounding like a question.

"Yeah, ummm, that's different," Bailey replied while lightly touching the left side of her head. "Did I say something wrong?"

"No! It's just a girl never asked me if she could touch my hair before, that's all. But, sure, you can touch my hair," Lynn said, shrugging her shoulders.

Bailey ran her entire hand slowly through the right side of Lynn's hair, causing the hairs on Lynn's arms to stand up. Then she pulled it slightly while removing her fingers.

"You're Puerto Rican, right?" Bailey asked as she bit her bottom lip.

"I am," Lynn said, looking surprised by what Bailey had just done.

Lynn took a small step back to maintain her composure because she was getting turned on.

"What?" Lynn chuckled nervously, fidgeting and placing her hair behind her ears. "You thought my hair was fake or something?"

"No. What made you say that, Lynn?" Bailey asked, staring at her without blinking.

Lynn felt her nipples getting hard once again. Bailey

noticed it but only smiled at her body's reaction.

Oh, I see what she's doing, Lynn said to herself. *She's trying to figure out if she's the reason my nipples are getting hard. Ahhhh! Now I know with one hundred percent certainty that she's flirting with me. I get it now. Bailey, you sexy weirdo! I see you, and I like it. But the joke's on you, baby! Don't get it fucked up. I dry humped a girl once or twice back in the day.* Lynn laughed in her mind.

Bailey walked over to a white Range Rover and opened the driver's side door.

"Oh wow! This is you?" Lynn asked, sounding impressed. "This is dope, girl!"

"Thank you, hun. Hop in, and lemme get you home."

"When did you get this car…yesterday?" Lynn asked her, grinning.

"No! Why you say that?" Bailey said, putting on her seatbelt and starting the ignition.

"'Cause, girl, it looks like you just drove it off the showroom floor! Chrome shining, no scratches, no dents, and it's hella white like it's never been driven outside! Shit, if I didn't know any better, I would swear you was a hustler or at the least a hustler's girlfriend."

"Nah…neither, baby. I don't do men, and I make my money legally," Bailey said, yawning and driving off the lot.

"No bullshit!" Lynn responded, surprised but not surprised.

She's too pretty to be a full-blown lesbian, she thought.

"Well, I'm impressed, girl, 'cause next to this…I'm driving the Mystery Machine," Lynn said, laughing loudly.

"The Mystery Machine? What's that?" Bailey asked,

frowning as she made an illegal U-turn.

"Oh, that's the van Scooby-Doo and his friends be riding in."

Bailey busted out laughing.

"Gurl! Now that shit was funny! You're funny. I like that," Bailey said softly, looking over at Lynn and then picking up speed. "You mind if I turn up the radio a little bit?"

"No, I don't mind. Unless it's a country music station," Lynn told her, chuckling.

"Country music?!" Bailey said, playfully widening her eyes, making them both laugh out loud.

"Don't sleep on country music, though. Some of that shit is nice!" Bailey said. "You ever heard of Shania Twain?"

"Yeah, I heard of her. She sings that song 'That Don't Impress Me Much' or something like that, right?"

"You're right."

"That song is okay, but I ain't trying to hear none of that right now."

"Awww, man!" Bailey said jokingly as she turned up the radio's volume.

Al B. Sure!'s "Night & Day" was just coming on.

"Oh, now that's more like it!" Lynn said, pointing at the radio as they both sang the lyrics together: but when the verse about running fingers through hair played, Bailey sang it solo, grinning while looking over at Lynn and making her blush.

Lynn was impressed with Bailey's driving skills, too. She whipped that road and turned those corners with one hand like a pro; Lynn thought it was kinda sexy. The ride was smooth, as well, despite that. She wasn't driving reckless and showing off like she had something to prove, and that was dope on all levels to Lynn.

"Make a right at the next light. My building is on the corner," Lynn told her.

"Oh! I know where you live…I remember when they were building these condos," Bailey said in a high-pitched tone. "I was in the process of buying one of the apartments, but they only had studios left when my number came up. But this is awesome. I can catch the highway at the end of your block."

"Yeah, I know, right?! It only takes me twenty…thirty minutes at the most to get to work," Lynn said in an excited tone.

When Bailey pulled up to Lynn's building complex, they exchanged numbers and said their goodbyes. Then Bailey took off down the street to the highway.

*****

Lynn had been eating at the park every day, except Friday because of the rain, hoping to run into Bailey, but she never did. She even looked across the street a few times at the building where Bailey worked, but she never caught her walking out. Lynn didn't want to call Bailey because she didn't want to look thirsty for friendship or just plain ole thirsty.

That Friday, Lynn left the office two and a half hours later than usual because she needed to finish closing deals. Afterwards, she collected her commission from those closings, logged off her computer, and left the office for the weekend. There was minimal traffic on the highway for some odd reason, so she arrived home in less than twenty minutes. She parked her black Volkswagen Jetta in her reserved parking space, went upstairs, took a shower, washed her hair, and put on her favorite cotton PJs. Lynn had eaten a satisfying lunch, so she didn't feel like eating dinner. However, she always had room for her favorite snacks—Twizzlers and popcorn. Leslie called her up and asked her if she wanted to hang out.

"Not tonight, girl. I'ma chill, pop me some Jiffy Pop popcorn in my new popcorn popper, and watch a movie. Where you going anyway?" Lynn inquired.

"One of my co-workers is throwing her sister a surprise birthday party at the strip club, girl! So, you know I said I was going! I got my dollars ready and everything, chile!" Leslie said, laughing hysterically on the other end.

"Well, you have yourself a good ole time and throw some fun in there for me!" Lynn said, chuckling. "I'll talk to you tomorrow, boo."

"Alright then, I'll call you tomorrow. Smooches!"

"Back at you, girlfriend. Later," Lynn said before they hung up.

Lynn decided she wanted to watch something on the Turner Classic Movie Channel, so she went into the linen closet, pulled out her freshly washed brown faux mink blanket, and plopped herself on the sofa. Lynn looked in the coffee table's drawer for the remote control and powered on the television.

"Let me see what's playing tonight. They're always showing something good on this channel," Lynn said, talking to herself as she took off her pajama pants because she was starting to get too warm.

"Oooh! This is a good one. *Play Misty For Me* is coming on with my man Clint Eastwood and Jessica Walter. Yasss! I used to watch this with my mom back in the day. She used to be smitten with Clint Eastwood."

I wonder if she knows it's on?

Lynn thought about calling her mother to let her know.

Nah! I got fifteen minutes before it starts, so let me set up the popcorn machine and go to the bathroom.

Lynn jumped up quickly from the sofa, humming a little tune on her way into the kitchen to put some corn kernels, salt, and butter into the machine. After turning it on, she pushed the machine all the way back on the counter in case it moved while it was popping. That way, she could use the bathroom without having to worry about it falling off.

Lynn finished in the bathroom, washed her hands, and went into the kitchen just when the last kernel popped. She took down her ceramic popcorn bowl, opened the top of the machine, and poured the popcorn into the bowl.

"Mmmm, you smell good even though some of y'all is burnt. But that's alright...gives more flavor to the rest of the boys," she said to her bowl of hot buttery popcorn while gently tossing it.

Once Lynn poured herself a glass of Welch's grape soda, she was ready to sit down and enjoy the movie. An hour in, Lynn dozed off.

*****

The next morning, the sound of the telephone ringing

scared Lynn awake.

"Damn!" she said, her heart racing.

She looked over at the clock on the cable box.

"It's eight o'clock in the morning! Who in the hell is calling me this early on a Saturday?" she said out loud before snatching up the phone from the coffee table and answering it.

"Hello?"

"Good morning, Lynn. What you doing today, girl?"

"Good morning…Who is this?" she asked, rubbing her eyes.

"It's me…Bailey. You forgot about me already?" she asked, chuckling softly.

Damn, her early morning voice is just as sexy as her nightfall voice, Lynn thought to herself, happy to hear from Bailey.

"Hey, lady! What's up with cha! I don't have anything planned today. I just woke up," Lynn said, stretching her arms and legs before sitting up on the sofa. "What are you doing up so early on a Saturday morning, Ms. Bailey?"

"I'm always up at the crack of dawn, girl. Listen, there's a black-owned salon and spa that just opened not too far from me. You interested in coming with me? I'm in the mood for a facial and a mani/pedi today. You down?" Bailey asked.

"Hell yeah! I can't remember the last time I had a spa treatment. Send me the address, and I'll meet you there. What time you trying to go?" Lynn asked her.

"You don't have to drive. I'll come and get you…say around ten-thirty?"

"Alright, bet! I don't feel like driving anyway. Plus, that'll give me enough time to shit, shower, and shave,"

Lynn said, laughing.

"You're funny," Bailey responded, softly chuckling. "Alright, doll, I'll meet you in front of your building at ten-thirty. Don't be late because I'm making us reservations for noon. They don't take walk-ins."

"Alright, no problem. I'll be ready at ten-thirty sharp! Ciao Bella," she said before disconnecting the phone.

Lynn was excited to see Bailey today; she hadn't felt this excited to see anybody in years.

Lynn turned on her Keurig and put in a pod while waiting for the shower water to heat up. She turned the radio to station WBLS, and the song "I Wanna Sex You Up" by Color Me Badd was on. Lynn started snapping her fingers and singing along.

Yasss! This record is the shit, Lynn said as she continued singing and dancing until the song was over.

Lynn agreed with the water temperature, so she got in the shower and lathered up her loofah sponge vigorously while saying out loud, "Today is gonna be a good day. I can feel it in my bones."

She finished her shower, dried off, and lotioned her body while trying to decide what she would wear. She wanted to wear something casual since it was a spa day. So, she pulled her freshly washed hair up into a ponytail and wore a denim baseball cap to pull her thick, curly puff through it. Lynn chose to wear a denim shirt dress with her designer brown leather slides. She put two gold ball studs in her ears' second and third holes while her heart-shaped bamboo earrings went in the first hole. Lynn draped a gold herringbone chain around her neck and slipped on a few gold bangles. Then she sprayed on some Calvin Klein

Obsession perfume and grabbed her matching designer brown leather bucket bag on the way out the front door, forgetting to eat or drink anything because she was so excited. Bailey was pulling up to the building when Lynn walked out.

"Hey, doll!" Bailey shouted out as Lynn got into the passenger side of the car.

"Hey!" Lynn said with a big-ass grin on her face while fastening her seatbelt.

Bailey was looking in her rearview mirror, applying that neutral-colored shiny lip gloss again. Her skin glowed like she had already been to the spa. Bailey wore a pair of distressed cuffed denim jeans that exposed her knees and a loose-fitting silk red top with three buttons open—just enough to reveal the top of her red lace pushup bra and firm breasts. A few gold chains adorned her neck in a cascaded manner, with them landing in the middle of her chest. Two gold rope chain bracelets jingled on her right wrist while a skinny gold Bulova watch sat pretty on her left wrist. A pair of red patent leather designer open-toe sandals were on her feet, with a matching clutch resting on the console.

She has some pretty feet, Lynn thought, looking down at them.

"You look nice, Lynn," Bailey commented, removing her sunglasses from the overhead visor.

"Thank you! You do, too," Lynn said, nervously adjusting herself in the seat. "How far is that salon from here?"

"Oh, we should be there in like thirty-forty minutes."

"Cool."

"Are you trying to make me obsessed with you, Lynn?" Bailey asked while looking straight ahead out the windshield.

"What?! Why you say that?" Lynn asked, looking nervous and confused.

Chuckling, Bailey turned to her.

"Relax, doll. I was joking. I said that because you're wearing my favorite perfume. CK's Obsession, right? Get it?" she said with a twinkle in her honey brown eyes.

"Oh!" Lynn said with a sigh of relief and faintly smiling. "Yeah, I'm wearing Obsession."

"You can turn on the radio if you want," Bailey told her while pulling off.

Lynn looked for the 101.9 jazz station. When she located it, Anita Baker's "Sweet Love" was playing. They both sat back in their seats and cruised, enjoying the smooth sounds of Ms. Baker's voice.

"Today must be our lucky day, doll," Bailey said, breaking the silence.

"Why?" Lynn asked with a quizzical look on her face.

"'Cause there's a parking spot right in front of the spa for us! Now how often does that happen on a busy Saturday afternoon, huh?" Bailey asked, smiling as she pulled in with one flick of her wrist like a G.

There was a 3-D gold blocked letter sign on the front of the black façade of the salon that read: HELLO, GORGEOUS.

"This is definitely a new spot," Bailey said, closing the car door and walking to the spa with Lynn directly behind her, pulling down her dress.

The ambiance inside was top-notch! Large gold

chandeliers were hanging from the high ceilings, and a variety of luxury beauty products—including expensive fingernail polishes—were on display within gold-trimmed glass curio tower cabinets in all four corners of the salon. The manicure stations were stark white and immaculate with clear acrylic customer chairs, and the pedicure stations had foot baths cast in gold with black suede technician chairs on gold wheels placed in front of them. The waiting area had white leather tufted couches and brass end tables with black and gold marble inlaid tops sitting on opposite ends of them and miniature waterfalls resting and flowing on top. Calming sounds of jazz music filled the air—not the tranquil Chinese garden variety type but the Ella Fitzgerald and Duke Ellington kind. The music resonated from the speakers embedded in the walls. The volume was loud enough for you to enjoy it but soft enough that you could hold a conversation. It was giving classy chill vibes.

A pretty young lady came from the back and greeted them.

"Hello, Gorgeous," she said, looking at both women with the friendliest smile on her face. "How can I assist you ladies today?"

Bailey and Lynn said hello to her at the same time.

"JINKS! You owe me a soda!" Bailey said, which made all three of them laugh.

"I have an appointment for two at noon. My name is Bailey."

"Sure. Follow me. I need to take a quick look at the appointment book," the receptionist said as she walked them through another door.

Behind this door were three white massage tables with women sitting at the head of them, waving and smiling as they passed, along with two facial tables. All were separated by a white curtain. There were also four white reclining massage chairs with chrome bases lined up against the wall with baroque-style mirrors in between them and pink potted peonies on each of the four accompanying marble-top chrome tables.

"This place is beautiful! And it smells like a mixture of lemons and roses," Lynn said out loud.

"Thank you. It's the essential oil diffusers we place strategically around back here," the young lady responded.

The young lady walked behind a huge acrylic desk with decorative golden hand sculptures resting on top. She searched through a large white leather appointment book for Bailey's name.

"Oh…here you are," she said, smiling. "You ladies are scheduled for facials, manicures, and pedicures. Is that correct?"

"Correct," Bailey and Lynn said in unison.

"Okay, we're all set," the young lady said, closing the appointment book. "Would you ladies care for a mimosa before the start of your treatments?"

"None for me, thanks. I didn't eat yet," Lynn informed her.

"Well, I'll have one," Bailey said, turning to Lynn. "Why didn't you eat something?"

"I wasn't hungry," Lynn told her.

Lynn didn't want to tell her the real reason that she hadn't eaten was because she was too excited to see her and had forgotten to feed herself.

The young lady raised her hand, calling over her colleague.

"Please bring over one mimosa for our guest," she told them.

"Here you go, Miss," the colleague said when she returned with the mimosa on a silver serving tray.

"Ooh, thank you," Bailey said, taking a sip.

It was a little too tart for Bailey's taste, so she put it on the acrylic desk and left it there.

"The types of facials we offer are outlined here," the lady said, pointing to the wall right above the desk.

"This is cute! They made it look like a restaurant menu," Lynn said.

"Yeah, that is cute," Bailey chimed in. "Okay, I see what I want. I'm gonna have the honey and turmeric facial."

"That sounds good," Lynn said. "And I'll take the blueberry and oatmeal facial."

"Good choices, ladies. Those are the two most popular facials we do here," the young lady told them.

"Really?!" they said, speaking at the same time once again.

"Great minds think alike, I see," the lady said, grinning while escorting them to the facial tables.

Lynn was so relaxed during the facial massage that she fell asleep, but a little snore woke her up.

"Oh shit," she said, looking around to see if Bailey heard her. "That's embarrassing."

The technician and Bailey were indeed laughing.

"Don't be embarrassed. People fall asleep and snore all the time here. After all, it's supposed to be relaxing. We massage all the kinks out for you, honey. That's why people keep coming back," the technician said with a wink.

Three hours later...

"Wow! This was one of the best spa treatments I've had in a long time! Thanks for inviting me, girl. I didn't know how much I needed this until I got it, for real," Lynn said cheerfully and softly tapped her cheek.

"Awww, you're welcome. Thanks for coming with me, doll. How does your face feel? It looks plumper, and your cheeks are extra rosy, too," Bailey commented.

"My face feels relaxed and tighter, too! I didn't even realize I was that tense," Lynn said, rubbing both cheeks this time. "How about you? Your face looks extra hydrated, and your eyes seem to have an extra glow in 'em."

"It must be the turmeric," Bailey said, batting her eyes playfully with a half-cocked smile on her face and her hands under her chin, wiggling her newly polished French manicured fingernails.

It should be a crime to be that fine, Lynn said to herself while slowly turning away to look out of the large spa window.

"What do they have to eat around here, Bailey? I'm hungry now."

"There's a Chinese restaurant up the street. I remember passing it on the way here."

"Cool. I can go for some Chow Mein," Lynn said.

"Oooh, yeah...that sounds good," Bailey said, licking her lips and rubbing her stomach before pulling out her black card to pay for their spa treatments. Thank-you, come again, the receptionist said after handing Bailey the receipt. Have a nice day, see you soon "Come on, doll. Let's go."

she said as Lynn waved goodbye.

Bailey pulled up to the restaurant, and they both went inside to order. After the gentleman in front of them put in his order and complimented them both on their beauty, they ordered their food and sat down. Lynn picked up a menu from the table and pretended to read it.

"Hey, Lynn," Bailey called out, "you trying to eat here, or do you wanna come back with me to my place and eat it there?"

Lynn looked up from the menu to answer her, and Bailey's eyes seemed to really be glowing now. They were piercing through Lynn and making her weak. She believed Bailey knew it, too, because she sat back in her chair and kept smiling at her. Lynn quickly looked away, acting as if she heard them calling her number to come and pick up their food.

"I don't mind going to your place," Lynn finally said, getting up from the table. "But I'ma order a spring roll to eat now, though."

"I can't wait. I'm hungry as hell!" she said.

"I wonder if we have the same taste," Lynn said, turning back to look at Bailey as she walked over to the counter to order the spring roll.

Lynn placed the order and returned to the table.

"Same taste in what?" Bailey asked, looking Lynn up and down.

"Hello! Yo food ready now," the Chinese woman behind the counter called out to them.

Bailey jumped up and walked over to pick up the food.

"The same taste in furniture and stuff," Lynn answered bashfully, shaking her head as Bailey walked back to meet her at the exit door.

"Oh, we have the same taste, doll. Most definitely," Bailey said, winking and simultaneously making a clicking sound with her teeth.

Lynn took the bags from Bailey, reached in the one that had her spring roll, and then placed the rest of the food on the floor in the back of the car.

"That shit smells so good. I can't wait to eat the rest of it," Lynn said, chewing on her spring roll as Bailey drove.

"I know, right?! I live about ten minutes from here, so it should still be hot when we get to my house," Bailey said while turning up the music.

"Fool's Paradise" by Meli'sa Morgan was playing, and both began singing along while snapping their fingers in between Lynn brushing off the crumbs that fell on her dress from the spring roll.

They arrived at Bailey's apartment complex, where she lived on the first floor.

"I don't wear shoes in the house, doll," Bailey said as she took out her keys and opened the door. "You can put your shoes in the wicker basket over there next to the fish tank."

"No problem. Oooh…you got angel and tiger fish. I think they're so cute," Lynn said, walking over to take a closer look.

Bailey's apartment smelled like Egyptian musk incense and was spotless! Lynn was impressed yet again. Each of her walls was a different color–one was red, another was yellow, one was orange, and one was blue. It was different but fly. She also had a lot of African art and various types of metal-framed hand mirrors hanging on the walls. The décor gave off shabby chic vibes for sure.

"I like what you've done with the place, Bailey," Lynn said softly.

"Thank you, doll!" Bailey shouted from the kitchen. "I'll get us something to drink. You like wine coolers, Lynn?"

"I never had one."

"What?! You never had a wine cooler before?" Bailey said, peeping her head out of the kitchen. "You're lying, right!"

"Nope. I never had one."

"How old are you?"

"I'm thirty-two, but that has nothing to do with it. I just never had one, that's all."

"Well, you're going to have one today," Bailey said, giggling and taking the wine coolers out of the fridge. "I'm glad you like my apartment, doll, and I hope you're making yourself comfortable out there. I think I might have to heat up the food a little, though."

"Okay, I can wait. And yes, I'm making myself comfortable," Lynn said as she walked over and sat down on the black leather sofa.

This sofa is very comfortable, she said to herself, bouncing lightly on it.

Bailey came into the living room with two wine coolers in her hand and wearing only her red lace pushup bra and jeans.

Damn, her tits look nice and firm, Lynn thought to herself.

"Yeah, I had to heat up the food. Look," she said, "you want the peach or the berry-flavored?"

"Ummmm, I'll take the berry one."

"Good, because I like peaches. It reminds me of something she said with a wink. You want to eat on the sofa, the floor, or at the table, doll?" Bailey asked as she put the bottle up to her mouth and took a sip.

"I'll sit at the table."

"Alright, come on. The table is over here. And, let me know how you like your wine cooler," Bailey said, taking another sip of hers. "Let me put on some music before we sit down because I don't like having to get up when I start eating. You wanna hear anything in particular?"

"No, I'll leave it up to you. We like the same music so far."

"Hmmm, let me see. How about some Whitney Houston?"

"Yeah, I like Whitney Houston, and I like the wine cooler, too. It's nice and fruity…not bad."

"Don't say I never gave you anything," Bailey said, making a funny face causing them both to laugh.

Bailey raised her bottle. "Cheers!"

"Cheers," Lynn said.

Bailey chose the song "Saving All My Love For You."

Wow, she's not subtle at all, and I like it, Lynn thought to herself. *I'm still not sure if she's just a flirty person or what, so I'm not going to jump to conclusions. Oooh, I'm feeling this wine cooler.* Lynn looked for the alcohol content on the label. *Bailey better chill 'cause this wine cooler got MY ass feeling a little flirty my damn self!*

Bailey came out shortly with the food on real plates.

Why though? Lynn thought, screwing up her face. *I eat Chinese food right out of the container it comes in. I thought everybody did that. Oh yeah, she had to heat the food up. Duh!*

That makes sense.

They sat down at the table and blessed the food before eating.

"How's your food, Lynn?"

"It tastes pretty good," she answered. "What about yours? You got shrimp fried rice, right?"

"Yeah. Let me have a taste of yours, and you can taste mine," Bailey said, grinning.

"Okay," Lynn agreed.

Bailey put a mountain of shrimp fried rice on the spoon, which caught Lynn totally off guard because she thought Bailey would put it on her plate.

"Come closer, doll," Bailey told her as she reached out to place her hand under Lynn's chin to feed her.

Her hands are so fucking soft, Lynn thought.

Neither one of them looked away during this exchange.

"Mmmmm. That tastes good," Lynn said, having to look away finally.

Bailey was turning her on so much that her stomach started doing flips.

"My turn. Where's mine?" Bailey said after taking a sip of her wine cooler and biting her bottom lip, looking at Lynn in that intense way again.

"Wait a minute," Lynn said in a playful voice. "Give me a second to put it on the spoon."

"Aht aht, I don't want you to use a spoon. I want you to use the same fork you were eating with and put THAT in my mouth."

"Ooooo. Alright then, open wide," Lynn crooned.

Lynn's hands shook a bit, but she managed to feed Bailey without spilling a drop of it. Bailey made sure her entire mouth wrapped around Lynn's fork, pulling back slowly while not taking her eyes off her.

"You alright, doll? Why is your hand shaking?" Bailey asked, chewing slowly.

"I'm good," Lynn answered softly, fanning herself. "It must be the wine cooler you FORCED me to drink." she said playfully.

"I forced you? Yeah, right. Okay," Bailey said jokingly.

"The Chow Mein tastes pretty good, but it's a little too salty for my taste. Other than that, the food is not bad at all."

Looking directly at Lynn, Bailey started singing along with Whitney while winking and smiling at Lynn and Lynn smiling back.

This wine cooler and Bailey singing to me like that is swelling my clit and driving my nipples crazy! Lynn thought to herself, sitting up straighter in the chair.

It felt like all the blood in her body was rushing to her clit and making it pulsate. Lynn had to cross her legs in order to put some pressure on it to calm herself down.

Bailey's phone rang, breaking the mood.

"Oh shit!" Bailey said, holding her chest as her breasts moved rapidly up and down. "That phone scared the shit out of me! Excuse me, doll. Hello? … Oh, hey, baby! Hold on a minute. I have company."

Bailey covered the mouthpiece with her hand and turned to Lynn.

"It's my girlfriend. Give me a minute, okay? I'll be right back," Bailey said as she walked to her bedroom and closed the door to take the call.

Her girlfriend? Lynn thought, raising one eyebrow.

Saved by the bell! I felt like those pretty-ass eyes were hypnotizing me. She almost had me wanting to do a striptease for her ass or some shit. Sheeed! If her phone didn't ring, I don't know what we would be doing right now. I'm feeling her, and it's been a long time since I let ANYBODY make me feel this way. Yo, this woman is so fucking hot. Word up!

Lynn's thoughts were interrupted when Bailey walked back into the room.

"Hey, Lynn, sorry about that, girl," Bailey said, putting the phone back on the base.

Lynn tried hard not to stare at her breasts that looked like they wanted to be freed from her bra.

"That was my girlfriend, Michelle. She works as a stenographer at the courthouse. She needs my help with something and wanted to come over around seven o'clock tonight. So, I'll drive you home when you're ready."

"Oh, okay. No problem. Let me use your bathroom first. Hey…can I ask you something, Bailey?" Lynn asked.

"Of course. What's up, doll?"

"When you said your girlfriend, did you mean girlfriend as in relationship or girlfriend as in friend? Because I remember you saying you don't do men, so I was just wondering…" Lynn asked, looking serious.

"Girlfriend as in friend, doll," Bailey replied, laughing. "Besides, she's not my type. Use the en suite in my bedroom."

Bailey began to clean off the table.

"What's an en suite?"

"Oh, that's when the bathroom is connected to the bedroom, baby."

"Got it! I'll be right back."

"Take your time, doll. No rush."

Bailey's bedroom smelled like Patchouli essential oils. The walls were light yellow, and the window blinds looked like they were made of straw, which let the sunshine peek through just a little. There was a small sitting area where she had a chair and ottoman with a reading lamp catty-cornered by the window. She also had a king-size brass bed smack dab in the middle of the room. The fluffy cream-colored down comforter had a burgundy paisley design on it, and many pillows were haphazardly thrown upon it.

It feels so romantic in here. Her bed looks so comfortable and inviting. It makes me wanna jump in it, Lynn thought, then laughed to herself.

Her bathroom flowed seamlessly with the bedroom—fluffy yellow bathmats on the floor, gold fixtures, pictures of sunflowers on the wall, and a huge walk-in shower.

This is nice. She has great taste.

Bailey was walking into her bedroom when Lynn came out of the bathroom.

"Oops! Girl, you scared me!" Lynn said in a somewhat startled voice.

"My apologies, doll. But, hey…I was thinking about something and wanted to ask you a question."

"Of course. What's up, Bailey?"

"I don't know how to say this, but umm…"

"What? You don't wanna hang out anymore or something?"

"No! Quite the opposite. Don't be so negative. Besides, that would be a statement, not a question."

Lynn busted out laughing.

"You right, you right. Okay, so what's the question

then?"

"Have you ever kissed a girl before?"

Lynn's heart skipped a beat.

"Umm, not really. I mean, I had a few flings with girls, if you can call them that, back in high school. But we didn't kiss or anything."

Bailey smiled as she bit her bottom lip while looking at her.

"So, you NEVER kissed a woman in a romantic way?" Bailey asked, walking closer to Lynn.

Damn, she looks like she's walking in slow motion. Am I bugging, or is the wine cooler finally kicking in?

Lynn's heart started beating faster, and her clit pulsated against the fabric of her panties.

"Do you have a boyfriend, Lynn?" Bailey asked seductively, tilting her head slightly to the side as she stood waiting for Lynn to answer.

"No," Lynn said, swallowing hard.

"Would it be alright if I kissed you in a romantic way then?" Bailey asked just above a whisper as she walked even closer. "Believe it or not, I wanted to kiss you the first day I saw you sitting at that picnic table."

Lynn noticed Bailey's eyes getting dreamy-like; she was giving Lynn bedroom eyes for sure.

I guess this is her "I wanna fuck" face, and I really want to fuck her, Lynn thought.

Her nipples got harder with every word Bailey spoke to her. She thought if she made the slightest move, her nipples would literally fall off.

"Your eyes are so beautiful," Lynn told her.

"You know why?" Bailey asked.

"Tell me," Lynn said, breathing heavier.

"Because they're looking at you, baby," Bailey said, slowly blinking her eyes. "You made my pussy cry every time I noticed your nipples getting hard for me. Did you know that?"

Bailey licked her lips while rubbing her hands up and down her jeans.

"I wanna kiss you. Can I kiss you in a romantic way, Lynn?"

"Yes," Lynn replied, her voice cracking a bit. "See? You got me all choked up."

Bailey took Lynn's hand and walked her over to the bed. Bailey removed her baseball cap along with the rubber band from her ponytail. Then she ran her fingers through her hair, gently grabbing a handful of it.

I see she's got a thing for pulling hair, and this shit is driving me crazy! Lynn thought.

Bailey took a deep breath in as she smelled Lynn's hair.

"Mmmm, I love the way your hair smells," she whispered, "I can still smell the Obsession on you, too, baby. I knew you were trying to make me obsessed with you, and it's working."

Bailey breathed heavier while gently brushing her face up against Lynn's cheek like a cat does when it's purring.

Oh my God, this is so fucking sexy! I want her so bad, Lynn thought as her breathing got heavier, too.

Bailey put her tongue in Lynn's ear, intermittently nibbling on her earlobe with her hand wrapped around the opposite side of her face. Lynn's body began to quiver with an intense desire to return the favor.

"Damn, you're good at this," Lynn said softly, getting

lost in her waves of sensations.

Bailey worked her tongue around to the front of Lynn's face, where she began kissing her eyelids and licking her lips slowly, allowing the juices from her mouth to coat them. Lynn couldn't help but moan in pleasure, opening her mouth so Bailey could put her tongue in it while simultaneously reaching out to caress her. But Bailey liked Lynn's response to the tease, so she gently pushed her hands down and kept bobbing her head up and down, licking and nibbling on her lips instead. The teasing was more than sensual to Lynn; it was unlike anything she had ever experienced before, and it was making her want to stay like this with Bailey forever. Bailey got up on her knees to the side of Lynn and gently pulled her head back. Lynn began licking her lips in anticipation of what was to come.

"Why you put it back in? Gimme that tongue, baby," Bailey said, looking at her with those honey browns leaning in to suck and nibble on that tongue before planting a sensually deep kiss in Lynn's mouth.

Lynn legit got weak in the knees. Thank goodness they were on the bed because Lynn would've fallen to the floor for sure. Lynn swore she saw fireworks and heard music playing when Bailey kissed her.

"Your lips are so fucking soft, and they taste sweet like that peach wine cooler you were drinking earlier. What time did your friend say she was coming over again?" Lynn asked softly.

"Let me worry about that, baby," Bailey said, resuming the kiss.

Grabbing two handfuls of Lynn's hair, Bailey pulled her closer while she put her tongue softly yet aggressively in

Lynn's mouth again.

"Damn, baby... you're so fucking sweet," Bailey told her, inhaling deeply. "I wanna do more than kiss you, baby. Take off your clothes."

Bailey sat back while biting her lower lip and taking off her bikini top and jeans to throw them across the room. Lynn's pussy dripped instantly because of how Bailey was ordering her around, and she didn't hesitate to take her clothes off either. Lynn felt very comfortable for some reason. It was almost like they had made love before, and it was thrilling. Bailey's body was glowing in the small rays of sun beaming through the blinds. Bailey's so beautiful, brown, and the epitome of sexuality. I love the way it looks on her, too, Lynn thought as she got off the bed to take her clothes off one article at a time as Bailey sat still watching her.

"Wow, baby, your body is beautiful with your nipples looking like Hershey kisses. Yum," Bailey crooned. "And that ass! Turn around. let me look at it. It's so fucking juicy." she said getting off the bed herself.

Bailey waved Lynn over and palmed both of her ass cheeks, squeezing them and watching them jiggle as she shook them.

"I'm really feeling how aggressive you're being with me. Your body is beautiful, too, baby," Lynn said, kissing Bailey softly as she placed her arms on her shoulders.

"Thank you. Now get on the bed, baby," Bailey told her as she stepped aside and moved the comforter to the foot of the bed while watching Lynn as she crawled on.

"Keep calling me baby. I like the way it sounds coming outta your mouth," Lynn said in a sexy voice, scooting back on the bed. "Your bed is as comfortable as I imagined it would be, too—smelling all good like Patchouli and shit."

Lynn lay up against the many pillows and rubbed her hand across the soft sheets. Bailey started crawling up next to her removing her panties along the way. She had a mountain of pubic hair, and Lynn liked how that looked on her. Bailey kneeled in between Lynn's legs, cupping both of her breasts in her hands and putting one nipple after the other in her mouth. She sucked on them softly and then more aggressively like those Hersey kisses were about to melt! Lynn's moaning was like music to Bailey's ears as Lynn had 'oh my God' on repeat. When Bailey opened her legs to straddle her, Lynn smelled the hint of pussy musk emanating from between her legs. Smelling that aroma turned her on in ways she couldn't explain.

"I think you're really beautiful. You know that, right?" Bailey said, her voice raspy and just above a whisper.

Bailey cradled Lynn's face in her hands and planted tender kisses on her lips while simultaneously grinding slowly on her thigh.

"You're beautiful too," Lynn whispered back while trying her best to lie down so she could return the grind.

Bailey's grinding was becoming faster, and her breathing was getting heavier, which made her pussy juices sticky and warm when it leaked all over Lynn's thigh.

This shit is so fucking hot, Lynn thought when she felt Bailey's juices flow, making her grip and slap Bailey's ass.

They began kissing, moaning, and licking each other passionately. Lynn thought Bailey's skin was as soft as a baby's ass while she rubbed on and sniffed her body.

According to Lynn, Bailey's body smelled like Pond's cold cream, peach cobbler, and pussy all mixed up together.

Damn! Lynn thought, continuing to sniff and rub on her.

Bailey removed her pussy from Lynn's thigh and pushed her down softly on the bed. She picked up Lynn's left leg and placed her body diagonally across hers, allowing their pussies to kiss while they grinded on one another. Bailey held onto Lynn's left ass cheek tightly during the grind and moaned sensually, throwing her head back.

She's hitting my clit with every move. How the fuck is she doing that? Lynn kept thinking to herself, enjoying every hit.

"What are you doing to me?" Lynn whispered to her, becoming stickier herself.

Bailey's moaning was the only answer she was able to give. Lynn had never felt anything remotely like this before; it was soft, sexy, and mind-blowing. Fucking fantastic!

Lynn lifted her body during the love grind, biting Bailey gently on her side because it was the only place her mouth could reach. They both got lost in their own world of total ecstasy, and it was like nothing else existed except the two of them. Bailey continued to moan while grinding slow and steady as if under a spell, making the flood gates to Lynn's pussy open and flow hard. Lynn squealed, grabbing Bailey's waist and resting her head on Bailey's side as she flowed.

"Oh shit…I felt that, baby," Bailey told her, coming out of position.

She pushed Lynn down, slowly licking and kissing her way to her stomach while her hands spread Lynn's legs open. Lynn helped, spreading her legs wider.

"Oohhh...you're ready, huh, baby?" Bailey said, her eyes practically closed. "Alright, it's time for me to make YOUR pussy cry."

Bailey began rubbing her face on Lynn's landing strip just like she did to her face moments earlier. She picked up both of Lynn's legs and placed them on her shoulders, slowly pulling her down to position her pussy closer to her mouth. Lynn gasped with anticipation from every kiss Bailey planted on the inside of her thighs.

"Oh my God, baby, you're driving me crazy," Lynn sang out.

"You want me to stop, doll?" Bailey asked her in between kisses while looking up at her with those honey browns.

"No...don't stop," Lynn said softly while squirming. "Please don't stop, Mami. Please...don't stop."

"Oooh...you speak Spanish," Bailey teased while nibbling on her thighs.

"You're sending shockwaves through my whole fucking body when you do that, baby," Lynn told her, squirming even more. "Ay dios mio, baby. Gotdamn."

Lynn reached for Bailey's head. When she found it, she ran her fingers through Bailey's hair and couldn't believe how soft her natural tight coils were.

"Your hair is so soft, baby. It's like I'm playing with a cloud. Ay dios mio, baby," Lynn continued to moan, tugging on Bailey's hair a little harder.

"Can I taste your pussy now, huh, baby?" Bailey asked

while licking her way up to Lynn's thighs. "Can I, baby? Can I taste…your…pussy…baby?"

"Fuck yeah," Lynn sighed, arching her back in anticipation with her hand still holding onto Bailey's hair.

"Am I the first woman you let taste your pussy?" Bailey asked while spreading Lynn's large lips apart to find her clit.

"MEOW! Look at you," Bailey said playfully to Lynn's clit as if she already had a personal relationship and was proud of it.

"Oh fuck!" Lynn said, her legs softly squeezing Bailey's head as her pussy gushed once again from Bailey sweet-talking her clit.

Bailey wrapped her mouth around Lynn's clit and deliberately paused, causing Lynn to gasp.

"Mmmmm…you like that. She's tasty, too," Bailey said, licking Lynn's clit and holding her legs steady. "Relax, baby. I got you. Your clit is jumping out of my mouth when you move like that, doll, and I want it all."

Bailey wrapped her mouth back around it.

"I'm trying my best to stay still…I swear, baby," Lynn said, grinding steadily on Bailey's face, "It's been a long time, baby. I almost can't help myself."

Bailey was now sucking on Lynn's clit rapidly, yet gently, like it was a watermelon Jolly Rancher. Lynn thought she was gonna lose her fucking mind! Nobody had ever made her feel this good before. Her juices were flowing like an open faucet into Bailey's mouth, who could care less about coming up for air. Bailey thoroughly enjoyed eating pussy, and she did it very well.

"Oh shit," Lynn sighed. "I'm floating, baby."

Letting go of Bailey's hair, Lynn grabbed the sheets with both hands as she softly climaxed. Oh my God was on repeat once more as Bailey had Lynn climaxing over and over again. Bailey was in heaven; she could literally eat pussy for hours without stopping. She drank up Lynn's juices with sheer and utter pleasure.

"What the fuck are you...doing...to...me.," Lynn cried out, grinding faster and harder on Bailey's face.

"Yessss, baby...cum. Keep cumming for me. Yeah, that's it, girl. I got you, baby. I got you. Let it alllll out for me," Bailey crooned, gripping Lynn's thighs as she talked and sucked on her clit simultaneously.

Bailey enjoyed the feeling of Lynn's cum slapping her in the face and wanted more.

How the fuck is she talking to me and eating my pussy at the same time?! This bitch got skills! Lynn thought, grinding on Bailey's face and pausing between her climaxes.

Bailey gently released Lynn's clit, kissing it and then crawling up beside her while purposefully running her nails up her legs. Bailey's nail strokes sent all sorts of sensations through Lynn's body, making her jerk slightly. The bed was damp with a combination of their sweat and Lynn's orgasms.

"Damn, doll. I had no idea you were a squirter, and I ain't mad at you either," Bailey whispered in her ear while reaching down between Lynn's legs to stimulate her pussy some more, kissing and biting her bottom lip slowly.

"Can you taste your pussy, baby?" Bailey asked.

"Yes," Lynn said softly, blushing.

"It tastes good, right?" Bailey asked her in a sexy tone, looking at the sticky liquid on her fingers once she removed them from between Lynn's legs.

Bailey began painting Lynn's juices on her lips like she did with her lip gloss, blinking slowly and hissing.

"You're...so fucking sexy," Lynn sighed, sliding her hand between her legs, squeezing her lips together, and pinching her clit as she continued to climax while watching Bailey.

"Nobody has ever made me cum like this before."

Lynn began breathing heavily. Bailey stared at Lynn with complete lust in her honey browns.

"You're welcome," stated Bailey as she sucked each of her fingers one by one.

This was blowing Lynn's mind on another level, making it difficult to speak because she was floating on a cloud named "Total Bliss."

"I enjoyed pleasing you, baby," Bailey said softly, bending down closer to Lynn's face, both of their eyes dreamy. "Now...I wanna invite YOU...inside my love. You think you have the strength to return the favor, baby?"

Bailey lay her body down alluringly.

"Say less, Mami, say less," Lynn told her as she rolled over and lay between Bailey's legs.

"Fuck! I can't wait to feel your mouth on me so you can know what I taste like, with yo' fine ass," Bailey whispered seductively with the tip of her French manicured pinky between her lips. "Oooooh, hold on, doll. Let me put on some music. I like to play music when I have sex, baby. I like how the instruments make love to me when I'm making love. I cum harder that way. You don't mind if I cum hard for you today, do you, baby?"

Bailey smiled seductively with her hands resting on her

knees after she sat up. Lynn rolled over to let her up.

"You mind, doll?" she asked, raising her brow while sliding to the edge of the bed and looking over her shoulder to see the reaction on Lynn's face.

"No, baby. Whatever floats ya boat," Lynn said, smiling. "Besides, I could use a bathroom break."

Lynn cheerfully hopped off the bed.

"That's what I'm talking about!" Bailey said, obviously pleased with her response as she, too, hopped off the bed, quick-stepping out of the room to select a song.

"Hey, Lynn!" Bailey shouted out. "Since I had you sexercising and wetting up my bed, would you like something to drink while I'm out here, doll?" she asked giggling.

"Oh shit! You got jokes!" Lynn yelled back, exiting the bathroom and laughing. "Yeah, I'll have some ice water, please."

"Okay, you got it, baby. Ice-cold water coming right up!"

Bailey came back into the room and handed Lynn the water before walking over to the window and pulling down the blinds a little more. She wanted the room a tad darker because music and a dimly lit room were the ambiances she was going for. Bailey climbed back into bed, and as soon as she laid down, The Isley Brother's "Between the Sheets" began to play.

"You like those quiet storm old school jams, huh?" Lynn said in a low voice.

Lynn put her glass of water down on the nightstand, then leaned down to kiss Bailey's sweet lips before sliding down into position between her legs.

"Sheeed!" Lynn said, softly kissing Bailey's thigh. "Me and this song are about to make you feel sooo fucking good, baby."

Lynn bent Bailey's legs up and spread them out slowly.

"Oh shit. You got my body tingling," Bailey whispered, breathing deeply with her hands in her hair.

Lynn slid her body up and placed her mouth close to Bailey's lips before spreading them open to kiss her clit.

"I can feel her growing," Lynn said as she closed her mouth around Bailey's clit so she could devour it.

Lynn began sucking on it, and Bailey whined.

"Suck that shit," Bailey whispered.

Lynn did as she was told and sucked and licked on Bailey's clit over and over again, but her jaws were beginning to get tired. She wasn't used to eating pussy or sucking on anything for an extended time. But she didn't dare stop; she just slowed down. She wanted to please Bailey the same way Bailey pleased her, and surprisingly, eating Bailey's pussy was getting her off. Bailey's moans started to sound like purrs, and that shit made Lynn reach down between her own legs to rub herself while continuing to suck on Bailey, allowing her complete enjoyment.

"Yessss, baby," Bailey panted, her legs now on Lynn's shoulders. "Yesss. Ummm-hmmm. Lick that clit, Mami."

Bailey grinded faster, laughing softly in that sinister tone Lynn's heard once before. Bailey pressed her pussy firmer into Lynn's face while she pulled open her lips as wide as they would go.

"Lemme help you out, baby," Bailey said, making Lynn rub on her pussy faster as her bangles jingled with the rhythm.

Lynn was moaning in sync with Bailey now, although her mouth was still gripping her clit as her tongue tickled it.

"I'ma need you to get all that pussy, baby," Bailey said loudly, grinding slow and then fast. "Suck it, baby. Ummm-hmmm. Suck it just like that, baby. Don't you dare stop. It's...right...there, doll baby. Don't move. FUCK!"

Bailey grinded faster while tossing her head from side to side. Her pussy was flowing like Niagara Falls.

GOTDAMN! Lynn thought, almost choking on the stream and feeling ready to climax herself.

Lynn knew she was hitting Bailey's spot because THIS cream tasted sweeter than the first batch that came down. You couldn't tell Lynn that honey wasn't dripping from Bailey's beautiful honey-brown eyes and pouring through her pussy, directly into her mouth. Bailey's high-pitched moans encouraged Lynn to move her tongue faster. Bailey reached down, grabbed Lynn's hair, and suction-cupped her mouth to her pussy.

"Oh, God! What the fuck! What the fuck, Lynn! Fuuuuuuck! You gonna make me cum, baby," Bailey said, arching her back and her fist pounding the bed as her legs squeezed Lynn's head.

"Damn, baby," Lynn said softly.

Bailey's body slightly jerked as she calmed down. Then Bailey started inching her way up the bed on her heels, trying to run away from Lynn's mouth. Lynn chuckled while gently grabbing her calves, trying to pull her back down.

"Wait...wait...I can't take anymore, doll," Bailey

whined, tapping Lynn gently on the head.

Lynn stopped but started kissing her way up Bailey's body instead. Bailey's body slowly twitched.

Hearing Bailey sniffling, she asked, "Are you alright, baby? Why are you crying, Mami?"

She sat next to Bailey with a look of concern on her face.

"I'm alright, doll," she said, leaning over to kiss Lynn. "Sometimes I cry when I cum. But don't worry; that's a good thing."

Bailey pinched Lynn's cheek and winked at her.

"I can't remember the last time I cried when I came, though," she continued, smiling. "Congratulations, baby doll! You did the damn thing!"

Bailey playfully tackled Lynn down on the bed, rolling around and smacking her ass.

"I can't believe you were never with a girl like this before," Bailey said, lying on her side and propping herself up on her elbow. "Are you telling me the truth?" she asked, smirking playfully.

"Yes, I am. I have never been with another girl, well… not like this; not even close." Lynn said, sitting at the edge of the bed and swinging her foot.

"Well, you sure know how to satisfy a woman; that's for damn sure, beautiful," Bailey said, kissing her arm.

"I guess you figure shit out when you want it bad enough, huh?" Lynn said, looking at Bailey lovingly.

"I guess ya do, baby," Bailey responded, leaning in to kiss Lynn on the lips before getting off the bed to use the bathroom.

"Hey, Lynn!" Bailey called out from the bathroom. "You wanna take a shower with me, baby?"

"Sure! I would LOVE to take a shower with you," Lynn said, skipping into the bathroom, smiling from ear to ear.

"Then let's go!" Bailey said, flushing the toilet.

Bailey pulled open the glass shower door with her firm breast bouncing and turned on the water.

"Come on, baby doll."

Bailey took Lynn's hand, and they walked into the shower. They stood under the rain shower and let the water pour over their beautiful naked bodies, wetting their hair and letting it cascade down their faces. Lynn closed her eyes while pulling her hair back from her face. When she opened her eyes, Bailey was staring at her seductively with those honey-brown eyes of hers glowing.

"Turn around. Let me wash your back for you," Bailey said, her voice low as she slowly reached over Lynn's shoulder to retrieve the thick bath sponge.

Bailey poured the Olay body wash on the sponge and began to slowly wash Lynn's back. Lynn tossed her hair to one side while placing her right hand lightly on her neck. With the two women now body to body, Bailey moved Lynn's hand away to kiss her neck. Bailey then moved the sponge to the front of Lynn, washing and squeezing the suds over her breasts. Lynn's clit was awakened by Bailey's tenderness. Lynn turned around slowly, took the sponge from Bailey's hand, threw it on the shower floor, and backed Bailey up against the shower wall with her hands extended above her head. Lynn kissed, licked, and bit Bailey's lips, hissing in between while looking into her eyes with every bite.

"I don't think your friend would appreciate having to wait," Lynn said in between kisses as she continued to look into Bailey's eyes.

"Damn...girl," Bailey said softly. "So...would I be correct if I said...today won't be the only day I get to have you in my bed?"

"Wild horses couldn't keep me away, baby," Lynn told her, bending down to take one of Bailey's nipples in her mouth to suck on it. "If you're a good girl, it'll be my bed next time."

Lynn pinched Bailey's nipple with her teeth and released her wrists while she backed away slowly.

"Wow! I'm looking forward to that shit," Bailey said, walking towards Lynn and grabbing her ass cheeks with both hands. She lifted her slightly, then released a cheek and smacked it.

"Okay, you better chill, or you'll be helping your friend out tomorrow instead," Lynn said, laughing.

"Oh! You ain't said nothing but a word, baby! Let me call her," Bailey said, pretending to leave the shower.

"Hahaha," Lynn said playfully. "I have to look over some paperwork this evening anyway, so go ahead and help your friend, baby."

They both washed their bodies, and as they dried off, Bailey decided to pop Lynn with her towel and run.

"Oh, hell no!" Lynn yelled, rubbing her upper arm and running after her.

Lynn caught up with Bailey in the living room, where she dodged Lynn on all four sides of the couch.

"Alright, I give up," Lynn said, walking back towards the bedroom.

"Awww...you give up too easy," Bailey said, relaxing as she began to walk into the bedroom herself.

"SIKE!" Lynn yelled, turning around and catching her.

"No fair!" Bailey yelled while Lynn began tickling and humping on her butt.

Bailey laughed hysterically.

They played around a little more before they had to get dressed so Bailey could take Lynn home.

"Did I make you happy today, doll?" Bailey asked as she adjusted the rearview mirror.

"You sure did, baby, and I'm looking forward to you making me happy again real soon," Lynn responded, grinning as she fastened her seatbelt.

"Ahhh shit now!" Bailey said, smiling as she pulled off.

They both laughed and talked about random things, occasionally listening and singing to whatever music was playing on the radio until they reached Lynn's condo.

"Can I call you tomorrow, doll?" Bailey asked while putting the car in park.

"What?! Your ass betta," Lynn winked, closing the car door and walking into her complex.

Bailey beeped her horn as she pulled off.

When Lynn got inside her apartment, she removed her clothes and got straight into the bed. She felt extremely relaxed but also sleepy as hell.

I guess climaxing multiple times takes a lot out of a girl.

She laughed to herself before dosing off.

*****

Brrring...brrring!

"Shit, that's loud!" Lynn said as she reached for the phone on the bedside table.

"Lynn! Lynn!" Leslie yelled on the other end.

"What happened?" Lynn answered, sitting up in the bed and rubbing the crust out of her eyes.

"You alright, girl?"

"Yeah, but why are you yelling," Lynn asked, frowning.

"Because I've been calling yo' ass since yesterday, and I just got you, THAT'S why," Leslie said sarcastically.

"Oh…my bad, boo," Lynn responded dryly, making kissing noises in the phone.

Lynn rolled out of bed and walked to the kitchen to make a cup of coffee before she used the bathroom.

"I went and had myself a spa day with a new girlfriend of mine, chile."

"A new girlfriend?! Where you meet her at? And why you didn't invite me?!" Leslie asked, obviously annoyed.

"What, you jealous?" Lynn asked her, chuckling while filling the water chamber of the coffee pot.

"Nah...well, kind of. Shit, I could use a spa day, too, you know."

"I apologize, boo. I just figured you'd be tired after that strip club party you went to last night," Lynn said, using that as an excuse. "Her name is Bailey, by the way."

"Girl, pick up your feet!" Leslie shouted.

"Damn, your ears are good. Anyway, I met her in the park across the street from my job. She's a paralegal at the law firm on the opposite side of the park," Lynn informed her. "Excuse me if you hear me peeing."

Lynn pulled down her panties and gathered toilet paper before sitting on the toilet.

"I've heard you peeing plenty of times when we go out, so that ain't nothing, girl. Bailey is a pretty name. Is she pretty?" Leslie asked.

"Real pretty," Lynn said, smiling.

"Oh…that's nice," Leslie said, obviously uninterested in any other information about her. "What you got planned for today, hon?"

"I have some paperwork to get to. What time is it anyway?" Lynn asked, wiping herself while holding the phone in the crook of her neck.

"It's seven o'clock on Sunday morning. Why?" Leslie asked.

"What?!" Lynn said, flushing the toilet and looking out of the bathroom window. "Oh shit! I've been sleeping since six o'clock yesterday evening! Get the fuck outta here!"

"You were knocked out, girl! I told you I was calling you all day. If you hadn't answered the phone this morning, I was going to call the cops and tell them to break down your damn door! That must've been one hell of a spa day, huh?" Leslie said, laughing at her.

"Wow!" Lynn said, shaking her head, still in disbelief as she dried her hands. "That new friend I went to the spa with yesterday."

"Yeah," Leslie said, hanging on to the edge of her seat, wanting to hear gossip.

"After the spa, we went and bought some Chinese food."

"Yeah, okay."

"Then we took the food back to her house and…I had sex with her," Lynn mumbled, taking a sip of her coffee.

"You did what? Speak up, Lynn. What you whispering for?"

"I said we had sex!" Lynn shouted.

"Oh shit! For real, Lynn? You lyinggggg!" Leslie screamed.

"Yup, we did. I'm not lying. Her pussy taste good, too!" Lynn said with a reminiscing smile on her face.

"Oh my God! I can't believe this!" Leslie continued screaming, "NO WONDER yo' ass was sleeping for hours! You haven't had sex in a minute! Good for you, friend! Tell me EVERYTHING."

Lynn chuckled bashfully.

"Wait...do I need popcorn for this?"

"Girl, please. All I'ma tell you is she's a fucking natural beauty with the most gorgeous set of honey-brown eyes I've ever seen. She drives a white Range Rover, has her own apartment, and the sex is the fucking bomb!" Lynn said, grinning from ear to ear.

"Damn, Lynn girl, I'm glad you're happy. It's been a long-ass time, too. So, it's about time somebody put a smile on your face, girl. I'm not surprised anyway, though."

"Why you say that?" Lynn asked, sounding surprised by Leslie's comment.

"Because when we were younger watching those re-runs of Charlie's Angels, you had a crush on one of them. You remember?" Leslie said, waiting on her response.

"Oh! I remember," Lynn said, snapping her finger. "That's right, the brunette Kelly Garrett! Jacklyn Smith's character! Yeah, I forgot about her. She was fine, too."

"And I saw how you was looking at Robin Givens, too. I just didn't say nothing," Leslie said, chuckling, "I don't give a fuck who you sleep with! But you know that already. Well, at least I hope you know that. Shit, if you like 'em, I love 'em."

"Oh yeah! I forgot to say she's also in my class!"

"Oh, word? That shit was meant to be then," Leslie said in a serious tone. "When am I gonna meet her?"

"I don't know yet. I don't wanna jinx it. It's still new, so it might be a minute," Lynn said, taking out an English muffin to toast it.

Beep...

"Hold on, Leslie. Somebody is calling me on the other line." Lynn looked at the phone and saw it was Bailey. "Hey, Leslie, I'll call you later. I gotta take this call. "

"Alright, boo! Tell Bailey I said hi!" Leslie said, laughing.

"I'll make sure she knows, silly."

Lynn chuckled as she switched over.

"Good morning, beautiful," Lynn said, smiling.

"Good morning to you, too," Bailey said in her sexy, raspy voice.

"What are you doing?" Lynn asked.

"Drinking coffee in my reading chair and thinking about you. Did you finish your paperwork?" Bailey asked, hoping Lynn said yes.

"You won't believe this," Lynn said.

"What, doll?" Bailey asked, taking a sip of her coffee while looking out her bedroom window.

"You put my ass to sleep, woman. I laid down as soon as I got in the house, and my friend, Leslie, woke me up this morning! I didn't even touch that paperwork," Lynn said, her eyes widened.

"Oh, I can believe that. Now you know who I am," Bailey said, chuckling softly.

Lynn couldn't stop herself from blushing.

"I'm just kidding, baby, but I'm glad I made you feel so relaxed that you slept through the night."

All Lynn could do was grin while listening to Bailey as she sat down and laid back on the sofa.

"What time did you finish helping your friend?" Lynn asked.

"Around midnight, so she just crashed here until this morning."

Starting to feel a little jealous, Lynn went silent on her.

"Hey, baby doll? You there?" Bailey called out.

"Yeah, I'm still here. Just thinking."

"Thinking about me, I hope," Bailey replied playfully.

"Yup, I'm thinking about you."

"Right answer, baby. Listen, I wanna come hang out with you at your place later, so call me when you finish your paperwork. Okay? Unless you don't wanna see me," Bailey said jokingly.

"I'd like that, and..." Lynn began to say something but decided to pause.

"And what, doll?" Bailey asked in a low voice.

"Oh, nothing. I'll call you when I'm done, baby."

"Alright, talk to you soon. Muah!" Bailey said before hanging up.

Oh my God! She didn't even trip when I didn't finish my sentence! I love it! Lynn thought as she went into the kitchen to put some butter and jelly on the English muffin.

She wanted to eat it and finish her coffee while doing the paperwork.

Two hours and three cups of coffee later...

"Hallelujah! I'm done!" Lynn said, dropping her pen on

the table. Let me make up my bed and season this chicken before I call Bailey, Lynn thought. Hold up...I'm in the mood for some music.

Lynn walked over to her music collection. She put on Marc Anthony's "I Need To Know" and started singing and salsa dancing to the music with her invisible partner.

WEPA!" she yelled out, dancing her way to the bedroom.

Lynn decided she might as well cook the chicken since she called Bailey and told her to come over. She seasoned the chicken with sofrito and put it in the countertop rotisserie oven while she rinsed and drained the pigeon peas for the Arroz con Gandules. Lynn then cut up her last green plantain to make tostones with a spicy garlic dipping sauce. Lynn was known to be a good cook, but she hadn't fed Bailey any of her food yet. She hoped Bailey thought so, too.

Bailey pulled into Lynn's complex parking lot in the section marked off for guests, then went inside the building and rang Lynn's intercom. In less than two seconds, the door clicked, and Bailey pushed it open. She walked down to the elevator, got on it, and pressed the number ten. Bailey got off the elevator and followed the arrows J-M, looking for apartment 10-K. By the time Bailey found the apartment, Lynn had already opened the door and was awaiting Bailey's arrival.

"Mmmm," Bailey said, sniffing the air and trying to locate the scent, which got stronger as she walked closer to Lynn's apartment. "What's that smell, baby doll? You cooked?"

"I did," Lynn said, walking over to Bailey and kissing

her while she closed the door behind her.

"Here you go," Bailey said, handing Lynn a dozen white roses and a grocery bag with two pints of vanilla Haagen-Dazs ice cream inside it.

"Thank you, baby!" Lynn said, smiling as she smelled the roses. "How do you manage to still be pretty wearing those overalls and that paperboy cap?"

"I just got it like that," Bailey said, chuckling and removing her hat to show off her naturally wavy ponytail.

"Well, if you're ready to eat, you can go wash your hands, and I'll fix your plate, Mami," Lynn told her.

"Alright. Where's your bathroom, doll?"

"Straight ahead, Mami. You can't miss it," Lynn said, walking into the kitchen to fix their plates and put her roses in water.

As Lynn put the last spoonful of rice & beans on the plate, Bailey stood behind her and wrapped her arms around her waist.

"Thanks for dinner, baby," Bailey whispered in her ear.

"You're welcome," Lynn whispered back with her bottom lip entirely in her mouth.

Bailey kissed her neck and released her before walking over and sitting down, her elbows on the table as she waited to be served.

"That smells good, baby," Bailey said, her eyes as gorgeous as ever.

Lynn brought the plates over and sat one before Bailey first and then herself before going to the living room to play "Ascension (Don't Ever Wonder)" by Maxwell.

"Damn, baby! This food is restaurant quality for sure! You put your foot in this food baby doll for real," Bailey said while dipping her tostones in the garlic sauce and sticking out her tongue to let the sauce drip on it.

Bingo! Lynn said to herself.

"I'm glad you like it, baby," Lynn replied, chewing and blushing.

They finished dinner, and Lynn asked Bailey if she had room for dessert.

"I have some Kahlua cream liqueur and pretzels that will go well with the vanilla ice cream you brought, baby. I can make us a couple of Kahlua ice cream sundaes that we can eat while we watch a movie," Lynn told her.

"Bet! I'll make some room 'cause that sounds delicious," Bailey said, burping. "Oops, excuse me, doll. Let me go use the bathroom. I'll be right back."

Bailey slid down the hallway on the parquet floors to the bathroom and returned to Lynn, putting the crumbled pretzels on the top of the sundae.

"Here you go, Mami," Lynn said, passing Bailey her sundae, then walked to the living room to turn off the music and turn on the television.

"What type of movie you wanna watch, baby?" Lynn asked as Bailey took a spoonful of her pretzels and ice cream.

"I'm not picky. I'll watch anything, baby," Bailey said, sucking on ice cream.

Lynn decided they would watch *Dead Presidents* with Larenz Tate and Chris Tucker.

They both finished their sundae and laid down together on the sofa, cuddling with Lynn's butt pressed up against Bailey's stomach as they continued to watch the movie. Shortly thereafter, Lynn heard Bailey snoring softly, and it lulled her to sleep, as well. Lynn was awakened by Bailey kissing her neck and sniffing her hair.

"So much for the movie, huh, baby doll?" Bailey whispered, squeezing Lynn tighter. "I wanna get in your bed."

Lynn stood up slowly, took Bailey by the hand, and led her to the bedroom. Once in the bedroom, Lynn turned around and began unhooking Bailey's overalls and leaning in to kiss her in the process. Next, she pulled Bailey's crop top over her head.

"Look at you. Always wearing pretty underwear," Lynn said while rubbing Bailey's body and getting lost in her honey brown eyes. "I wanna touch the inside of you today."

"Well damn," Bailey said while Lynn led her over to the bed, both crawling up and getting in it.

Lynn removed Bailey's panties without resistance, kissing her lips deep and long.

"You need some music, Mami?" Lynn asked, looking at her lustfully.

"Touch my pussy," Bailey said, spreading her legs, her eyes practically closed.

Lynn's touch made Bailey gasp.

"Oooooo, did I do that?" Lynn teased while rubbing it.

"You did, and no, I don't need any music right now, baby," Bailey said, opening her eyes.

With her eyes closed, Lynn slowly sucked Bailey's juices off two of her fingers. Then she opened her eyes and placed those same fingers gently but deeply inside Bailey's canal. Bailey reached up and grabbed onto Lynn's back as she tried to catch her breath. When she caught it, she proceeded to ride Lynn's hand like it was a mechanical bull.

"This feels so fucking good, baby."

Bailey's walls were opening and closing rapidly, squeezing Lynn's fingers as her body rocked back and forth on them.

"Damn, baby. It's so warm in here," Lynn whispered, going deeper while slowly moving her fingers in and out.

Lynn kissed Bailey with all the passion she could muster. Bailey whimpered as her juices began to pool on Lynn's fingers seconds before her explosive climax. Lynn removed her fingers when the cream's flow paused and placed them in Bailey's mouth. Bailey began sucking and licking between Lynn's fingers, ultimately turning Lynn over and penetrating her. Lynn started grinding on Bailey's fingers fast and begging her to put one more inside.

"Shit, baby," Bailey moaned, her head down as she put one more finger in, moving faster to keep up with Lynn's grind.

"This about to be quick, baby," Lynn said softly. "I'm about to cum, baby."

Lynn gently bit down on Bailey's shoulder.

"Don't stop, Mami," Lynn panted. "Oh God, I'm cumming, baby."

Lynn's body slowly jerked while she squeezed Bailey tight until her body could relax.

"You're fucking awesome," Lynn said, kissing her and rolling over to snuggle.

"Ditto, doll," Bailey said, wiping the sweat from her brow returning the kiss, their lips sticking together.

"I need some water, baby," Bailey told her.

"Me, too."

Lynn chuckled as she got out of the bed to get them both something to drink.

"I hope you like grape soda," Lynn said, walking back into the bedroom with two glasses of grape soda in her hand.

"I don't care what kind it is, baby. I'm thirsty," Bailey said, reaching out for her glass.

She drank the soda down in three gulps.

"You weren't bullshitting. You were thirsty. I gave that pussy a workout, huh?" Lynn said, laughing loudly.

"Yes indeed. You fed me, fucked me, and let me fuck you. What more could a girl ask for?" Bailey said with a wink, then laid down and pulled the sheet up over her.

"You have work in the morning?"

"I sure do, baby. Why? You trying to get rid of me already?" Bailey asked jokingly.

"Girl, please. You don't have to leave at all as far as I'm concerned," Lynn said.

"I didn't bring any work clothes. Otherwise, I would stay. Maybe next time?"

Lynn convinced Bailey to take a plate of food home because she cooked way too much for one person, so she did. Lynn fixed Bailey a plate while she got dressed to go home. Bailey tongue kissed Lynn goodnight at the door before she opened it.

"I'll call you when I get home, baby," Bailey told Lynn, giving her a quick peck.

"Alright, Mami. Drive safe. I'll talk to you later," Lynn said, leaning her face against the edge of the door as she watched Bailey walk down the corridor.

Lynn hoped in the shower then went into the kitchen to put away the food when the phone rang. She ran to pick it up because she knew it was Bailey, but it wasn't. It was her friend, Leslie.

"Hey, girl, what you doing?" Leslie asked her.

"I'm getting ready for tomorrow. What's up?"

"Nothing. You talked to Bailey today?" she asked.

"Umm-hmm. As a matter of fact, she just left," Lynn said, smiling.

"Ooooh, she did? Y'all was fucking again?" Leslie asked, laughing and being noisy.

"We sure did," Lynn said, busting out laughing.

"Good for you, girl. Shit, at least one of us is getting it," Leslie said in a serious tone.

"Alright, boo, I'ma call you tomorrow. I'm sleepy, but I'm waiting for Bailey to call me to let me know she got home safely."

"She knocked your ass out again, I see. Alright, nite nite," Leslie said, hanging up the phone.

The phone rang just when Lynn put it back on the base.

"Hey, doll, I made it home, and I'm about to turn in. I'm sleepy as shit," Bailey said.

"Ooooh, I got YOU sleepy this time, huh?" Lynn said.

Chuckling, Bailey replied, "Sweet dreams, baby. Muah!"

"Sweet dreams to you, too. Smooches," Lynn said softly.

"Talk to you tomorrow," Bailey said before hanging up.

*****

Four months passed, and Lynn and Bailey completed

their Economics class and received their credits. They took a weekend trip to the Poconos to celebrate and purchased a timeshare together because they enjoyed it there so much. They threw a party at their cabin and invited a few of their closest friends for the last hurrah before it got too cold. During that time, Lynn introduced Bailey to Leslie, and the two hit it off like they've always known each other.

"Hey, Lynn," Leslie called out, cocktail in hand, "if I got down like that—you know, with women and everything––you would have some competition on your hand, girl, 'cause Bailey is FINE."

"I'm keeping my eye on your ass now," Lynn said, looking over at her and chuckling. "All jokes aside, though. I'm in love with her."

"I know, friend. It's written on both of y'all faces. She's in love with you, too. I see the way she stares at you with those pretty eyes of hers. She doesn't look at anybody else like that. I've been checking her out. Umm-hmm, mark my words," Leslie continued, "that woman's in love with you, too."

Some of the guests were hanging out in the Jacuzzi. Some were playing Jenga, and the rest were singing karaoke.

"It's my turn," Bailey yelled out, walking over and picking up the microphone. "Alright, everybody…sit back and enjoy the show."

Bailey began laughing loudly as the music started to play, and everyone snapped their fingers when they recognized the beat. Then Bailey began to sing the lyrics to SWV's "Weak".

When the song ended, Bailey took a bow, and everyone

there cheered for her.

"Please, please. You're too kind," Bailey said playfully, then ran over to Lynn, picking her up and swinging her around while kissing her on the cheeks.

The two of them decided they wanted some alone time. So, they snuck off down to the lake, where they started a fire. Lynn sat on Bailey's lap while she sat on the Adirondack chair; they looked up at the stars while holding each other and thinking.

"It's really beautiful out here tonight, right, baby?" Lynn said, looking at Bailey.

"It is, baby doll. You think I should go and get that U-Haul now?" Bailey said in a serious tone, staring at the fire.

"A U-Haul?" Lynn asked, looking puzzled.

"Yeah…a U-Haul, baby. Isn't that what they say when two women fall in love?"

"Huh?" Lynn said, sitting up, still obviously confused.

"Yeah, baby…when two women fall in love, they rent a U-Haul 'cause they're supposed to be getting a place together. I'm shocked you never heard that," Bailey said, smiling as she smoothed down Lynn's fly-away hair strands with her hand.

"Wait," Lynn said, getting up slowly, "are you saying you love me, baby, and you wanna move in together?"

Lynn's eyes got wide, and she placed one of her hands over her mouth.

Bailey stood up and took Lynn's free hand in hers. "That's exactly what I'm saying. I love you, Lynn. But we don't have to move in together right away, even though I'm open to the idea if you are."

Bailey looked at Lynn lovingly, her eyes twinkling like

the stars. Lynn pulled her hand away and threw her arms around Bailey's neck.

"I love you, too, baby," she said, sniffling while holding Bailey tight.

"Awwww, baby doll," Bailey whispered, her eyes closed as she lightly rocked Lynn in her arms.

Lynn held on to her tighter and continued to sniffle.

"Come on, baby," Bailey said, kissing her on the cheek and moving her hair behind her ears. "Let's go back inside before somebody comes out here looking for us, saying we're bad hosts."

"Okay," Lynn said, releasing her arms from around Bailey's neck.

Lynn kissed her on the lips and took her hand as they walked back to the cabin.

"Why are all the lights off upstairs?" Bailey asked, ascending the log staircase with Lynn in tow. "Oh, shit, baby. Everybody went to bed already," she said softly, raising her eyebrow as she looked at Lynn.

"Well, that's our cue," Lynn said, breaking away and running to their room.

She tried to slam the door shut before Bailey got there.

"Ahhhh! Too fast for ya, huh!" Bailey shouted softly, holding the door open with one hand, pretending to be a superhero.

Bailey pushed it shut in a dramatic fashion, then grabbed Lynn and dived on the bed.

"You wanna play, huh?" Bailey said while tickling Lynn and rolling all over the king-sized bed.

They play fought and took turns finger-popping each other before taking a shower together and falling asleep underneath the huge, white fluffy down comforter.

*****

The following morning, Lynn, Bailey, and their friends gathered for a family-style breakfast in the large dining room. There was music, laughter, and tons of food. Each person paired up to prepare something different. They cooked grits, scrambled eggs, poached eggs, omelets, country ham, bacon, sage sausages, biscuits, home fried potatoes with green peppers and onions, cinnamon rolls, orange juice, coffee, and hot chocolate. They had the dopiest straight and gay friends anybody could ever wish to have.

Hours later, they all helped clean up and then left the cabin in separate cars and trucks, heading back to the concrete jungle. Except for Bailey and Lynn—they drove up together with Lynn in the driver seat this time. They held hands the entire trip home, listening to the O'Jays CD. When "Stairway To Heaven" started playing, there wasn't a dry eye in that car. They had to stop and pull over just to hug and kiss each other. It was so romantic.

"I hope this never ends, baby," Lynn whispered. "It's usually only this beautiful when love is new."

"Hey, look at me, baby," Bailey said, her beautiful eyes glowing. "Our love will always be new. Remember that, okay?"

"I really love you, Bailey," Lynn said, her eyes moist.

"I really love you, too, Lynn," Bailey said, hugging and kissing her again before they continued on their journey.

Once they arrived in Yonkers, Lynn parked the car to

let Bailey out.

"Come with me upstairs for a minute, baby. I've been wanting to give you something for a while now," Bailey told her.

"Okay, baby," Lynn said while unfastening her seatbelt, her heart skipping a beat as she helped Bailey with her luggage.

What she gotta ask me? Lynn repeated in her mind, her palms getting moist as they walked down the corridor to Bailey's apartment.

Bailey opened the door, and they both stepped inside. Bailey went into her bedroom while Lynn went into the kitchen for a glass of water. Bailey came out with one hand behind her back.

"Doll?" Bailey called softly.

Lynn placed her glass in the sink and turned around to face her.

"Yes, baby?" Lynn said nervously.

Bailey smiled as she walked closer to Lynn, her hand remaining behind her back.

"I had this made a few months back, and I wanted to ask you then, but…I wasn't sure if you were ready. So, I'm asking you now," Bailey said, looking sincerely into Lynn's eyes.

"Yes, baby? You're killing me here!" Lynn said, shuffling from one foot to the other while wringing her hands.

"Okay, baby…hold on," Bailey said, chuckling in a low tone. "I wanted to ask you if you would do me the honor of…"

TO BE CONTINUED…

The Escort

Dr. Muhammad, please call extension 2755, 9 North Nurses' Station. Dr. Muhammad, extension 2755, 9 North Nurses' Station.

"I need another J-O-B," Allison said. "Having one job ain't cutting it right now, Jackie. I got plans. Do you know any places hiring, girl?"

"Not off the top of my head," Jackie said, then snapped her fingers as if suddenly remembering something. "Wait a minute. I do know somebody—a nurse who runs her own registry. I'll call her and see if she can hook you up with something."

"That'll be dope! But I can't have Uncle Sam up my ass, girl. So, ask her if she has any off-the-book private duty cases," Allison said, crossing her arms. "I really want to buy my dream home this year if I can."

"I hear you, and I'm not trying to be all up in your

business, but doesn't your man own that barbershop on the avenue?" Jackie asked.

"What's your point, friend?" Allison said as she took a piece of Juicy Fruit gum out of her uniform pocket, rolled it up, and put it in her mouth.

"My point *IS*, friend, why do you have to work so hard if you got a man? Not to mention he has his own business."

"True that, but here's the thing—I wanna put a hefty down payment on my dream home. *AND* my boyfriend doesn't own the barbershop; his father does. He just works there sometimes and helps him with the books. He also doesn't have the same dream I have, so this relationship may be short-lived. I'm alright hustling to get my own money, though. That way, I don't owe nobody shit. Okaaaay," Allison said, smirking.

"I'm feeling that!" Jackie said, pulling out her phone. "Check this out; I'ma call Gloria now and see if she has anything."

"Who's Gloria?" Allison inquired.

"She's the nurse who owns the registry. My bad," Jackie replied with a chuckle. "Hold on. Her phone is ringing. I don't want anybody listening to my conversation out here in the lobby. Let's go over to the café," she suggested.

"Oh, they're open?" Allison asked, her eyebrow raised. "That was fast, but I'm glad 'cause it's nice to have somewhere else to eat besides the hospital cafeteria, especially when it gets cold outside."

"Alright, hun, I'll let her know. Thanks a lot," Jackie said before ending the call. "Okay, so Gloria said there are a few wealthy patients who prefer to pay cash directly to the nurses."

"That's great!" Allison squealed.

"Yeah, but you have to give her a percentage when you get paid, though."

"That shouldn't be a problem. How much of a percentage is she looking to get?"

"You'll have to discuss that with her, friend. Here's her number. She said to call her in about two weeks. She's expecting to have some new patients by then," Jackie told her.

"Thanks a lot! I hope her percentage is reasonable, friend. Otherwise, what's the point, right?"

Allison folded the napkin the number was written on and placed it in her pocket.

"What about working some overtime in the meantime, Allison? A lot of nurses work overtime."

"I did some overtime recently. I thought I told you," Allison said, looking confused. "Guess I didn't. Anyway, Uncle Sam kicked my ass in taxes because of my single status. So, it was like working all those hours for nothing! Not doing that again. Not to mention, my CPA told me to chill because if I make too much money again this year, I might wind up owing instead of breaking even. Now ain't that some shit!"

Allison popped her gum and rolled her eyes.

"I hear you, friend. Come on, walk me back to my post," Jackie said.

Just then, her walkie-talkie went off.

"Roger that," she said into the handheld device.

"They're calling you to see where you're at, huh?" Allison asked, chucking.

"Yeah," Jackie responded, then the two started lightly

jogging the rest of the way back.

"Where did you go?" her fellow officer asked once Jackie reached her post.

He appeared to be a little upset about her disappearance.

"I'm sorry. I had to use the bathroom so bad that I forgot to let you know I was leaving my post," Jackie said, looking remorseful.

"You can't let that happen again, Jackie."

"I won't. Again, I'm sorry."

"Alright, I'll be in the office if you need me," her fellow officer said as he walked away, shaking his head.

"Yikes!" Allison said playfully. "Well, since I gotta wait two weeks before I can call Gloria, there IS something I've been thinking about doing for a while now."

"Tell me more," Jackie said, standing behind the podium and tapping her fingertips on it. "Speak up, girlie. What might that be? Do tell!"

"Nah, never mind," Allison said.

"ALLISON! Don't do that. You know I can't stand it when you do that shit! You better tell me. I'm not playing with you."

"Alright, alright," Allison said, pretending to clear her throat. "I'm scared to tell you, though."

Allison looked away and bit off a hangnail.

"What?! Come on now. Stop it. You're scared to tell me? What kind of shit is that? I thought we were best friends?"

"We are. We are," Allison assured her.

"So, why would you stand here and fix your mouth to say that to me?" Jackie said, pointing to her chest. "You're bullshitting me, right?"

Allison stood there blinking and popping her gum.

"Would you stop popping that damn gum? It's starting to get on my nerves. I can't even believe you right now," Jackie said, throwing her hands up in disbelief, then made an about-face and started walking away.

"Jackie. Jackie, come back here. Where you going? You better stay your ass here before you get in trouble again," Allison said, laughing.

"You're so funny I forgot to laugh," Jackie shot back sarcastically, turning around.

"Okay, okay. Fine, I'm sorry for saying that, but I'm scared you're gonna judge me after I tell you," Allison said in a childlike tone.

"Gimme a freggin' break, Allison. For real? I'm probably the least judgmental person you know. Stop playing and tell me, girl."

"Alright, I'll tell you, but it's going to have to be after work, though. What you doing after work?" Allison asked, still popping her gum.

"You're kidding me, right? You're gonna leave me hanging like that? Come on now, Allison! You for real?"

"Yeah, I'm for real. I don't know how long YOUR lunch is, but I gots to get back to my floor, girl. I got people to keep alive!"

"You play too much. You got me begging you and shit, knowing you gotta go," Jackie said, sucking her teeth in annoyance. "That's fucked up how you did that."

"I'm sorry, friend, but my lunch hour is over," Allison said, blowing air kisses.

"Alright then, I guess I have no choice but to wait. You make me sick. I need you to know that," Jackie said, chuckling.

"I'll meet you in the lobby at five o'clock," Allison said.

"Cool."

"Hey, Jackie?"

"Yeah."

"You better not judge me," Allison told her while running to catch the elevator.

"Girl, knock it off! I'll see you at five," Jackie said, smiling before assisting a visitor.

Allison gestured the okay sign with her fingers, then got on the elevator.

*****

It's ten minutes after five. What in the world is taking this girl so long? Jackie thought as she compared the time on the lobby's clock to her wristwatch.

The elevator bell dinged, making Jackie turn around.

"Oh, there you are. What took you so long, Allison?"

"I had to change out of my work clothes, friend. Let's go to the lounge around the corner and get something to eat and have a few cocktails," she said, grinning. "I don't feel like cooking tonight, and I need some liquid courage before I tell you what I've been thinking about doing. Shit, YOU might need a drink after I tell you!"

"Oh damn, this must be serious. I can't wait to hear this!" Jackie said, hurrying to keep up.

*****

"Dang! Does everybody have a story to tell tonight?

Why's it so crowded in here? It's only Wednesday, for God's sake," Jackie said in a frustrated tone while looking around the lounge.

"I have no idea," Allison responded. "Oooh, look. There's a table right next to the jukebox in the back over there."

"It's next to the bathroom, though."

"Shit, who cares! Let's hurry up before somebody else sees it."

They got to the table just as a couple was about to snatch it up.

"Ya slow, ya blow," Allison mumbled, pulling out her chair.

Jackie heard her, and they both laughed.

"I love the atmosphere in this spot. Doesn't it kinda remind you of that movie *Cooley High* a little bit, Jackie?"

"Oh snap! You're right. It does—minus the crapshoot in the back."

"Right!"

They both high-fived while laughing.

"Hey, Jackie, go order the food for us, and I'll get the drinks, bet?"

"No problem. Where's the menus?"

"Oh, you never been here before?"

"Nah, I heard of it, though. I take it you forgot I live in Brighton Beach, right?"

"No, I didn't forget, but you didn't always live in Brighton Beach, Jackie. Your ass used to live right up the street, so stop playing yourself," Allison said, laughing. "Not only that, but this spot is open during lunchtime, too. So, I assumed you came in here for lunch sometimes since it's right up the street from the hospital."

"Well, I haven't," Jackie stated sarcastically.

"Ewww, what you getting mad for?"

"I'm not mad," Jackie said, looking away.

"Whatever... Anyway, you place the orders on the other side. You can look at the menu while you're over there, but I already know what I want," Allison told her.

"Oh, word! Okay, so what you ordering?"

"I'm going to have the smothered pork chops and cabbage with white rice and gravy. But tell them to put a little bit of gravy on my rice. Otherwise, they'll put too much, and don't forget to ask them for the cornbread. It's like the water in here—if you don't ask for it, they won't give it to you."

"Alright, I won't forget. Those smothered pork chops sound good, but I have a taste for chicken. Do they have smothered chicken?"

"They should," Allison responded, shrugging her shoulders.

"Alright, if they have it, I'm gonna get me some smothered chicken, mashed potatoes with gravy, and some creamed corn."

"That'll work," Allison said, chuckling. "What you want to drink?"

While Allison waited for Jackie's answer, somebody put a dollar in the jukebox and played a song by Fatback called "Backstroking". Jackie two-stepped to the other side while telling Allison to get her a strawberry daiquiri.

"My poor friend," Allison said to herself while laughing and dancing her way to the bar. "Hey, bartender. What's going on? How you doing?"

"I'm fine. Thanks. What will it be, young lady?" the bartender responded, smiling.

"Let me get a Strawberry Daiquiri and a Fuzzy Navel, please."

"Sure, no problem. Will you be drinking at the bar, or do you have a table?"

"I have a table."

"Where? I'll bring them to you."

"Oh, okay. Right over there next to the jukebox."

"Alright. You can go have a seat, and I'll bring your drinks right over to you," the bartender said, winking and putting down the towel she had been using to dry the glasses.

"Thank you," Allison told her, then thought, *She's kinda cute. If Jackie was single, I would try and hook those two up.*

Jackie returned to the table twenty minutes later, but she was empty-handed.

"What's up? I was just about to put an APB out on your ass. Let me find out you had to cook the damn food!" Allison said, obviously irritated. "What took you so long, girl? I'm almost finished with my drink."

"That line was long as hell, girl. You see all these people up in here? Stop playing."

"Well, I hope it don't take that long for them to bring the food out. I'm hungry as fuck!"

"This my drink?" Jackie asked, pointing to the other glass on the table.

"Yeah."

"Thanks. I could use this drink right about now." Jackie picked up the glass and took a sip. "Mmmm! This shit tastes good! It's the perfect combination of strawberries and rum. Not everybody can get this right, you know."

"I need to order me another one of these," Allison said, swirling the ice around in her almost empty glass.

"What's your drink called?"

"A Fuzzy Navel. It's sweet, but it sneaks up on your ass. So, I'm only ordering one more. It's small, but it's mighty," Allison told her with a chuckle, then added, "By the way, the bartender is a cutie."

"Word? The bartender is a female? No wonder this drink tastes so good. Let me see," Jackie said, turning around to get a good look at the bartender. "Oh yeah, she's unquestionably my type for real."

"Uhhh huh, I know, but don't go getting yourself in no trouble. You already got a girlfriend, and she's pretty, too. So, don't go fucking that up," Allison said, sucking on her ice cube. "How's Lola doing anyway?"

"Excuse me, ladies."

Allison and Jackie looked up, and there stood the waiter with the food.

"Finally!" Allison exclaimed, causing the waiter to chuckle at her reaction.

"Who got the pork chops?"

"Right here," Allison said, pointing to the space on the table in front of her.

"You must have the chicken then?"

"Yes. Thank you," Jackie replied.

"Enjoy, ladies, and sorry for the wait. It's starting to get busy in the evenings, as you can see."

"Yeah, we realize that. Is there something special going on tonight?" Allison asked him, cutting into her pork chop.

"No...nothing special. I guess people like the way the

new chef cooks," the waiter said as he began walking away.

"Excuse me!" Allison shouted.

"Yeah, what's up?" the waiter asked, heading back.

"Can you bring us two glasses of water, please?"

"No problem. I'll be right back."

"Thank you!" the two women said in unison.

"This food is the bomb, Allison! Wow!" Jackie commented, smacking her lips.

"It's almost as good as my momma's, girl! Maybe the new chef is somebody's mama," Allison replied jokingly, making Jackie roll her eyes.

As both women continued enjoying their food, Allison suddenly realized no music was playing. She wiped her mouth and got up from the table to put money in the jukebox before somebody else beat her to it. She selected En Vogue's "Giving Him Something He Can Feel" and then returned to the table.

"Friend, you in love," Jackie teased while sucking on her chicken bone.

"What you mean? That song is dope. I don't know what you even talking about, Jackie," she said, grinning slightly. "Anyway," Allison continued with a wave of her hand, "it's a lounge—not a club, girl. You're supposed to chill, talk, eat, and drink here. Even the lights are dim. Get a clue, friend."

"Yeah, you're right," Jackie said, finishing her mashed potatoes.

"But hey, you never answered me."

"Answered you about what, friend?" Jackie asked.

"About your girlfriend Lola? How's she doing?"

"I guess she's okay," Jackie replied with a shrug of her

shoulders while slurping on her drink.

Allison placed her fork down and looked up from her plate.

"Say what now? You guess she's okay? What's up with that?" Allison asked, raising her eyebrow. "Don't tell me y'all arguing again. Y'all always breaking up to make up."

"Nah, not this time. I officially ended it, Allison."

"What?! Why? When? What happened, Jackie?" Allison said, leaning in to make sure she heard every word.

"Her kids are what happened, friend," Jackie responded while buttering her piece of cornbread. "I love Lola and her kids, but they bad as hell for real. You remember *Bebe's Kids*?"

Allison busted out laughing, spitting out some of the food she was eating.

"Oh, shit, girl! My fault. Let me get that," she said, reaching for her napkin. "But, yeah, I remember *Bebe's Kids*."

"That's alright. I got it," Jackie said, wiping her arm herself. "Well, Lola's kids are worse than that! They jump all over my furniture and break my shit."

"What?!" Allison said, her eyes wide.

"Yup, they be doing all kinds of shit. Lola don't say a damn thing to them either, and to top it off, she argues with me if I try to chastise them about it! Bitch, that's MY shit!" Jackie said, looking for Allison to agree while she shook her head. "I don't want to be in a relationship with a woman who disrespects me like that. I had enough of that shit."

"Damn, friend. Ummp! Lola fucked up losing you 'cause you're a good-ass catch," Allison said, biting the inside of her jaw.

"I appreciate that, friend, because she had me wondering if it was me sometimes. Hmph. You know, I really didn't want to date a woman with kids in the first place."

"Yeah, I remember you telling me that," Allison said, chewing on her ice.

"But she was fine as hell with that fat ass and those big-ass titties," Jackie said, using her hands to outline the female form in the air.

"Yeah, she's a brick house. No doubt about that," Allison agreed.

"I knew it was officially over when I stopped wanting to have sex with her, though. Shit, I remember the days when I would run home from work to make love to that woman."

"Word! You used to tell me about your sexcapades AND your arguments with her all the time," Allison said, chuckling.

"Yup, but not no more 'cause ME not wanting pussy! Yeah, that relationship is done," Jackie said as she wiped the cornbread crumbs off her mouth.

"I hear you, friend. How long ago did y'all break up?"

"Oh, it's been about a month now."

Allison's mouth dropped open in surprise.

"Wow! And you never said anything to me about it?"

"I know, friend. I figured you might be tired of me complaining about my relationship to you all the time. Plus, I was so relieved to have those kids out of my life that I didn't want to jinx it by saying anything," Jackie explained with a chuckle.

"I know that's right! It beez like that sometimes—it

really does," Allison said, shaking her head and chuckling softly.

"Alright, enough about me. Tell me your big secret. I know you think my ass forgot why we came here."

"Alright, friend, but wait… Let me order another drink first," she said while waving over the bartender. "You want another one?"

"Nah, I'm good."

Once the bartender approached their table, Jackie asked her, "How you doing, beautiful?"

"Why, thank you. You're beautiful yourself," the bartender replied with a smile before turning to Allison. "What can I get for you?"

"Can I get another Fuzzy Navel, please… and your phone number?" Jackie interjected, smiling.

Allison kicked Jackie's foot under the table.

"What the fuck," Jackie said softly.

The bartender noticed and thought it was cute. However, after thanking Jackie, she informed her that she was in a committed relationship.

"I'll be right back with your drink," the bartender told Allison before walking away.

"What you do that for, Allison?"

"Because your ass needs to chill. You just got out of a relationship a month ago. Chill for a minute. Damn, friend."

"Wait a damn minute," Jackie said, resting her elbows on the table and talking with her hands. "Hold up. Stop the muthafuckin' presses! Who are you, the pussy police? I don't tell you how much dick you should be sucking, so back up with your pussy restrictions on my ass! Okay, puhlease." Jackie rolled her eyes extra hard.

"Pussy restrictions! Ha!"

They looked at each other and busted out laughing.

"Your ass is funny, but you got that," Allison said.

"Shit, my tongue don't need no rest. You betta ask somebody," Jackie added, grinning.

"In-knee-way…you ready for my secret?" Allison asked anxiously.

"COME ON! Spit it out, damn it!" Jackie said.

"Okay, okay. Have you ever seen that movie *Pretty Woman*?" Allison asked her.

"I think so. Is it that movie with Julia Roberts and that guy who played the gigolo? What's his name again?" Jackie asked, tapping the table, trying to remember.

"His name is Richard Gere," Allison told her.

"Yeah! That's his name," Jackie said, smiling. "I saw it. Julia Roberts played a prostitute, right?"

"No, she wasn't a prostitute. She was an escort," Allison told her.

"Same shit. What does that movie have to do with anything, though? I'm not following you, friend," Jackie asked, frowning.

"Well…that's what I want to do," Allison said, her voice just above a whisper.

"What? Be an actress like Julia Roberts?"

"No, stupid. I wanna be an escort."

Jackie choked on her saliva.

"Wait, wait…you wanna be a what?! Get the fuck out of here! You're playing, right?"

"See, that's why I didn't wanna tell you. You're judging me already," Allison said, crossing her arms over her chest.

"No, wait, wait. Let me wrap my head around this shit, Allison."

"Ummm, okay."

"So, you telling me you wanna be an escort, right?"

"Yes. It's the same thing as a gigolo but the female version."

"Who the fuck told you that?!" Jackie asked, looking confused while shaking her head and shrugging her shoulders.

Allison rolled her eyes at Jackie's response.

"Well, that's what I wanna do. I have an appointment for an interview at the agency on Friday, and I need you to come with me."

"You got an interview for this shit, too! Woooowww! This shit is deeper than I thought! Wait, what about your man?" Jackie asked.

"What about him? He's not giving me the money I need for my house, and what he doesn't know won't hurt him. This is my business. Besides, we're not married and probably won't be, so let's keep him out of it."

"Well, if this is what you want to do, and you understand what you're getting yourself into, what can I say? Shit, you're grown. I got your back and am not judging you one bit, but I don't understand why you wanna do this, though. You're a nurse, Allison," Jackie said, trying her best not to make Allison feel bad.

"I know I'm a nurse, Jackie. So what, am I not supposed to want to do different shit? Everything ain't for everybody, friend," Allison said sarcastically. "Look, I'm done talking about it...but are you still coming with me on Friday or what, Jackie?"

"Yeah, I'll go with you on Friday, Allison," Jackie said with a sigh.

Allison jumped up and rushed around to Jackie's side of the table, giving her a big hug and a kiss on the cheek.

"Thank you!" Allison shouted, jumping around.

"You're welcome, FREAK," Jackie said, laughing.

"I LOVE YOU, bestie!"

"I love you, too," Jackie replied, then thought to herself, *I can't believe this girl wants to be an escort. Out of all the shit she could do, why she chose this is a mystery to me.*

"You finished with your food, Allison, 'cause I'm ready to go, girl? I gotta be in early tomorrow. One of the officers called out."

"Yeah, I'm ready. Where did you park? I'll walk you to your car."

Allison treated Jackie to dinner and paid the bill. Then they left the lounge and walked to Jackie's car parked across the street.

"Can you believe this shit?!" Jackie shouted.

"What?"

"I got a fucking ticket! I can see it from here! FUCK!"

"Aww, man, I'm sorry," Allison said.

"This is some bullshit, and it's seventy-five dollars! Ain't this about a bitch! Alright, girl, let me go. I'll call you when I get home," Jackie told her.

They hugged and kissed each other goodbye.

"Drive safe."

"I will. Night," Jackie said, waving her hand out the window as she drove off.

*****

"It's Friday—your big day. You ready, Allison?" Jackie asked after they exited the hospital.

"Friend, I'm getting a little nervous," Allison told her.

"You don't have to go through with this, you know. Nobody's got a gun to your head, friend," Jackie told her.

"I know, I know. Let me shake this feeling off. I'll be alright once I get there. Let's go," Allison said.

They walked to the corner and waited for the light.

"What's the address to this agency, and what time is your appointment anyway?" Jackie asked.

"I wrote it down in my address book. Let me see."

Allison rummaged through her purse and pulled out her address book to look for the information.

"Here it is. It's at 720 Fifth Avenue, and my interview is at seven o'clock. What time is it now?"

"It's five-thirty."

"Alright, cool. I don't feel like getting on nobody's train right now, so let's catch a cab," Allison said, stepping off the curb and a few feet into the street to hail one.

"You don't want me to drive you there?"

"You'll never find parking this hour in midtown, friend."

"Well, I'll pay for parking 'cause I'm not coming back up here to get my car. That doesn't make any sense."

"Yeah, you're right," Allison said as she followed Jackie to her car.

Surprisingly, Jackie found a parking space a block away from the agency.

"I hope this is a good sign," Allison said, still a little nervous as they entered the building.

The agency was located on the ground floor of a well-kept, high-rise office building. The receptionist buzzed them in. Once they reached the receptionist's desk, the white woman sitting behind the desk looked at them as if they were in the wrong place.

"Can I help you?" the woman asked, looking them both up and down.

"Good evening. My name is Allison, and I have a seven o'clock appointment with Mindy."

"Oh!" Her whole demeanor changed quickly.

I guess she realized we were in the right place, after all, Allison thought.

"Sure. Let me tell her you're here."

"Thank you."

"Hello, Mindy. Allison, you're seven o'clock, is here... Okay, I will." Once she placed the phone's receiver back on its base, she told Allison, "Please have a seat. Mindy will be out in just a moment. You can help yourself to some refreshments while you wait. We have coffee, tea, and water."

The woman pointed to the refreshment station.

"Okay, thank you," Allison said while walking away.

"This office looks more like a modeling agency. I thought an escort agency would look a little more playboy-ish," Jackie commented.

"Playboy-ish how? Like what?" Allison asked her, feeling quite relaxed now.

"Shit...I don't know. Just not like this, Allison."

A short, stocky white woman with shoulder-length blonde hair called out Allison's name as she walked towards the two. Allison gave a quick wave.

"Hello, I'm Mindy," she said as she reached out to

shake Allison's hand. "What a beautiful young lady you are. I'm glad you could make it this evening. Come with me."

"Hi, Mindy. It's nice to finally meet the woman behind the phone," Allison said, smiling. "Excuse me a moment, Mindy. Jackie, I'll be right back. It shouldn't take long. Check out one of those fashion magazines 'til I get back."

Jackie stuck her tongue out playfully at Allison and picked up a magazine.

Ten minutes later…

"Yeah, that's about right," a young black woman standing in front of the receptionist desk said.

The receptionist handed the woman an envelope, which she placed in her black designer bag hanging from her shoulder by its gold chain.

Struck by the woman's beauty, Jackie almost fell out of her seat, and she could only see her side profile! Her wavy jet-black hair was pulled back in a chignon-style bun. She wore a short black mink jacket on top of a camouflage catsuit that showed off all her curves and a pair of fly-ass black stiletto boots with silver heels!

Oh my god! I'm glad Allison asked me to come with her down here tu-day. Gotdamn it! Jackie thought to herself. *Is she an escort, too? If so, escorting can't be a bad thing; it just can't be. Damn, she's fine. I got to get to know her.*

The woman turned around in Jackie's direction, sporting a pair of matching monogrammed designer sunglasses but removed them when she noticed Jackie staring at her.

Her face! That beautiful cocoa brown skin is as flawless as they come.

A bright red lipstick adorned her full lips, and her newly-applied eyelashes hovered over top a set of gorgeous Diana Ross-esque eyes with no need for eyeliner. She looked like she had just stepped out of the movie *Mahogany*.

My goodness! I can tell when a woman takes care of herself because it shows in the way she walks, talks, dresses, and smells. And the scent of her expensive perfume… Mmmm!

The woman nodded and smiled at Jackie while walking towards the exit door. Jackie quickly stood up and hurried over to hold the door open for her.

"Hey, how you doing? My name is Jackie. Can I get your name, love?"

"Hello, Jackie. My name is Nina. Nice to meet you, and thanks for opening the door for me," she replied softly, then asked, "You work here?"

Jackie chuckled and replied, "No. My friend is on an interview right now. She asked me to come with her for moral support, and I'm certainly glad I did."

"Wow, Jackie," Nina said, giving her a once-over as she held one of the arms on her sunglasses in her mouth. "You're damn sure pretty enough to work here. Does your friend look anything like you?"

"Nah, she looks like her," Jackie responded, smiling.

"Oh! I see," Nina said, raising an eyebrow and softly chuckling. "I like a woman with a sense of humor, and you seem like a nice friend to boot."

Nina put her sunglasses back on.

"Come with me to the bathroom upstairs. I need your help with something," Nina told her, then walked out the door without waiting for Jackie's reply.

"Say no more." Jackie walked quickly behind to catch up.

They arrived at the empty bathroom upstairs and down the hall. It was clean, had a sitting area, and a bathroom attendant, to who Nina handed her mink jacket after removing it. Then she walked over to the sink to wash her hands. Jackie followed like a puppy.

"Can you help me with this?" Nina asked while looking through the gold-gilded mirror hanging above the sink.

"Sure, love. What do you need my help with?" Jackie asked.

Nina smiled seductively. "My zipper, sweetie. I can't reach it. I need you to unzip me, please."

Jackie stood close behind her. *She smells so fucking good,* Jackie thought as she unzipped the woman's catsuit slowly while looking back at her through the mirror with one eye over her right shoulder. Nina pretended to be bashful by looking downward for a moment, then gazed back up slowly while simultaneously removing her arms from the catsuit, revealing a sheer beige brassiere that introduced her 38C's with silver-dollar-sized nipples. Jackie had the urge to bite or at the least kiss Nina's neck, but she refrained. It was too risky to be that bold. Jackie's mouth began to water, and she licked her lips to keep from drooling. As she took a tiny step back, Nina turned around, having Jackie believe she was about to be kissed. But…

"Excuse me," Nina said softly while deliberately brushing up against her as she passed to go into the stall.

"Ummm, mmmm, mmm," Jackie said out loud as she watched Nina's every move. "Why are you being such a temptress?"

Nina didn't answer and continued to walk to the stall. Once at the stall's door, Nina pulled her catsuit down to her ankles, revealing her pantyless cheeks, and looked back to ensure she had Jackie's undivided attention.

I can't believe this. Is this really happening to me right now? AND she isn't wearing panties! Damn, girl, Jackie thought, shaking her head slowly.

"My lips would be the perfect addition to them cheeks, you know that?" Jackie stated out loud.

Nina just smiled.

Shit, I wish I was the middle seam of that catsuit. I would love to be swimming in her juices all fucking day, Jackie thought while continuing to watch Nina and fantasizing about touching her until she finally disappeared inside the stall and closed the door.

I forgot the bathroom attendant was even in here with us. Oh, what the hell. She's probably seen a WHOLE lot of shit. Look where we at! She's not paying us no damn mind.

Jackie chuckled to herself as she walked out and sat on the brocade loveseat in the waiting area. She thought it would be better than standing by the stall area like a perv. A few minutes later, Nina came out drying her hands off with a paper towel, looking more stunning than she did going in.

Damn, Jackie thought.

Nina smiled at her before putting her designer shades back on. She walked towards Jackie, who stood up to greet her, and then realized…

"Oh shit! I gotta go back downstairs, love. I forgot all about my friend. She's gonna kill me," Jackie said as a couple of young ladies were entering the restroom.

"Excuse me," they said softly, walking in between them.

"Can I take you out to dinner sometime, Nina?" Jackie asked while moving towards the exit.

"Sure, you can take me to dinner, but I don't like Mexican food, just so you know," Nina said, smiling.

"Yes!" Jackie responded while she punched the air.

"Oh!" Nina responded, clutching her invisible pearls and blushing.

"So, how would I get in touch with you, love?" Jackie asked, pausing in the doorway.

Nina opened her purse, pulled out a silver business card holder, and opened it. Walking closer to Jackie, she placed one of the cards in her hand.

"Here you go."

Jackie read the card out loud. "Nina Hampton, freelance model. Call for rates."

Nina's number was also listed on the card.

"Freelance model, eh?" Jackie chuckled lightly. "Okay. I wanna know more about this 'modeling thing' you got going on," she said with a wink. "I'll call you tomorrow. Is that okay, love?"

"Yes, of course. I look forward to hearing from you, sugar," Nina said.

"Okay then, I'll speak to you tomorrow," Jackie told her, then gave her another wink before jogging away.

Nina quickly removed her shades.

"No kiss?" Nina shouted.

"Oh, word! I can get a kiss?" Jackie asked, speed walking back to her.

"I saw you admiring my lips, so I thought… You know what? Never mind, come here," she said, putting her shades on her purse chain.

Nina met Jackie halfway, reaching out to caress the left side of her face. Moving in slowly, she closed her eyes before planting a tender kiss on Jackie's lips. Jackie returned the kiss, contemplating if she should throw in some tongue. She didn't.

"I like how soft your lips are, Jackie," Nina complimented Jackie.

Then with her eyes still closed and her hand remaining on Jackie's face, she went in for another one.

"Wow," Jackie said, gently removing Nina's hand and holding it as she stepped back. "You just made my night, you know that? But I really gotta go now, love."

"I know. Go to your friend, sugar. I'll talk to you tomorrow," Nina said, putting her shades back as they both exited the bathroom and went their separate ways.

*****

"Where in the hell have you been, Jackie?" Allison shouted, standing outside the agency's doors. "I thought your ass left me! I was paging your ass and everything! Yo, I was getting pissed."

"I apologize, friend, and I left my pager in the car," Jackie said, giving her puppy dog eyes. "You know I would never leave you like that, but I had to use the bathroom right quick."

"Well, damn, are you constipated or something?" Allison asked, genuinely concerned. "'Cause I've been waiting out here for you almost thirty minutes, friend."

"You funny. How did your interview go?"

"I think it went well."

"Alright, what type of questions did that lady Mindy ask you?"

"Oh, just stuff like if I have any objections being a companion to males as well as females. You know, questions like that."

"Well, do you?" Jackie inquired.

"Not really. As long as I don't have to sleep with her, I'm cool," Allison replied.

"You'll sleep with the men, though?" Jackie asked her in a serious tone, her hand on her hip.

Allison shrugged her shoulders.

"Well, did she tell you how much you'll be paid?"

Allison shrugged her shoulders again.

"Alright, friend, I'ma leave you alone. Let's go get in the car," Jackie said. *Fuck it. It's her life. Besides, I got Nina on my mind.*

Once in the car and while staring out her window, Allison said, "Mindy told me that somebody will reach out to me next week."

"Hmph! The ole 'don't call us, we'll call you', huh?"

"I wouldn't say it like that, but I hope they call me, though." Allison lowered her head as if disappointed.

"Well, you wanna go and get a drink or something?" Jackie asked her.

"Nah, just take me home. My boyfriend should be there waiting on me."

"Okay, not a problem, friend. I'll have you home in twenty minutes tops!" Jackie said, picking up speed.

The following day...

Brring... brring....

"The party you are trying to reach is unavailable right now," the female operator's voice announced. "Would you like me to send this person a message for you?"

"Yes, I would."

"Okay, you can start talking when you're ready."

"Hey, Nina love, it's me...Jackie. Call me back when you get this message. I would really like to talk to you. Ummm. There's a fabulous restaurant I would love to take you to for dinner tonight. Alright, love. Looking forward to speaking to you soon."

"Okay, will that be all?" the operator asked.

"Oh snap! Yeah, there is one more thing. I forgot to leave her my phone number," Jackie said with a chuckle.

"Yeah, that *is* important," the operator said, chuckling with her.

Jackie gave her phone number to the operator and thanked her before disconnecting the line.

One hour later, Jackie's phone rang, and she rushed to answer it.

"Hello!" Jackie answered, slightly out of breath.

"Hey, Jackie, it's Nina. Sorry I missed your call earlier. I had to run some errands."

"Hey, love," Jackie said, blushing. "Thanks for calling me back."

"Of course. So where is this *fabulous* place you want to take me for dinner?"

"Have you ever been to the Vintage Room restaurant?" Jackie asked.

"No, I haven't," Nina replied.

"Okay, that's where we're going tonight then. Would you like me to pick you up?"

"I don't have a problem meeting you there. Where is the Vintage Room anyway?" Nina asked.

"It's in Manhattan on West 57th Street."

"Oh, I can walk there! I live on West 60th Street," Nina told her.

"Do you now?" Jackie said, sounding impressed.

"Uh-huh, I do," Nina responded, chuckling softly.

"Your laugh is so cute. Alright, love. Shall we make it dinner at eight?"

"Dinner at eight it is, sugar."

"I'll see you then, love," Jackie told her.

"I'll be the woman in the little black dress."

"I can't wait to see you in it either," Jackie replied with a nice visual in her mind of how Nina would look in the dress. "See you soon, love. Later."

"Alright, later," Nina said, smiling as she hung up the phone.

*****

Jackie arrived early and parked her car in the underground garage adjacent to the restaurant. She didn't want to risk getting another ticket by parking on the street like the last time.

Jackie went inside the restaurant to wait for Nina. Twenty minutes later, Nina arrived and was greeted by the hostess.

"Are you dining alone tonight, Miss? Can I show you

to a table?" the hostess asked her.

"No, thank you. I'm meeting a friend for dinner. Oh! I see her," Nina said, pointing to Jackie, who was facing the entryway and waving at her.

Nina walked over to the table, leaned in, and gave Jackie a peck on the cheek. Nina wore an off-the-shoulder little black dress, patent leather stilettos, and a clutch to match. Her diamond tennis bracelet and diamond stud earrings sparkled brightly in the dimly-lit restaurant.

"I'm scared of you!" Jackie said, grinning from ear to ear.

Nina did a little twirl so Jackie could get a full view.

"You look absolutely beautiful tonight, love."

"Thank you, sugar. Stand up and let me have a look at you," she said.

Jackie stood up and twirled around herself.

"You have on a little black dress, too! Don't you look stunning! My, my, that dress fits you like a glove! Aht aht, not the seams in the back of your stockings! Check you out," Nina said, grinning. "I can certainly appreciate a good-looking woman in a dress."

Nina slowly took in all of Jackie with her eyes.

"You smell nice. Is that Gardenia by Russo?" Jackie asked while taking her seat.

"Ahhh, and you know your perfumes, too, I see. Yes, it's Gardenia. I'm glad you like it," Nina said, obviously impressed by that, taking a seat herself. "And you're wearing…Sandalwood by Kirsty, correct?"

"Yes! Now would you look at that? We both have good taste in perfume," Jackie said.

The maître d came over to assure them that their waiter

would be with them shortly. Moments later, the waiter brought over the breadbasket and an ice bucket stand that contained a bottle of champagne. He greeted them with the menus, then proceeded to fill their glasses.

"I didn't see you order any champagne," Nina said, looking at Jackie quizzically.

"I took the liberty of ordering the champagne when I arrived."

"Wow, you sure know how to treat a lady," Nina said, smiling seductively while toying with her napkin.

Jackie raised her glass to Nina for a toast; Nina followed suit.

"What shall we toast to?" Nina asked.

"To a wonderful night."

"To a wonderful night indeed!"

"Cheers!" they said in unison.

"Ooh, that tickles," Nina said, smiling.

Jackie couldn't help but smile at her remark. They both looked over the menus and decided what they wanted to order.

"Are you ladies ready to order?" the waiter asked when he returned. "Or do you need more time?"

Nina glanced at Jackie, then took another sip of her champagne and looked off into the distance. The non-verbal exchange was loud and clear. Therefore, Jackie placed the order for both of them.

"Okay, we'll both have the Vintage Room house salad, and she'll have the pastry-wrapped salmon with onions, mushrooms, and mixed vegetables with a side of carrot and raisin herbed rice pilaf. I'll have the red wine braised beef short ribs with the thick noodles tossed in some mushrooms and black truffle cream sauce."

"Very well. I'll be right back with your order," the waiter said as he collected the menus.

"So, Nina, are you from New York?"

"I'm not. I'm from a little place called Grand Island, Nebraska," Nina responded, taking a breadstick from the basket.

"Really? I don't think I've ever heard of that place before," Jackie replied, seemingly perplexed. "What brought you to New York?"

"Work. I gave you my card, remember?" Nina said, winking and biting the breadstick.

"You like it here?"

"Yes! I love it!" she responded, scoping out the restaurant.

"Well, that's good to hear. I don't need you leaving me so soon," Jackie said with a chuckle before having another sip of champagne. "How long have you lived here?"

"I've only been in New York for nine months now."

"Oh, okay. How long have you lived on 60th Street?"

"I lived on 60th Street ever since I landed, sugar," Nina answered right as the waiter placed their food on the table.

For the next few hours, they ate, talked, and laughed as they got to know each other. When they finished with the champagne, dinner, and dessert, Jackie summoned the waiter over to pay the check, and then they left the restaurant.

"Hey, love, I know you live within walking distance from here, but let me drive you home. My car is parked in the garage," Jackie offered, pointing to it.

"I'd like that," Nina responded.

"Awesome! Follow me, love, but wait up here for me because the hill down to the garage is steep. Don't want you to chance breaking your ankle walking in those stilettos."

"I'll be waiting right here for you," Nina responded.

Jackie gave the agent her ticket, and the garage attendant drove around Jackie's two-seated red sports car. After driving up to street level, she got out to open the passenger side door for Nina.

"Awww, you're so sweet, but I could've opened the door for myself, sugar," she said.

"I know, but I wanted to, love," Jackie told her, then closed the door and walked back around the car to get in the driver's seat.

"I like your style," Nina told her.

"Thank you, love. I like yours, too," Jackie said, quickly looking over at her while changing lanes.

"My building is right over here, sugar," Nina pointed.

Jackie pulled up to the luxury-style apartment building and double-parked the car.

"This is nice, love," Jackie commented as she unbuckled her seatbelt.

They both sat there for a moment in silence before Jackie decided to lean over and kiss Nina. This time, Nina put her tongue in Jackie's mouth. This kiss was the sweetest—long and gentlest, yet ravishing.

"Your mouth has such a pleasant taste to it, sugar," Nina said, looking at Jackie alluringly while reaching behind her for the door handle but not opening it. "Hey, do you want to come up for a nightcap? I'm not ready for this night to end yet."

"I would love to come up and have a nightcap with you, love. Shit, I'll have a daycap with you, too!" Jackie said, grinning.

Nina laughed as if it was the funniest thing she'd ever heard.

"You make me laugh. I like you. I haven't met anybody like you since I left Nebraska. You're different."

"I hope I can keep it up," Jackie said, winking and holding Nina's hand.

"Does your building have a garage, love?"

"It sure does, sugar."

"Hot damn!" Jackie said, making Nina chuckle once again.

Jackie pulled around the corner and parked her car in the underground garage of the building, then followed Nina through the side door to the elevator inside the building. The doors to the elevator opened.

"Good evening, Ms. Moore," the elevator man said before turning to tip his hat at Jackie.

"Good evening, Glenn," Nina said, and Jackie concurred.

They got off on the twelfth floor and walked down the freshly vacuumed hallway towards Nina's apartment.

"We're herrrre," Nina playfully said as she opened her apartment door. "Welcome to my home, sugar."

The first thing Jackie noticed was the floor-to-ceiling windows greeting her with a scenic view of the Manhattan skyline through the open white vertical blinds.

"This shit is magnificent, love! You're living large," Jackie said, smiling.

Nina had a chunky, navy-blue velvet, tufted nailhead

sofa and loveseat set in the living room. A white fur shag area rug covered the floor with a glass coffee table in the middle of it and two matching side tables. One side table was next to the loveseat; the other was on the side of the sofa adorned with two black mini chandelier lamps—all resting on the grey and white marble floors. A floor lamp with a white ostrich feather shade was in the corner next to a gold bar cart. Her kitchen was small but neat, without dirty dishes in the sink, and equipped with state-of-the-art appliances—stainless steel refrigerator and stainless-steel stove and microwave combo. The short galley didn't provide enough room for a kitchen table. So, there was a breakfast bar with just enough space for two white leather and chrome high stool chairs where she could sit and eat.

I'm impressed.

"Come, sugar. Let me show you the bedroom," Nina said, leading her to it.

"This is nice, love," Jackie said, taking it all in.

There was a king-sized bed with black leather tufted head and footboard, burgundy satin sheets on the mattress, and a leopard fur throw resting on it. A large crystal chandelier hung from the tray ceiling, and two black lacquer side tables with white crystal knobs were on each side of the bed. Each table had a crystal lamp on top of it with black ostrich feather shades. A vintage-style vanity table and bench with a silver tri-fold mirror and plenty of expensive perfumes adorning it sat against the wall. Her bathroom had lingerie hanging up everywhere! She had painted the walls white with gold trim, and a gigantic, beveled mirror hung over the stand-alone sink.

"You need to come and decorate my place," Jackie

joked.

"Sure, I can help you out, sugar. I used to be an interior decorator in Nebraska."

"Really? Well, it's not hard to tell. I might have to take you up on that offer because I suck at decorating," Jackie said, chuckling.

"Just let me know when, sugar, and I'll be there," Nina told her, smiling.

Where has this woman been all my life? Jackie thought while looking at her.

After the tour, they went into the living room and sat on the sofa that faced the skyline's breathtaking view.

"Would you like a drink?" Nina asked before sitting down.

"Sure, love. I wouldn't mind having a glass of white wine if you have it. Thank you."

"White wine coming up! And I'll have a glass with you."

Nina handed Jackie her wine, then sat down next to her on the sofa.

"So, tell me more about your *modeling* job, love," Jackie said, taking a sip of her wine.

"You know exactly what I do," Nina said, rolling her wine glass between her palms as she looked out the window. "Your friend was interviewing for the same job."

"True. Tell me, do you only date men for the agency?" Jackie asked.

"No, sugar, I'm a companion for women, too," she responded, tapping her nails on her wine glass.

"Do you have sex on those *companion dates*?"

"No. Well, not all the time. Why? Would that be a

problem for you if I did?" Nina asked, looking over her glass.

"Well, I knew where I was when I met you. So, no, that doesn't bother me at all, love."

"You see, that's why I let you take me out. I knew you were different. You're not like anybody else I've met. Not everybody can handle what I do for a living, sugar. Alright, let's cut to the chase. I want to have sex with you...tonight," Nina told Jackie, smiling seductively.

"It would be my absolute pleasure to have sex with you tonight, but here's the thing, love," Jackie said, reaching for Nina's hand. "I don't have any of my stuff with me."

"You mean a dildo, don't you?" Nina said with a half-cocked smile.

"Yes, that's exactly what I mean," Jackie responded softly while blushing.

"Well, worry no more, beautiful, because that's not going to be your problem any longer. I'm sure I have one that'll fit you just fine. Come with me, sugar."

Once again, Nina led her into the bedroom. She turned the dial on the wall next to the light switch.

"Oh shit...not the red lights. I wasn't expecting that," Jackie said in a low sexy voice, turning to look at Nina.

"You must not want me to leave here tonight, huh, love?"

Nina didn't respond. Instead, she took off her dress, allowing it to fall freely to the floor. She was wearing a sheer nude-colored strapless bra and panty set. She kept her stilettos on.

Jackie swallowed hard and began following suit until...

"Aht, aht, turn around," Nina commanded. "Let me

help you out of that dress, sugar."

Jackie turned around and could feel the warmth of Nina's breath on her neck as she pressed her body up against hers and slid down while simultaneously unzipping her dress.

"Ooooooh, la la, sugar. Mmmm. Your stockings look even sexier with this garter belt holding them up," Nina said, gently running both hands up the sides of Jackie's thighs. "You're so fucking sexy."

Nina blew a puff of air into Jackie's ear and unsnapped her garter one leg at a time, body to body while breathing heavily on Jackie's cheek. Jackie moaned, her breath shallow as she squeezed her breasts. Nina reached out and slapped her on her ass.

"Now kiss it. Kiss my ass, baby," Jackie whispered.

"With pleasure," Nina said, sliding down and slowly licking Jackie's back along the way.

Then she kissed, licked, and bit each of Jackie's cheeks. Both women moaned in pleasure as Jackie put a hand between her legs.

"Like this, baby?" Nina asked while placing soft kisses all over her cheeks.

"Yes, just like that," Jackie responded, trying to keep her balance.

"I have you falling for me already," Nina playfully said, holding Jackie up.

Nina took one last bite before she stood up and paused.

"Hold on, sugar. I'll be right back," she told Jackie.

Walking over to her nightstand, she opened the bottom drawer where she kept her dildos. Nina chose the strap and dildo she wanted Jackie to wear and handed it to her.

"Wow, baby, you can handle all this?" Jackie asked, stroking the dildo as her eyes admired its girth.

Nina remained silent, staring at Jackie with those gorgeous eyes as she walked back towards the bed. Jackie stepped into the dildo holster and fastened it as tight as she could take it. She wanted to make sure it didn't get loose while she was putting her back into it.

"This is cyber-skin soft, nice and heavy," Jackie said while licking her lips.

She watched as Nina placed one of her hands between her legs and the other one around her neck.

Nina's facial expressions were a cross between passing out and extreme lust.

"You want me to suck you off?" she asked seductively, still touching herself.

"Dayum," Jackie said, rubbing on the dildo and making her pussy wetter. "Fuck yeah. Come and suck me off, baby."

Nina slowly dropped to her knees and crawled over to Jackie. Placing both hands around the dildo, she sucked on it like it was the last on the market! The dildo was pressed flush up against Jackie's clit, allowing her to feel every sensation when Nina moved her mouth. Jackie couldn't take her eyes off her. Watching Nina swallow the dildo was driving her ass crazy. Nina's mouth was stuffed, her saliva oozing down the sides of the dildo. She took it out of her mouth, spit on it, and then slurped it back up.

"Oh my god, baby. That's so fucking nasty," Jackie whispered as she held Nina's head to keep it steady. "Fuck, baby! Don't take your hands off it. I want you to deep-throat it for me. I wanna hear and see you gag on it."

"Errrgh... Errrgh...."

"Yeah, that's it. Right there, baby. Gag on it for me. Oh. My. God," Jackie whispered, looking down on her. "Now, I wanna see tears fall from those pretty eyes. Uhm hmm, there you go. There you go. Yeah, baby, there goes that tear. That's a good girl."

Jackie slowly backed away, letting the dildo fall out of Nina's mouth.

"Okay, baby, can you get on the bed for me?" Jackie asked, rubbing the dildo and smiling.

Nina picked herself up and walked slowly over to the bed, kicking off her stilettos along the way. Once she crawled onto the bed, she lay on her back.

"No, baby, I don't want you to lay down. Get on all fours and crawl down to the foot of the bed for me, mama. I'm gonna get behind you. I want you to ride me doggie style."

"Mmmmmm, I like the sound of that," Nina said, pulling on her nipples and crawling to the foot of the bed nice and slow, opening her legs wide with her ass in the air.

"A fucking work of art," Jackie said softly as she climbed on the bed and straddled Nina from behind, planting soft, wet kisses up and down her spine.

Nina arched her back, moaning sensually with pleasure and waiting with bated breath as she felt the head of the dildo resting at the peak of the crack of her ass. Jackie placed her hand on Nina's head and gently pushed it down while spreading her legs wider.

"Damn, baby. Oooooo, look at what I did—strawberries and cream," Jackie said, licking her lips and lightly tapping Nina's clit, making her body jerk as she looked back at Jackie with her eyes, barely open.

Nina reached back and spread her lips open wide enough for the dildo to have easy access to the entrance of her vagina.

"I need you all up in there. What are you waiting for, baby?" Nina pleaded.

"Here I come, baby," Jackie said as she slid inside Nina's vagina.

Slow and deep strokes made Nina gasp in ecstasy. Her head dropped, and her hands grabbed the sheets. Jackie continued to stroke Nina long and deep, both women moaning in pleasure. Nina lost control and began bouncing her ass up and down on the dildo, encouraging Jackie to spank her, which she did quick and hard. Nina's cream spread all over the dildo as Jackie stroked her faster, holding on to her waist as they both received pleasure with every stroke.

"Yes, baby, back it up for me. FUCK!" Jackie cried, her hands now pressing down on the top of Nina's ass for leverage. "You're sooo fucking wet."

Jackie reached out and grabbed Nina's breasts while simultaneously stroking her.

"You're fucking amazing! You're fucking amazing! I love this shit!" Nina yelled. "Oh shit, you're hitting my spot, baby! Don't stop! Please don't fucking stop!"

"Shiiiiitttt, girl." Jackie's strokes were now slow and deliberate. "Uhhh huh…ummm hmmm, I'm about to cum."

Jackie shut her eyes tightly.

"Come on, baby. Let's cum together," Nina said as she grabbed Jackie's ass and held it steady against her as they both climaxed hard.

Jackie remained inside Nina while she sat up slowly, her vagina still gripping the dildo as she wrapped both of her arms around Jackie's neck.

"Oh, you want some more?" Jackie whispered in Nina's ear and squeezed both of her breasts. "Here you go, baby."

Jackie began stroking her so hard and deep that the headboard was now hitting the wall.

"Go deeper, baby. Take it! Just take it!" Nina yelled, reaching for the footboard as she climaxed over and over again.

"Baby! FUCK! I'm cumming," Jackie said, her head dropping on Nina's back before she slowly withdrew the dildo and fell back on the bed sweaty and satisfied. "Whew! That was so good."

Jackie removed the strap and let it fall to the floor in a loud thump while Nina leaned over to give her a sweaty but sweet kiss.

"I'll be right back, baby. I need to use the bathroom," Jackie told Nina, rolling off the bed.

"I'm not going anywhere, beautiful," Nina responded, blowing her a kiss and then laying down spread eagle.

When Jackie returned, Nina rolled over and patted the spot in the bed next to her, gesturing for Jackie to get in. They both looked at each other lovingly, kissed, and minutes later, Nina fell asleep on Jackie's chest.

*****

It had been a year, and Nina and Jackie were still going strong. They had been on vacations to Turks and Caicos, went on a cruise to San Juan, Puerto Rico, and even visited New Orleans just because Nina wanted some Gumbo and Beignets. They enjoyed spoiling one another.

Nina still worked for the agency, and Jackie was still cool with it. Jackie's friend, Allison, never got the job at the agency, but she did get those private patient cases and made enough money to put down an even larger deposit on her dream home. She also snagged a new boyfriend.

It was autumn in New York, and Nina decided to throw a dinner party with just a few of their close friends. She had food catered from Dom's and Nick's because Jackie loved their Prawn and Gorgonzola pasta, and she ordered Jackie's favorite dessert, caramel pecan mini cheesecakes, from Georgia's Bakery. She also had Jackie's favorite flowers, white calla lilies, spread throughout the apartment and a case of Brut Rosé Champagne.

Everyone arrived at Nina's apartment on time, and there was plenty of food, conversation, drink, music, introductions, and laughter. Nina wore a white satin evening gown that had a side split, small rhinestone spaghetti straps, and cut just low enough in the back to tease. Jackie wore a white satin double-breasted jacket dress open just enough in the front to show some cleavage, and they both wore silver rhinestone stilettos.

Frankie Beverly and Maze's *Golden Time of Day* played softly in the background. It was a very sophisticated evening, and everyone could see how much Nina and Jackie cared about each other by the way they laughed and spoke to one another. People also commented on how good- looking they were and how well they complemented each other.

The song "Flowers" by the Emotions was interrupted by the sound of metal tapping on a glass.

"Excuse me. Excuse me. Can I get everyone's attention for a moment, please?" Nina asked.

Everyone stopped talking and gave her their undivided attention.

"I want to propose a toast to my best friend, my lover, and my confidant…Jackie."

Jackie was shocked and happy at the same time. *What's this all about?* she thought but could only stand there and listen like everyone else.

"Jackie…I just want you to know how happy I've been since you came into my life that day at the agency. I want to thank you for sharing your gift of love with me. Thank you for accepting ALL of me without judgment. Thank you for never finding the need to compete with me. Thank you for not trying to change me. Thank you for putting up with my crazy-ass mood swings."

Nina paused to flash a smile, and the crowd chuckled.

"But, most of all, baby, I want to thank you for not needing me but for wanting me just like I want you."

The crowd oohed and aahed as Jackie stood there blushing.

"I am so happy you found it easy to love me, because I don't usually let people in. Most people find it hard to love me and give up on me. But you…you're a cut above the rest, baby. You found the easy route to me, and I want to let you know, in front of everybody here, that I love you."

"Here, here!" someone shouted out.

"I love you, too, baby," Jackie said, trying to hold back her tears.

Nina slowly walked over to Jackie, holding out her manicured hand.

"May I have this dance?" she asked.

Jackie took her hand, and Nina led her to the middle of the room, where they danced to "I'm Ready" by Tevin Campbell. Everyone stared at the couple with admiration as Jackie spent and dipped Nina while holding the small of her back. When the music stopped, everyone clapped; some were even wiping their eyes. They both couldn't help but blush because they forgot they weren't alone—just like that time in the agency's bathroom when they first met.

Nina took a step back and lovingly looked Jackie deep in her eyes.

"Jackie, baby?"

"Yes, Nina," Jackie responded, dabbing away an escaped tear.

"Will you…"

TO BE CONTINUED…

Intermission: Toni & Lily

Toni: "Baby, I thought you said you would be home for my birthday this time. What happened?"

Toni whined as she spoke, her voice full of sorrow.

Lily: "I know, sweetheart. That was the plan, but my flight was canceled. They put me up at the airport's hotel, and I'll catch the first flight out in the morning. Please don't be mad at me. I promise I'll make it up to you."

The soft sounds of Toni weeping were tearing Lily apart.

Lily: "Aww, baby, come on now. Don't cry, okay? Listen to me for a minute. I wanted to surprise you when I got home with this, but I can't stand hearing you cry. So, guess what?"

Lily knew what she was about to tell Toni would cheer her up.

Toni: "What?" she asked, her voice soft and low.

Lily: "You sound so sexy right now, baby."

Getting aroused, Lily unbuttoned her blouse and ran her hands across her large breasts while blowing kisses to Toni through the phone.

Lily: "You're gonna be happy to hear this, I swear. Okay?" she told Toni in a comforting tone.

Toni: "Alright, baby, I'm listening. What is it?" she asked, sniffling as she wiped away her tears.

Lily: "I bought us tickets to the Cannes Film Festival. Didn't you always say you wanted to go?"

Lily smiled as she walked over to the dresser and looked at herself in the mirror.

Toni: "You did, baby?! Oh my god! When do we leave?!" Toni's sad tears had turned into tears of joy.

Lily: "Two weeks from tomorrow," she replied, chuckling at Toni's excitement. "I rented us a three-bedroom villa at a place by the sea. It's close to the festival, shopping, and everything, baby."

Lily grinned from ear to ear at how happy Toni sounded.

Toni: "I can't believe this!" she shouted, twirling around like a ballerina.

Lily: "That's right. Nothing but the best for my baby," Lily told her, chuckling once more. "Oh yeah, I also booked us a sightseeing tour of this famous castle, too. It's about an hour away from the villa. I know how you like that art deco stuff. So you happy now, baby? Did I make it right?" she asked, licking her lips and smiling, impressed with herself.

Toni: "Yes! I'm ecstatic! Baby, you always make me happy. I just miss you and was expecting to see you on my birthday, that's all."

Toni's voice cracked as she tried not to cry again.

Lily: "What room are you in right now, baby?"

Toni: "I'm in the living room. Why?" she asked, blinking away a residual tear as she lay across the suede lavender chaise.

Lily: "What you got on?"

Lily spoke softly while removing her blouse.

Toni: "My surprise birthday outfit. Why?" she seductively responded, crossing her legs slowly.

Lily: "Mmm…go in the room and get your Rabbit. I wanna play with you for a while."

Toni: "Ooh, we haven't had phone sex in a minute. I like that," she said softly, then stood up from the chaise and walked into the bedroom.

She looked on the top shelf of the closet and took down the green lacquer box where she stored the Rabbit.

Toni: "Okay, baby, I got it. You wanna FaceTime so I can do a striptease while you watch me play with myself?" she asked, putting her finger playfully in her mouth.

Lily: "That sounds so naughty, baby, but no. I wanna use my imagination; it's more fun this way. Put your earpiece in, though. I want your hands to be free. Is the Rabbit charged, baby?" she asked while removing her pants and watch, placing them on the valet stand.

Toni: "Let me turn it on and see. I haven't needed to use her in a while."

Buzzzzzzzz…

Toni: "Oh yeah, baby, it's fully charged, and I'm raring to go," she said, opening her robe and lying across the bed.

Lily: "Damn, baby, that charge is strong. Don't cum too quick on me now."

Lily giggled at her own comment while taking off her bra.

Toni: "I'll try my best not to," Toni said, her tone alluring.
Lily: "You know what, baby?"

Toni: "What, my love?" she said while playing with the ties on her robe.

Lily: "I bought a vibrator when I landed in Dallas. It's in the shape of lipstick. It's cute and very discreet."

She took it out of her bag and admired it.

Toni: "Really? What made you do that?" she asked, curious.

Lily: "Because I knew I wouldn't be home in time for your birthday. So, I wanted to be already prepared for when I asked you if we could have phone sex tonight."
Lily's hands were now between her legs.

Toni: "Well, it's the next best thing to you being here with me, baby. Now we can both cum harder," she whispered. "Oh, wait. I forgot something," she said, sitting up slowly.

Lily: "What did you forget, baby?"

Toni: "I got us a bottle of that Cognac you like, and I don't want it to go to waste," she said, laughing seductively.

Lily: "Yass! I like how you get when you drink that. We're gonna have some fun tonight. Go get you a glass and hurry your ass back to the phone, baby."

Toni: "Baby?" she replied, chuckling softly.

Lily: "Why are you laughing?" she asked while playing with the nipple of her left breast.

Toni: "Because, silly, I can still talk to you while I get a drink. You told me to put my earpiece in, remember?"

Lily: "I'm so glad I married you," she said, kissing Toni through the phone again before slowly crawling onto the hotel bed, wearing only her boy shorts. "Describe to me in detail what you have on. Wait! Before you do that, have I seen you in this birthday outfit before?"

Toni: "No, but you bought it for me when we went to that expensive-ass boutique in Denver two months ago. You remember the black and white satin panty set with the matching robe?"

Lily: "Oh yeah, how could I forget? We were only supposed to be passing through, but you just had to go shopping," she responded, laughing.
Toni laughed with her at the memory.

Toni: "You loved it, don't front she chuckled. Well, that's what I'm wearing. I was hoping you would be taking it off me tonight, but as they say, there's more than one way to skin a cat. Ain't that right, baby?" she purred.

Lily: "Here, kitty, kitty," she called out softly. "Take a sip of your drink for me."

Toni took a sip and closed her eyes as she swallowed the Cognac, indulging in its smooth, warm texture.

Lily: "Damn, even the sound of you swallowing is turning me on. Take your panties off for me, baby."

Toni: "I took them off already," she replied seductively. "Now take yours off, open your legs, turn on your vibrator, and put it on your clit. I want to hear you."

Lily: "Aww shit, baby," Lily moaned, her voice vibrating from the tiny jolts the sex toy was giving her. "Take another sip, then put the Rabbit on your clit. I want us to cum together. Fuck… I feel like I wanna nut already, baby," she said, her tongue protruding slightly out the side of her mouth.

Toni: "Yass… you hear mine? Baby. Fuck. This. Shit. Is. Strong," she said, her voice vibrating, too.

Lily: "Umm-hmm, that's right. Slide it up and down on your clit with me, baby," she instructed, her voice mellow.

Toni: "I don't think I can hold it much longer, baby. This. Shit… Oh God…"

Toni's voice trailed off as she climaxed.

Lily: "Oh shit, baby," Lily called out as her voice trailed off, as well.

Her body jerked forcefully, the movements causing her to drop the phone and vibrator on the bed. She shut her eyes tightly while she climaxed.

Both laughed at each other for climaxing so quickly.

Toni: "Wow! That was short but sweet, huh?" she said, still trying to control her laughter

Lily: "I know, right! That shit had my ass drooling a little bit. Now I need a cigarette," she responded, chuckling softly.

Toni: "Me too! I wasn't gonna say anything because I was embarrassed," she expressed while laughing. "But what's up with wanting a cigarette, though? You don't smoke, babe."

Lily: "I know. It just seemed like the right thing to say at the time."

Lily laughed as she pulled the covers over her body. Just then, the phone in the hotel room rang.

Lily: "Who's this?" she asked herself out loud, grunting as she reached over to answer it. "Hold on, baby. Let me see what this is about," she said and picked up the phone.

As Toni walked in the bathroom to clean off the Rabbit, she wondered who it could be calling Lily in her hotel room.

Lily: "Oh wow! Okay. When does it leave?" she asked the person on the other end of the phone. "Alright, good. I have an hour. Thanks so much!"

She disconnected the line, sprung out of bed, and grabbed her blouse before picking up her cell phone to continue her conversation with Toni.

Lily: "Hey, baby."

Toni: "Hey, babe. What was that about?"

Lily: "That was the front desk," she said cheerfully while zipping up her pants.

Toni: "Oh, yeah? And what did they want?"

Lily: "Somebody canceled their flight, so I'll be home in four hours, baby!"

Toni: "YAY!"

Excited, Toni jumped up and down and then started twerking in the bedroom.

Lily: "Yay! I'm happy, too, baby," she said, grinning. "Remember when people used to tell us our relationship wouldn't last 'cause two feminine women couldn't hold each other down?"

Toni: "Hell yeah, I remember! They tried like a son of a bitch to convince us it wasn't gonna work. I'm glad we have minds of our own, and our love was stronger than those naysayers. Plus, half of them ain't even together!
Toni shook her head as she reminisced about all those who bet against them in the beginning.

Lily: "Look at us—eight years in. I love you, baby, and Happy Birthday."

Toni: "I love you, too, baby. Wait! You didn't forget to buy me a present, did you?"

Lily: "I'm not suicidal, baby," she replied, chuckling.

Toni laughed. Lily's sense of humor was one of the things she loved about her most.

Toni: "You know I'm just messing with you, right? Now hurry up and get your ass home. I miss you!" she yelled playfully, then repeatedly blew kisses into the phone until they ended the call.

Hazel Blue

I wish I had met my mother, but she died after giving birth to me. The Madame and the man I call Daddy brought me to 4200 Kenmore Avenue in Chicago, Illinois, from the hospital—right to the room where I was conceived and where my mother entertained her gentlemen callers. Because my mother brought in the most money, Madame gave her the largest room on the second floor of her six-story brownstone. It had a wood-burning fireplace and a washroom with a working toilet. Of course, the room was changed into a nursery by the time I arrived.

All the young ladies working in Madame's house doted over me. It didn't hurt that I was a cutie either. They took turns feeding and changing me in between servicing their gentlemen callers, and when they weren't available, I belonged exclusively to Madame. I was the first and only child to be brought into this house, not to mention raised there.

I was never left unattended, and I never missed having a mother's love. On those cold winter nights that Chicago is known for, either Madame or one of the ladies would make sure I ate a hearty meal. Then they would light the fireplace in my room, dress me in my footed onesie pajamas, sit me on their lap in the rocking chair my daddy bought for me, and read me stories until I fell asleep. Sometimes, I would wake up to either Madame or one of the ladies cradling me in their arms just like a loving mother would. I felt so loved and protected that I'd go right back to sleep.

Hi, my name is Lovely Eva James. Yes, my birth name is Lovely. It was one of the first words out of my daddy's mouth when the nurse handed me to him. Eva was my mother's name, and James is Madame's last name. How they pulled that off is anybody's guess, but nobody calls me Lovely anyway, though. They call me by my nickname, Hazel Blue. Why, you ask? Well, it's because I have one hazel eye and one blue eye. My hair is a mound of tightly wound reddish-brown locks with golden blonde edges. My complexion is the color of a lightly toasted piece of bread, so Madame and my daddy decided I was black because my mother was black, you see. I grew up to be the spitting image of my mother, too, just without the gap in my front teeth.

Madame calls me her little trick baby because no one has any idea who my biological father is. Bobby, the man I call my daddy, spoils the shit out of me. Bobby was a big-time hustler from Michigan Avenue who was in love with my mother. He just knew I was his baby when my mother told him that she was pregnant.

Since Bobby refused to let my mother work while carrying me, he made sure Madame was paid every week so she could stay in that room. He looked after my mother throughout her entire pregnancy, and he was there at Madame's when she went into labor. He wouldn't let anybody call the ambulance because he wanted to be the one who drove her to the hospital. Bobby was a 6'5" tall, muscular, extremely handsome dark-skinned man who dressed to the nines every single day! Bobby prayed to God that I was his kid. Well, he knew his prayers hadn't been answered when he saw me up close and personal.

"Let me see that baby. Aww, if I didn't know any better, I would think she was my blood," Madame said.

Madame didn't have any children of her own, and she was what black folks called a high yella gal. She had green eyes, salt and pepper semi-curly hair she always wore in a French twist, a heavyset build, and stood around 5'5" tall. Although it was obvious I wasn't Bobby's, he still went ahead and signed my birth certificate, promising to love me just the same.

Daddy made sure I didn't want for nothing. I never had to second-guess how much he loved me, even though he had two biological sons, Stanley and Marcus. Stanley lived with his mother in Arizona, and Marcus lived with his mother in Mississippi. They both would come to Chicago in the summer months, but they had to stay with Daddy at his place on Michigan Avenue. Madame didn't want any boys around me at all! They loved looking after their little sister when they WERE allowed around me, although they had to be supervised. They often tried to carry me around and feed me even though I could walk and feed myself.

"Put that girl down! What did I tell y'all boys about picking her up?! She can walk, and she ain't handicapped! So, stop picking her up. I'm not gonna tell you again!" Madame would yell at them.

Both Madame and Daddy kept me away from their lifestyle as best they could by hiding me away upstairs and chauffeuring me to schools miles away. I went to Madison Park Elementary School from kindergarten until the 8th grade. Then I went to Adlai E. Stevenson High School for the talented and gifted because I was a mathematical genius. I was smart, quiet, and very shy as a young girl, so my daddy made it his business to put me in a martial arts academy when I turned ten. I had to go four times a week!

He would say, "You're pretty but too timid, so people are gonna fuck with you, baby. Me and your brothers ain't always gonna be around to protect you, Lovely, and I don't want you growing up thinking you have to wait on a motherfucking niggah to come around and save you. You have to learn how to protect yourself, ya hear me?"

"Yes, Daddy," I would say in a shy tone.

"That's my girl. Now give your daddy a kiss. I gotta go and make this money, baby."

I reached up for him to pick me up like he always did, but he didn't.

"Aht, aht. You're too big for that now, baby."

He bent down to kiss me instead, and I pouted but kissed him back.

"Bye, Daddy. I love you," I told him with puppy dog eyes and a sad tone.

Daddy would let me know he loved me more and then

give me some money before being on his way.

When I turned twelve, I wanted to hang out with my friends more often, but Madame and Daddy didn't trust anybody. If I wasn't with them, my brothers, or in martial arts class, I would be upstairs in my room doing my homework, watching television, or talking to a classmate on the phone. Whenever I heard that loud music turn on and grownups laughing and carrying on downstairs, I knew what time it was. That commotion indicated it was time for those gentlemen callers to choose a woman they wanted to spend the evening with. I'd tell my classmate I had to go, and I would turn down the television or stop doing my homework before tiptoeing slowly to open that heavy-ass wooden door to my bedroom. I would walk out of my room, bend down, and peek through the thick banister spindles to watch what they were doing down there. The ladies would be all dressed up in their finest boudoir clothes, smoking cigarettes held in one of those long cigarette holders while standing in a row waiting to be chosen by one of the men. I could smell the booze they were drinking all the way upstairs.

"Drink up, gentlemen," Madame would say as the ladies played with the men.

Some ladies sat on the men's laps laughing, and others slow danced to the music. I wasn't too young to understand what was going on. I could hear them in the room sometimes, but I never said anything because there was an unspoken rule in Madame's house—stay in a child's place. I only needed to be popped once, so I knew better to say anything. Sometimes Madame would look up and see me peeking and pretend not to see me. Then there were other times when she would shoo me away. Of course, I'd run back to my room like the obedient girl I was and continue to do whatever I was doing prior.

When I turned sixteen, I was already 5'8" and 155 pounds. I started going to the salon to have my hair blown out, and it hung midway down my back. This was also the time my curves decided to make an appearance. Although I had soft facial features, I was considered androgynous-looking to most, but my breasts were 38DD, and my waist was 24 inches while my hips were 36 inches. My blossoming into a woman was becoming a problem for my daddy.

It's at this time that he bought me my first car, a midnight blue Coupe. He said I was too fine to be walking, but I knew that was bullshit because I didn't have my driver's license yet. He just didn't want anybody looking at or talking to me. But, yeah, I gotta agree with my daddy, though. I *was* too fine to be walking. Madame and Daddy asked me if I had a boyfriend on occasions, and I couldn't help but laugh.

"What's so funny?" they both would ask me.

"Oh, nothing. I don't have a boyfriend, but y'all will be the first to know *if* or *when* I do. I promise," I said, chuckling as I walked away.

If they knew how much I was checking Pinky out, they would probably lose their fucking minds. Pinky was the most beautiful lady in Madame's house. She was a voluptuous, caramel complexion, soft-spoken woman who always wore a feather boa around her neck. Her roller-set shoulder-length black hair cascaded to one side, held by a large crystal barrette. She wore bright red lipstick and a demure personality that was the epitome of sensuality. I loved that about her, and I guess the men did, too, because they always chose her the most out of all the ladies.

One evening, Madame told me to come upstairs to her room because she needed to talk to me about something important.

"Alright, I'll be right there," I yelled from the bottom of the wide staircase.

As I walked up the stairs, Pinky was walking down. She smiled and winked at me but kept going as there was no small-talking with me allowed. My stomach flipped when she winked at me; I thought she was the prettiest woman in the whole wide world! *Mmm mmm.*

When I arrived at Madame's room, she told me to shut the door and sit down.

"Hazel Blue baby, I need to tell you something."

"Yes, ma'am," I said, sitting on the bench at the foot of her bed.

"You must promise me that you won't tell anybody what I'm about to show you."

I assured her that her secret was safe with me.

Madame walked over to the left side of her bed.

"Hand me that poker from the fireplace, baby."

I did as I was told, and Madame commenced to pull up four of the floorboards.

"Come a little closer, baby," she said, gesturing to me with her hand. "Look here."

Madame pointed to the hole.

"I've been saving my money in these floorboards since you were born 'cause I don't trust banks. I'm not sure how much is in here, but if anything should ever happen to me, this money is yours. Take it and get the hell out of here. The only person you can tell is your daddy because I trust him to do right by you."

"Yes, ma'am," I said, my eyes wide.

"ONLY you're daddy. NOT your brothers or Pinky."

"What!" I said with a look of shock.

"Oh yeah, baby girl. Madame don't miss nothing around here," she said, shaking her head and chuckling.

How in the hell…? I thought, totally confused.

"Okay, I won't tell anybody but my daddy, Madame. I swear."

"I believe you, baby, I believe you. Promise me one more thing, baby, before I let you go."

"Sure. Anything," I said.

"Continue to go to school and become a lawyer or something. This life ain't for you, honey. You're better than this shit," she said, rubbing my left cheek softly with the back of her hand.

"Yes, ma'am, I will. I'll go to school and become a lawyer or something," I said bashfully and looked down at the floor.

Madame chuckled. "That's my trick baby." she said pinching both of my cheeks. I didn't like being called a trick baby because that shit was disrespectful, and it hurt my feelings a little. But I never said anything to Madame because she was too good to me. Hell, she gave me her last name, for God's sake!

By the time I turned seventeen, I was a third-degree black belt, and my brothers had moved to Chicago permanently to live with my daddy. Daddy had Stanley and Marcus out there hustling right alongside him. Stanley was five years older than me, and Marcus was seven years older. But they had more brawn than brains. I would hear Daddy cursing them out when I came to visit.

"You muthafuckas must have shit for brains or something! Y'all be giving dope away like government cheese out here in these streets! You not cutting the shit enough! Motherfuckers are OD'ing out here. Damn!" he'd say, slamming his fist down.

"I know, Pops, but when somebody OD's, everybody wants some of the same shit they got," Marcus told him.

"Yeah, Pops. They won't stop coming. The shit is crazy," Stanley said, shaking his head, agreeing with Marcus.

"You're right, but I can't have them out here dying on me, man. It'll bring too much unwanted attention our way if you know what I mean."

When the yelling stopped, their attention was focused on me. Stanley would challenge my martial art skills from time to time to see if I still had it. I guess he was trying to prove to me that he wasn't a sucker, but I would kick his ass every time. Marcus kept trying to convince me that I needed to know how to handle a gun, but I didn't want anything to do with a gun at all!

On the streets, my brothers were a force to be reckoned with. Nobody fucked with them because they were even bigger than my daddy.

Every Friday night, without fail, Daddy would call Madame's and tell me to get dressed because he was on his way to pick me up. He always took my brothers and me out to eat somewhere on Fridays.

"Come on, Hazel Blue! Your daddy is outside, baby

girl," Pinky would yell upstairs to me.

"Tell him I'm coming, please," I'd yell back with either one foot in a boot or one arm in my coat while looking for my designer leather bucket bag.

I was so excited because I couldn't wait to finally get out of the house. I'd go outside, and as usual, Daddy would be driving a black Town Car and not his convertible. I guess the convertible was too small for all of us to fit in, especially with Stanley and Marcus' long-ass legs.

"You look beautiful, Lovely," Daddy told me.

"Stanley bought you a silver fox, and you are wearing it well, baby girl," he crooned.

"Thank you, Daddy," I said while blushing and reaching for the back door to get in, but Daddy would stop me dead in my tracks.

"What you doing? You ain't a whore. I thought I taught you better than that, Lovely. Get in the front seat where you belong, baby girl."

Daddy came around the car and opened my door for me because my brothers were joking and talking shit in the backseat, not paying me any mind.

Daddy would either take us to the steakhouse at the Paradise Room on 85th because I adored the panoramic views of downtown Chicago while we were eating or the Chestnut Room downstairs in my favorite upscale department store if he was taking me shopping.

During dinner, Daddy would ask me how I was doing in school. if I needed anything, if anybody was fucking with me, and of course, the boyfriend question would come up. He would wait for my answers, too! My daddy was amazing, but he would take me directly home after dinner because he was either going back to the streets or going to spend time with one of his many girlfriends. I always hated when our time came to an end. I would pout and refuse to get out of the car when he pulled up to Madame's.

"Come on now, baby. Don't look like that. You know I would take you with me if I could, right?"

"Yeah, I know, but I don't wanna go home yet. It's boring," I would whine.

Daddy would sigh, give me a wad of money, and walk me to the door with his one arm around my shoulders. Then he would give me a kiss and tell me he would call me in the morning while jogging back to his car.

"Bye, Daddy. Bye, Stanley. Bye, Marcus," I'd yell while slowly walking backwards into the doorway.

"Bye, big head," they would both shout out as Daddy pulled off.

Beep! Beep!

"You got a big head," I'd yell back, but they didn't hear me.

Those big heads spoiled my ass, too! They bought me nothing but the best of everything! Clothes, furs, jewelry, you name it. I had about five fur coats: one full-length black mink coat, a white mink three-quarter jacket, a chinchilla jacket, and a full-length silver fox. Let's not talk about jewelry! I could open my own jewelry store with all the jewelry they bought for me. I guess they needed something to do with their money. At seventeen, what the hell did I need with half of this shit anyway? But I didn't refuse any of it, I bet you that! I was observant and extremely humble. Half of my humbleness came from my personality, and the other half was from the discipline I learned in martial arts school and the life lessons Madame and Daddy taught me. They had that shit on lock! They made sure I was book smart as well as street smart. They didn't sugarcoat a damn thing. They gave it to me straight with no chaser. Sometimes the shit they were laying on me was a bit harsh to hear, but I'm pretty sure I'm going to need those lessons at some point in my life. I just know it.

*****

Madame passed away from a massive heart attack when I was eighteen. It happened two months before I graduated high school, and it broke my heart because she was the only mother I had ever known. I think I cried for two months straight. Daddy, on the other hand, didn't know how to handle her passing or how to comfort me. So, he did what he knew best—he bought me presents and gave me money. He made sure to take me out more so I wouldn't have to be alone in the house that much. If he couldn't take me himself, he saw to it that either Stanley or Marcus did.

I know Madame's passing hurt Daddy even though he tried to act tough about it. I would see his eyes get watery when we would talk about her, but I let him be and never mentioned I saw it.

After the funeral, the lawyer read the will, and Madame left everything to me. I couldn't believe that! My high school guidance counselor encouraged me to apply to law school. I did and was accepted on a full mathematics scholarship to a law school in New York. Madame would've been so proud of me. My brothers, the ladies, and Daddy threw me a huge graduation party. I even got a kiss on the lips from Pinky that night!

"Congratulations," she said, smiling after kissing me.

I thought I would faint! Daddy saw her kiss me, but he just shook his head. He didn't seem fazed by it.

He thought it would be a good idea for me to put the house up for sale since I would be going to college in New York. He also suggested that he and my brothers move with me since I've never been away from home before. Not to mention I was only eighteen, so I agreed.

I sold the house but not before I got the money from under the floorboards in Madame's room. Madame had over five hundred thousand dollars! Add that with the three hundred thousand I had saved through the years from my daddy plus the two million dollars from selling the brownstone. My ass was rich! I gave Pinky twenty-thousand dollars, and she started crying so hard I thought she was gonna pass out. Snot was coming out of her nose and everything!

"Nobody has ever been this good to me before…and for nothing," Pinky said, blowing her nose and shaking her head in disbelief.

She threw her arms around my neck so tight that my reflexes made me grab her around the waist. She backed up, looked me in my eyes, and thanked me again. Then she gave me another kiss!

"Wow," I said bashfully, "It's all yours, too, Pinky. You don't have to give anybody a cut of it."

"You've always been such a beautiful young lady, Lovely, inside and out," she said. "You have no idea how much I appreciate this, baby girl. Thank you from the bottom of my heart."

"Well, I couldn't leave my girl out in the cold, now could I?" I said, winking at her.

"A smooth talker with pretty eyes, too, I see," she commented, smiling while reaching out to give me another hug before she left.

I sure wish I could take her with me instead of them boys, that's for damn sure, I thought to myself.

I didn't tell Daddy about the money I gave Pinky, the money Madame had left me under the floorboard, or the money I had saved. I only told him about the money from the sale of the house, and that wasn't even the whole truth. Shit, that was my business.

Stanley, Marcus, Daddy, and I moved to Sugar Hill in Harlem, New York. Since I was used to living in a big house, I purchased a three-story brownstone in Hamilton Heights on 147th Street between Convent and Amsterdam Avenues. The first floor was for daddy, and the second floor was for me because it had more space. I hid my money in different locations throughout my section of the brownstone in the event one of my brothers got greedy and tried to steal some of it. This way, I would know it was missing and hopefully prevent myself from losing it all. The third floor was for Stanley and Marcus.

The university was within walking distance of the house, and thank God, too, because I didn't know a damn thing about New York yet. Daddy didn't have to go back to the streets if he didn't want to, but it was in his blood. So, he reached out to his New York connections, and it was like we never left Chicago. Nobody ever knew I existed because

I was accustomed to being hidden and keeping a low profile, but Daddy relied on my math skills a lot. So, I got to learn the business on the down-low.

During my junior year at the university, I fell for one of my law professors. Her name was Francis. Francis was a soft-spoken, curvy, middle-aged, married black woman who wore cat eyeglasses. She often wore pencil skirts, medium high heel pumps with bow blouses, and her signature vanilla perfume. She had a fair complexion and wore her naturally curly auburn-colored hair in a short, neatly cropped style. There's something about a soft-spoken woman that turns me on. I'm not sure why, though. Francis would deliberately rub on my arm whenever she returned one of my graded papers. Once after class, she requested to see me, and I obliged her.

"Lovely," she said.

"Yeah, what's up, Francis?" I answered nonchalantly, not wanting to sound too eager.

"I wanted to know if you would like to get coffee with me sometime," she said softly.

"Sure. I like coffee, Francis. When you wanna go, sweetheart? Oh, and I'm the type of person who doesn't like to hold long, unnecessary conversations or waste time. So, how about right now?" I asked.

"Alright, ummm, there's a coffee shop around the corner. We can go there," she said, blushing and pretending to fix her hair.

She grabbed her purse, I picked up my books, and we walked together to the coffee shop. We ordered two cups of coffee, an apple turnover for her, and a cranberry muffin for me. While we waited for our coffee to cool off a bit,

Francis started the conversation by informing me about her inability to have children, which was why her husband was cheating on her.

What a fucking icebreaker! Sorry, but I'm interested in her, not her husband or their marriage.

Besides, I wasn't taking courses to become a marriage counselor, so I changed the subject to *us*. She said she wanted to get to know me better, so I gave her some bullshit story about my life.

After that day, we went for coffee a few more times and engaged in more small talk while continuing to flirt with each other. One day, I told her that I wanted something more than just coffee and muffins, so I asked her if she wanted to go for dinner, and she said yes. I picked her up in a Town Car the following afternoon at the corner of the coffee shop and took her to Ralph's Seafood Restaurant in the Bronx. We laughed and told nasty jokes over lobster bisque, shrimp scampi, and a bottle of Pinot Grigio.

After dinner, she said she wanted to have sex, and I damn sure wasn't gonna make her wait! That wine went straight to her head, and I wasn't complaining. She didn't have to say another word. *CHECK, PLEASE!*

I called for another Town Car and instructed the driver to drop us off at the Stover Motor Lodge on Underhill Avenue. It was the closet motel from the restaurant, and I couldn't wait to see what she was working with. Francis had other plans, though. She decided she wanted a little something right there in the backseat of the cab. She grabbed my hand and shoved it under her skirt!

"Oh shit," I whispered, looking at her. "Is it me, or is it the alcohol, sweetie?

"A little bit of both," she said, grinning.

"I ain't mad. Shit, anything that gets you in the mood like this is alright with me, but damn, baby, you want it right now?" I asked, working my hand between those thick thighs and up to her panties.

"Wait a minute, baby. Let me take my ring off. I don't want the diamonds to scratch you, because my hands move fast once I'm up in that, mama."

She blushed and looked away. *Shit, don't get shy now,* I said to myself while looking at her as I put the ring in my pocket.

"Alright, baby, where were we?" I asked, giving her wet kisses on the lips.

I rolled over slightly to my left side so I could put my arm under her back and around her waist while I laid my head on her chest for leverage. I wanted to prevent her from moving too much because I was about to finger pop the fuck out of her pussy.

"Ooh, look what I found," I said, sticking my tongue out the side of my mouth as I put my finger deep in her vagina and began popping it fast and hard.

Francis started squeezing and hugging my head, making so much noise that the driver slowed down to look through his rearview mirror.

"Hey! What's going on back there?"

I laughed at his dumb-ass question and slid down to my knees to bury my face in her stomach while my fingers continued assaulting her pussy. His ass knew what was going on, and I wasn't fucking stopping either. I had a rhythm going.

I love this freaky shit she got me doing! He's just mad he can't get none.

"Mind your business and keep driving," I told him through my "yeah, baby" whispers.

He sucked his teeth but did as I said.

"Gurlllll, you don't even know! Wait until I get your fine ass in that room," I said while slowly finger-fucking her pussy and dropping more wet kisses on her lips.

We pulled up to the motel, and before we got out, I told the driver to wait for us. We went inside, and I paid for the room. When we got on the elevator, I cupped Francis's ass cheeks the entire time. Once we got to the room, I was completely turned off! It wasn't clean, and it smelled like sex, cigarettes, stale liquor, and weed. Nah, I wasn't going anywhere near that bed. I don't know what I was expecting from a motor lodge anyway. I should've known better.

"We're leaving, baby," I said, grabbing her hand and exiting the filthy room, I didn't even bother getting a refund.

Once we got back in the car, I finished Francis off and had the driver drop her off around the corner from the coffee shop where she parked her car. I gave her a kiss goodnight and then directed the driver to my house, where I took my ass to sleep.

Francis's never-ending stories about her marriage were getting old and turning me the fuck off. I never got the opportunity to have sex with her the way I wanted to anyway, so I bounced and never entertained the thought of being with her again.

Now here's Nicki. I met her at the park on 145th Street and Lenox Avenue while playing handball with a couple of my guy friends from college. She walked over to the court and introduced herself as I dried the sweat off my face. A girl who is bold enough to walk up to another girl and introduce herself is sexy as hell to me! I was intrigued by her confidence, so I didn't mind kicking it with her.

Our game was over, so I told the guys I'd see them later and then started a conversation with her. Nicki was cute—not my usual type, but cute. She was brown-skinned, about 5'5" tall, had shoulder-length brown hair, and skinny with a decent taste in clothes. I usually like a woman with some meat on her bones because grinding on a skinny woman can be painful at times, but because she had a cute face and was bold as hell, she piqued my interest.

I took her roller skating, bowling, and to the movies, but I preferred going out to eat. We had sex like four times at her place—if you can even call it that because all we did was grind and tongue kiss. And yes, grinding on her made my pussy bone sore as shit! That's all she wanted to do, though! She said she didn't like the way fingers felt inside her pussy. *Say what!* I didn't even get to taste her because she would climax so quick from the grinding! No finger popping, no pussy licking, no bootie nibbling, none of that. *This shit is whack!* But she obviously enjoyed herself because she started being all clingy and demanding more of my time. Nope, I don't find needy or pushy women attractive, so I stopped going around her.

Then there was Barbara Jean, a pretty-ass, light-skinned, big-boned young lady from South Carolina. She stood about 5'4" and had freckles. She had a slight overbite, wore her hair in flat twist pulled up in a high ponytail, and always had that fresh out the shower smell.

Barbara Jean had her own apartment but was an

exhibitionist; she preferred fucking outside. She would take me to the rooftop of her apartment building, where I would hem her up next to the exit door with my tongue down her throat and fingers in her pussy. Barbara Jean loved the idea of getting caught with a girl. Shit, she had my ass getting excited about getting caught, too! After about two months, though, I had to stop seeing her because she was loud and talked about people too damn much. I don't like women who carry themselves like that. She never asked me for money or anything, but I knew she needed some since she had recently lost her job. I paid her rent for about six months and gave her five thousand dollars for groceries and other stuff until she got another job. I didn't come around anymore after that. She had my number, and I told her to use it if she needed to, but she never did.

I played hard, but I studied even harder while at law school and managed to graduate magna cum laude, receiving my law degree at the ripe old age of twenty-six.

"Madame, this is for you," I said while looking up towards the heavens when called on stage to receive my degree.

Daddy was diagnosed with rheumatoid arthritis three years after I graduated, but things got worse a year after that. Both of my brothers got locked up, but I couldn't represent them in court due to our relationship, even though we weren't blood relatives. That shit is crazy, right?

Daddy's fingers and the joints of his knees had become so deformed and painful that he couldn't take care of himself, let alone hustle. I had to hire an around-the-clock nurse to help him with his daily needs. Plus, I had to buy all his medications, and that shit wasn't cheap! Then I had to turn around and bail those two knucklehead brothers of mine out of jail, which cost me a whopping fifty thousand dollars each despite it being their first offense. Of course, I knew I was getting ripped off, but there wasn't a damn thing I could do about the shit.

I made decent money as a lawyer, but I wasn't representing any big-time clients yet. So, I was dipping into my savings most of the time. You don't pay attention to money when you're getting that shit hand over fist. It's not until you're not getting it like that anymore that you notice you gotta chill spending reckless. My money was going fast! So, I hung up my lawyer's hat for a minute and got out there to work it like my daddy taught me. I got the brains and the brawn, so my brothers better get used to having a new sheriff in town. Hell, I gotta make sure me and Daddy are straight! I know Madame is turning over in her grave right now because I'm out here hustling, but I don't have much of a choice right now. I'll just do it for a little while until I can stack my money up again.

A few weeks later…

"Stanley, take the west end corner of 138th Street on Convent Avenue by the supermarket. Marcus, you take 138th Street and 8th Avenue so you can catch the stragglers coming down the hill. I'm gonna work the corner by that payphone on 7th Avenue and 143rd Street. Page me if you need me, and I'll call you back from that number. Better yet, I'm gonna page you from that number, so write it down 'cause that's the phone I'll be using while I'm over there. Alright?"

"Alright, sis. We got this," they both said.

I was making a killing! I was in those streets whether rain, sleet, or snow. It didn't matter if it was a heatwave! My ass was out there just like the postman. Only I was prettier. I was able to recoup my funds and then some in no time! But hustling is addictive, so I told myself that I would only do this for a little while longer.

I can't mess with any women while I'm out here either because I gots to stay focused, and beautiful women are like kryptonite to me. They distract my ass way too much! I had a Thursday ritual that kept me sane, though. I needed something to take my mind off the streets every now and then. Every Thursday afternoon at two o'clock, I would drive down to 125th Street and 8th Avenue and buy my periodical from Mr. Pepper's newsstand on the corner. Then I would go into the soul food restaurant and order my favorite dish—chicken and waffles with a glass of ice-cold milk. I liked to sit in a booth so I could spread out with my editorial excellence and read it comfortably and uninterrupted while waiting for my food.

I looked around for Rita, the waitress who usually takes my order, but she may have been in the back somewhere because I didn't see her anywhere on the floor.

Oh well, she'll come over when she notices I'm here, I said to myself.

I picked up the paper and started to read it, when suddenly…

"Excuse me," a soft-spoken woman said.

When I lifted my head from the newspaper to respond, I literally gasped. *Who is this essence of beauty standing before me, looking so sweet and innocent in her green and white waitress dress with the riffled apron?*

I nearly knocked over the salt and pepper shakers sitting on the table. *Damn, she's one gorgeous woman.* My mouth was ajar for a minute. She was most definitely Janet Jackson's doppelganger, and she was rocking the same curly hairstyle from Janet's *Velvet Rope* album!

"Hello, my name is Lark," she said with the sincerest smile while placing the menu on the table. "I'll be your waitress today. Are you ready to order, or do you need a minute to look over the menu?"

"Hey, Lark," I said, clearing my throat and looking around, acting like I was still searching for Rita. "Rita isn't here today, huh?"

"No, Rita doesn't work here anymore," she replied.

"Oh really! Is she alright?" I asked with concern.

"I'm not sure. A lot of people have been asking for her, though. I just started today, so I didn't know her."

"Hmmm, alright then. I hope she's okay," I said, raising my eyebrow.

I folded my newspaper and gave Lark my order.

"I'll have the chicken and waffles with an ice-cold glass of milk, please."

"Okay, got it. Are there any specific pieces of chicken you want?"

"Yes, I'll take a breast and a leg, please."

"Sure. I'll be right back with your order," she said, picking up the menu.

"Okay, thanks. By the way, has anyone ever told you that you look like Janet Jackson?"

"Yes! I'm told that practically every day," she responded with a chuckle. "I wish I had Janet Jackson money to go along with these looks," she said, still smiling, "I'll be right back with your order."

This woman had me mesmerized. I felt my mouth hanging open and had to close it yet again.

A short while later, Lark returned and placed the syrup on the table, then sat down the milk with a straw.

"Here you go," she said, putting my chicken and waffles in front of me.

"Thank you, sweetheart," I said.

"You're welcome."

"Can you bring me some extra napkins, a straw, and a glass of water, please?"

"Sure, but ahh, I gave you a straw with your milk," she replied, a confused expression on her face.

"I know, sweetheart, but I don't like using the same straw from my milk to drink my water. It makes the water cloudy."

"Oh! I didn't think of that. I'll be right back," she said, hurrying behind the counter.

"Here you go. Will there be anything else I can get for you?"

"No, I'm straight. Thank you, sweetheart."

"You're welcome."

While eating, I watched this woman's every move like I had never seen a woman before. *Damn!* I said to myself, cutting my chicken to put on top of my waffle. *It's been a while since I've been with a woman, and I do miss the affection of one. Hell, I might have to reconsider having relations. I'm gonna ask her which days she'll be working because those are going to be the days I come back here to eat!*

"Hey there!" Lark said, walking towards my table all

chipper. "Was the food to your liking?"

"Indeed, it was, sweetheart. Thanks for asking," I said, wiping the milk from my top lip.

"Can I get you anything else, or are you ready for the check?"

"You can bring the check. Thanks."

"I'll be right back." When Lark returned with the check, she asked, "Will you be paying with cash or charge?"

"Cash. Hey, do you mind if I ask you a question, Lark?"

"Yes…I mean, no. Sure, you can ask me a question."

"Which days are you scheduled to work here?"

"This week, I'll be working through the weekend, and next week, I'm scheduled to work Tuesday through Thursday."

"If you don't mind, what are your hours?"

"No, I don't mind at all. I work from two o'clock till closing, which is around ten o'clock, but we can't leave until eleven o'clock because of the cleanup."

"Good. I'll be in tomorrow around six o'clock for dinner and every day after that when you're scheduled to work. I like looking at you, and I want to see more of you if that's alright," I said, raising an eyebrow.

"Sure…okay," Lark said, smiling while playing with her apron strings. "Heck, everybody's gotta eat, right?"

"Cool," I said, smiling and putting my newspaper under my arm.

Lark had the sweetest smile. *She's so fucking cute.*

"Here's the money for the check, and here's a little something for you. Thank you for the great service."

"Twenty dollars! Wow, thank you. That's so sweet of you," Lark said as she put the tip in her apron pocket.

"Sweets for the sweet. See you tomorrow," I said, winking on my way to the door.

Lark waved goodbye.

The following morning…

Oowee! It's cold in here! I quickly rushed to put on my thick terrycloth bathrobe after getting out of bed. *What time is it anyway?*

When I went to turn the heat up on the thermostat, I looked at the time.

It's only seven-thirty in the morning? Damn.

Wanting to compare the temperature in the house to the temperature outside, I opened the door and stepped out my brownstone.

Yikes! It's cold for real, for real.

Slamming the wrought iron door shut, I quickly came back inside and turned on the television for the weather report.

Hmmm, no wonder it's so cold in here. It's only twenty-four degrees right now, and the high is only going to be thirty-two. Shit!

After turning off the TV, I walked into the kitchen where the nurse was cooking oatmeal and making a fruit bowl for Daddy.

"Good morning, Nurse Enid. How's Daddy doing this morning?"

"Good morning, Lovely. He's doing as well as can be expected. I'm going to give him a warm Epsom salt bath and a massage. I'll sit him up in the chair after he eats breakfast."

"Alright, I'll be in to see him before I leave."

"Alright, dear," she said, leaving the kitchen.

I made myself a bagel with cream cheese and jelly and a cup of hot chocolate. When I finished, I ran upstairs to get dressed. I decided to leave my hair out, tucked behind my ears, and wear my workwear brown designer overalls with the matching sweatshirt and knit cap. Then I threw on my wheat construction boots and cream-colored leather puffer jacket with the detachable red fox hood.

My knucklehead brothers had already left, so I'll talk to them on the block.

"Good morning, Daddy. How you doing?" I asked, walking into his bedroom and kissing him on the forehead.

"Hey, my Lovely! I'm in a little pain, but I'll be alright, baby. The nurse is taking good care of me."

"You need me to bring you something when I come back?"

"No, baby. The nurse got me," he said, pulling on the hem of the nurse's skirt.

I just shook my head and mouthed "sorry" to the nurse. She nodded her head, gesturing it was alright.

I gave Daddy another kiss and left the house.

Shit, the nurse blocked me in. That's alright; I'm not gonna make her move her car. I'll drive the Jeep today. It matches the color of my jacket anyway.

*****

Stanley and Marcus had two new dudes they wanted me to put on, so I had to designate them a post. I instructed my brothers to teach them how *we* do things.

"Oh shit! It's seven o'clock. Y'all got this, right? Because

I gotta leave," I asked them.

"Yeah, we got this, Haze."

"Okay, call me if you need me for something," I told them while jogging to my Jeep.

There's no way I was gonna miss seeing my girl Lark tonight.

"Yeah, no problem, Haze," they said, knowing better than to call me sis outside.

I got to the restaurant around 7:30 p.m. and parked on the corner by the liquor store to go inside the restaurant.

Oh good, a booth is available.

I hated sharing a table with people when I came here because the place isn't that big to begin with. I just can't get comfortable.

I took off my jacket and blew into my hands to warm them up.

"Hey, you!" Lark softly shouted as she walked across the dining room floor. "I thought you stood me up."

Lark smiled at me, making me smile back.

"Nah, I'll never do that to you, sweetheart."

"Good," she replied, blushing.

The only thing I could think about while looking at her blushing was how much I wanted to spoil her. Let's keep it real, though; I would first have to know this woman for at least thirty days before I started spoiling her. (LOL!)

"Do you want a menu, or do you want me to tell you about our Friday special?" Lark asked.

"Sure, baby, tell me about the Friday special," I said, still blowing into my hands. "But can I get a hot cup of tea first, sweetheart?"

"Of course. I'll be right back."

Once Lark returned with the tea, she told me about the day's special.

"On Fridays, our special is fried fish."

"I like fish. Go 'head."

"It's fried porgies or whiteys, macaroni and cheese, collard greens, and your choice of hush puppies or candied yams."

"That sounds good. I'll have it all!"

"You want both types of fish?" Lark asked.

"No, lemme get the whiteys because I don't like fighting with my food. Porgies have too many bones, sweetie," I said, frowning.

"Fighting with your food…that's funny. Okay, I'll be right back," Lark said, then walked away to put in the order.

"Wait a minute, sweetie. Can you bring me a glass of water and another cup of tea before you put that order in?"

"No problem. I'll be right back with your drinks."

If I'm not mistaken, I swear she skipped off when she left to put in my order. That's a good sign. Please, Lord, let her be single.

When she returned, I told Lark the food was delicious as we engaged in small talk in between her taking other orders.

"Hey, Lark, I need to ask you something."

"Sure, you can ask me anything," she said, smiling.

"Are you single, sweetheart?"

She giggled and replied, "How did I know you were gonna ask me that? Yes. I'm very single."

"Well, that's good news," I said, pretending to wipe sweat from my forehead with the back of my hand, "So, what time do you get off tonight?"

"I get off at ten o'clock, but I won't walk out the door until eleven, remember?"

"Oh yeah. Please forgive me, sweetheart. I have a lot on my mind. Well, I enjoy talking with you and was wondering if we could continue our conversation later? Can I come back when you get off?" I asked after eating the last piece of fish on my plate.

"Of course, you can come back. I like talking to you, too," Lark said, smiling.

"Cool! I'll see you at eleven then."

"See you at eleven," Lark said, wiggling her fingers and smiling before clearing the empty plates from the table.

Yes! I thought, excited that I would get to see her outside of her place of employment.

Look, I have some moves to make before coming back to scoop up Lark, so I'm going to let my homie take over and tell my story from here.

*****

Lovely made sure she was outside in front of the restaurant when Lark walked out the door because she didn't want her waiting outside in the cold. Lark was prepared, though. She wore a chunky green turtleneck sweater, a matching beanie knit hat with a pom-pom on top, and a pair of jeans stuffed into black lace-up combat boots with a long black hooded snorkel coat. She was cute as she wanted to be.

Lovely unlocked the door from the inside, and Lark climbed in.

"Mmmm, I like the smell of cherry-scented air

fresheners," Lark said, breathing in deeply.

"I'm glad you like it, sweetheart. 'Cause if you didn't, I swear I was gonna throw it right out the window."

"You're so silly."

"I just thought of something, Lark. It's late. How do you usually get home, sweetheart?"

"Oh, I take the train or the bus."

"How far do you live from here?"

"I live in the 96th Street projects."

"Nah, you're not taking the train OR the bus tonight. I'm taking you home."

Lovely paused to look over at Lark's expression. She didn't want to seem pushy.

"If that's alright with you, of course," she added.

"Hell yeah, that's alright with me. You feel how cold it is out there?!" Lark said, making them both laugh.

Lovely pulled off and found parking under a streetlamp in front of a church on the next corner.

"Hey, I didn't want to say anything at first because I know everybody compliments you on your eyes, but…I think your eyes are so pretty and wildly sexy," Lark said, blushing.

"Thank you, sweetheart. I'm told they're beautiful a lot for sure, but nobody ever called them "wildly sexy before," Lovely said, also blushing, which was a first since she only blushed for her daddy.

"Well, they are," Lark told her. "By the way, you never told me your name."

"My name is Lovely, but everyone calls me Hazel Blue for obvious reasons."

"Well, can I call you Lovely? It fits you. Don't get me

wrong, Hazel Blue fits you, too, of course. But I think you're lovely, as well."

"Aww, that was sweet. So, for you, I'll let you call me Lovely, but only you, though," Lovely said, winking, "So now that I have you all to myself, tell me more about yourself. Wait. Hold that thought. Are you warm enough, or do you want me to turn the heat up a little bit?" Lovely asked as she reached for the knob.

"No. Actually, I was just about to take off my coat," Lark said, fanning herself and dabbing the sweat from her upper lip. "I didn't dress for a car today."

"Sorry about that. Let me turn the heat down then. I can't turn it off, though, because the windows will fog up from our body heat."

"I understand," Lark said.

"Okay, is this temperature better for you?" Lovely asked.

Lark placed her hands in front of the vent.

"Yeah, the temperature is fine now," Lark replied, removing her coat anyway.

"No doubt. I want you to be comfortable. Go ahead, sweetie. I'm listening. Tell me about yourself," Lovely told her.

"Okay, well, I'm twenty-six and originally from Baltimore, Maryland. I have two younger sisters, Karen and Stacey, and we all live with my mother and stepfather. I write poetry and paint a little bit. I even won five hundred dollars once for a poem I submitted to a popular black magazine a couple of years ago."

"Really?! Wow! I never met a real poet before. Okay, so now I'm intrigued. Tell me more," Lovely said, smiling and making Lark blush.

"Right now, I'm working at the restaurant so I can save up enough money to get my own place. It's too crowded at my mom's house. It's a three-bedroom apartment, and I share a room with Karen, my middle sister, and my baby sister Stacey has special needs so she's gotta have her own room because of her medical equipment and stuff."

"Wow," Lovely said, hanging on her every word.

"You're probably thinking I'm too old to be living with my mother, huh?"

Before Lovely could answer, Lark continued.

"It's expensive out here. Plus, I help my mother out with Stacey when I have free time so she can get a break."

"Nah, you're helping your mother out with your sister, and that's admirable. Don't concern yourself with what other people think about you living with your mother at your age, 'cause they don't shit what you eat, baby. Besides, you could be out here doing worse things."

"You have a way with words, don't you? Oh wow! When the streetlight bounced off your face, your left eye glowed like a cat. See, there goes that 'wildly sexy' I was talking about," Lark said, smiling.

Lovely laughed. "Yeah, I've been known to glow sometimes, sweetheart."

Her response made them both laugh.

"I like your sense of humor. Mmm, I'm going to read one of my poems at a poetry slam tomorrow and wanted to invite you. It's on the lower east side in Hell's Kitchen. I know it's the last minute, but—"

"Hold on. Slow down, sweetheart," Lovely said, chuckling. "I would be honored to listen to an award-winning poet recite her poem at a poetry slam. I'd be crazy to miss that. Thanks for the invite. What time does it start?"

"Yay!" Lark said, clapping her hands like the toy monkey with the cymbals. "I go on at eight o'clock, so I'm going to leave my house at five."

"No problem. I'll be there with bells on," Lovely said, pretending to ring a bell. "How are you getting there?"

"I'm taking the train."

"Not if I'm around. There will be no more mass transit for you, young lady," Lovely said, playfully shaking her pointer finger at her. "I'll pick you up at around…I wanna say five-thirty."

"I like the sound of that! I'll be ready at five-thirty on the dot."

"Alright, sweetheart. Let me get you home," Lovely said, pulling off but was stopped by a red light.

"Lovely, you didn't tell me anything about you. No fair," Lark said, folding her arms and pretending to pout.

"You look so cute making that face, but let's save talking about me for another day, okay?" Lovely asked, half-smiling.

"Okay, another day then," Lark said, unfolding her arms. "It's a casual atmosphere, by the way. So, you can wear jeans."

"Cool. I was just going to ask you about that," Lovely said.

Just then, a car behind them blew their horn.

"Well, damn! What's the rush, mister? The light just turned green. Goodness!" Lovely vented, looking in her rearview mirror to check out the car.

During the drive to Lark's mother's house, Lovely was

smitten with Lark because she seemed kind, patient, had a sense of humor, and was easy to talk to. This made Lovely wonder if Lark could be the one that makes her fall in love.

"I'm the second building on the left, Lovely."

"Cool. Alright, I got you home safely," Lovely stated as she double-parked the car. "Good morning, sweetheart. I'll see you at five-thirty this evening."

Lovely unlocked the passenger door for Lark.

"Good morning?" Lark said, raising her eyebrow. "Oh shit, I just realized it's quarter to two in the morning! Alright, but just so you know, I felt like time stood still while we were together."

"Aww," Lovely responded, her hand on the clutch.

"Alright, see you at five-thirty. And, Lovely, thanks for driving me home."

"You're welcome, sweetheart."

Lovely waited for Lark to walk inside the building before she drove off.

*****

"Coming to the stage from the upper west side of Manhattan, let's give a warm welcome to our next poet… Lark!"

"Good evening. Thank you so much for having me," Lark said, adjusting the mic stand. "Tonight, I'm going to recite one of my newest poems. I call this one 'The Connection'."

They said the eyes are the window to the soul
Is that why you look at me like that?
Like you recognize me

I turn around so my back would be to you
But your stare is piercing my flesh
And I can hear you call my name
But when I turn around, your mouth is shut
My soul decides to answer
How do you know my name?
Perhaps, you followed me here
Stop looking at me like that!
Open your mouth
I wanna hear the sound your voice makes
When you call my name
Did you follow me here from another lifetime?
I'll come to you without hesitation, no delays
You can see my light glowing from within,
Can't you?
Wait! I can see your light glowing, too
Reach for my hand
I swear I'll take it
You
Feel
Familiar
I remember!
At last, you found me!
I forgot I was lost
Oh, how I've missed you
I'm staring at YOU now
My mouth is shut
I call your name and
Our souls begin to dance
As we embrace
We're finally home, and I'll never leave you again

"Bravo! Bravo!" Lovely yelled as she stood up, clapping wildly while the others snapped their fingers.

The audience's applause was like music to Lark's ears. She took a bow, then located Lovely in the crowd and walked over to the table to join her.

"Wow, sweetheart! That was beautiful! Now I see why you won that contest with the magazine. You're the truth, sweetheart—the absolute truth!"

"Thank you," Lark said, blushing while looking into Lovely's face. "I wrote that poem about two years ago, but I didn't have a reason to share it until I met you. I know it's early, but there's something about you."

"Stop it. You're kidding me, right?"

Lark lowered her head.

"I know. That sounds stupid, right?"

"No, sweetheart. That doesn't sound stupid at all. For real, though, that's how I got you feeling right now? Wow! You're nothing short of amazing, you know that?"

Lovely reached out and took Lark's hand.

"Can you still feel that? Does it still feel familiar to you, baby?"

"Yes," Lark answered sincerely.

"Okay, let's get out of here. Go get your coat, sweetheart. I know a nice quiet place where we can get a drink and talk some more. How does that sound?" Lovely asked softly.

"That sounds like...what are we waiting for? I'll be right back!"

Lark ran backstage to get her coat while Lovely waited by the exit door for her. When Lark returned, Lovely reached out for her hand and held on to it a little bit tighter as they walked out of the poetry slam.

"It got colder tonight, didn't it? This wind ain't no joke!" Lovely said, shivering as she noticed that Lark was wearing the same black snorkel.

"Go back inside, baby. I'll bring the car around."

"No, I wanna walk with you," she said in a playful voice.

"Aww, you do? Come on then. I parked around the corner."

Lark put on her hood, and Lovely pulled down her grey sheepskin aviator hat snug to her head, then put her hands inside the pockets of her matching grey sheepskin coat.

Lark hooked her arm with Lovely's, and they hustled down the block towards the car. They stopped in front of a champagne-colored sedan at the corner. Lark thought they were waiting for the light to turn until Lovely opened the passenger side door for her.

"This is yours?!"

"Of course, it's mine, baby. Get in," Lovely said, smiling.

"You see, that's why they named you Lovely," Lark said softly.

Lovely hustled over to the driver's side and turned up the heat once she slid behind the steering wheel. Then she pressed play on the CD player, and Keith Sweat's "Nobody" started playing.

both singing in unison, then looked at each other sweetly with smiles on their faces as Lovely drove off.

*****

"We're here, sweetheart. See over there?" Lovely said, pointing, "This is the place I was talking about. It's called Treks."

Treks was a dimly lit bar-restaurant located at 120th Street on Manhattan Avenue. They walked inside and checked their coats before choosing their seats next to the bar.

"Good evening," the waitress greeted. "Would you ladies be having dinner, drinks, or both?"

"We'll just be having drinks tonight," Lovely told her.

"No problem. What can I get you?"

"I'll have a Black Russian," Lark said

"And I'll have a White Russian," Lovely replied.

"Okay then, I'll be right back with your drinks."

Freddie Jackson's "Love Is Just a Touch Away" played softly in the background. Lark took the initiative and reached across the table to take Lovely's hands in hers after sliding over the floating votive candle placed in the center.

"Is it my turn to learn something about YOU now, Lovely?"

"Of course, sweetheart," Lovely said, clearing her throat. "Alright, here it goes. I was born and raised on the west side of Chicago. My mother died after giving birth to me, so—"

"I'm sorry, baby," Lark whispered while rubbing the top of Lovely's hands with her thumbs.

"Aww, that's alright, sweetheart. I was raised by my dad and a woman affectionately known as Madame. I never missed a mother's love. They made sure of that, so don't feel sorry for me, baby. I'm okay," Lovely said, half-smiling. "I have two stepbrothers from my dad. I'm thirty years old, and when Madame died, my dad, my brothers, and I moved to New York because I was accepted to law school. I graduated from law school when I was twenty-six and passed the bar on my first try."

"Wow! You're a lawyer?"

"I am," Lovely replied, nodding her head proudly.

"That's impressive, Lovely! Congratulations!"

"Thank you, sweetheart."

The waitress returned with their drinks, briefly interrupting their conversation.

"Here you go," she said, giving the Black Russian to Lark and the White Russian to Lovely.

"Thank you," they both said, taking a sip of the drinks.

They continued getting to know each other better and laughed at each other's jokes for the next three hours.

"You ready to go, sweetheart?" Lovely asked.

"Yeah, I'm nice and warm. I feel like I know you better now."

"Yeah, you're nice alright," Lovely responded with a chuckle.

Once in the car, Lark asked Lovely, "Can I kiss you?"

"Of course."

Lark leaned over, and they French kissed slowly over the center console.

"Wow…I feel butterflies in my stomach," Lark said softly.

"Believe it or not, so do I, sweetheart," Lovely said as she picked up Lark's hand and kissed it while they waited for the car to heat up, "What are your plans for tomorrow?"

Lovely continued to hold Lark's hand against her lips.

"I usually go to church, unless you have other plans for

me."

"Nah, go to church, baby. I'll come through when you get home. Just call me, and I'll swing by and pick you up. Okay?"

"Okay, I will. I really enjoyed our time together tonight, and thank you for coming to my show and making me feel special, Lovely."

"It was my pleasure," Lovely said, looking over at her.

"Can I get another kiss before you drive off?"

"Absolutely."

However, this time, Lovely pulled Lark closer to her, gripping the back of her neck and giving her a deeper, more passionate kiss—heavy breathing and all.

"Damn, girl. You got my lips on fire," Lovely told her, biting her bottom lip. "Let me take you home before you wind up somewhere else—like in my bed." she said pulling off.

Lark laid back with her eyes closed until they reached her building. She had just a tiny bit too much to drink.

"Alright, baby, you're home safe and sound," Lovely announced as she pulled into a parking space.

She looked over at Lark, who was opening her eyes very slowly.

"Are you okay, sweetheart? You need me to walk you upstairs?" Lovely asked her, unbuckling her seatbelt.

"No, I'm okay. I was just resting my eyes, but I guess I fell asleep, huh?" Lark said, chuckling softly.

"Okay, baby, I'll see you tomorrow after church. Good night."

"Good night, and thank you again for a fantastic evening," Lark said, winking as she got out of the car.

*****

The following day, Lovely received the call from Lark telling her that she was home. So, she dropped everything and rushed over to pick her up and drive out to the mall in Union City, New Jersey.

"Hey, Lovely," Lark called while looking out her window at the "Welcome to the Garden State" exit sign.

"Yeah, sweetheart, what's up?"

"Why did we come out here?" Lark asked with a look of confusion on her face.

"Well…we're here because I'm taking you on a shopping spree today, baby."

"Oh my god!" Lark yelled but quickly covered her mouth with both hands. "Sorry. I never went on a shopping spree before. Thank you, Lovely! Why are you doing this for me?"

"Because I can AND want to, sweetheart," Lovely replied as she pulled into the mall entrance. "Come here."

Lovely grabbed Lark's hand while leaning in to plant a kiss on her forehead.

"Don't ask so many questions when you're with me. Just enjoy yourself, baby. Okay?"

"Okay," Lark said, practically jumping out of the car.

Lark bought so much stuff that they needed customer service to help them push the four shopping carts out to the car.

"It's a good thing I drove my Jeep today," Lovely commented, laughing as she helped put the bags inside.

She enjoyed making Lark happy, and money was no

object. Sixty-five days had gone by, and Lovely dated Lark exclusively, including picking her up every night from work to drive her home. But on Lark's days off, Lovely dropped those streets to spend time with her. They went to the movies, museums, shopping, out to dinner, and even did horse carriage rides through Central Park.

After dinner one night, while waiting at a stoplight, Lovely turned to Lark and said, "I told myself that I would wait at least thirty days before I asked you to be my lady. The first day I laid my eyes on you, I couldn't believe nobody had snatched you up yet," Lovely said, grinning. "I wanna make love to you so fucking bad, baby. You just don't know! I daydream about us making love all the time, but because I have so much respect for you, I didn't want you to think that was all I wanted from you. That's why I courted you and waited sixty-five days instead."

"Aww, baby," Lark said, her hand resting gently on her chest as she hung on to Lovely's every word.

"Let me pull over so we don't get into an accident out here," Lovely said, pulling over on the side of a park. "I want to get to know more about you so that I can fall in love with ALL of you—the good, the bad, and the ugly. I wanna break up to make up with you, girl. I want you to be my lady, baby."

Lovely looked into Lark's eyes as she said the final line.

"Hell yeah, baby! What took you so long? I wanna be YOUR lady, and I want YOU to be mine," Lark said, smiling from ear to ear.

"I'm gonna make you the happiest woman alive, baby," Lovely told her, kissing Lark's lips ever so softly.

Lark continued to blush and smile uncontrollably.

Lovely knew it was time for her to make some major moves now. So, she decided it was time to move Lark out of her mother's apartment. She wanted Lark lying in her arms every night, but Lovely wouldn't even think of bringing Lark to the brownstone because her family and that street life were off-limits.

Not wanting Lark around any of that, Lovely purchased a four-hundred-and-eighty-one-thousand-dollar two-bedroom duplex on Riverside Drive on the 3rd floor of a six-story prewar building that had the most amazing architectural façade she'd ever seen. There was a large courtyard with a huge birdbath fountain just before you entered the building, and there was a friendly 24-hour doorman who greeted you upon entering the building's grand entryway. The lobby had luxury marble flooring with a medallion inlay in the center of it and two large-scale chandeliers hanging from the cathedral ceilings. There was a set of highly polished brass elevators to one side and residential mailboxes to match on the other side while a concierge service was in the center of it all. Inside the apartment were 14-inch ceilings with Corinthian-style crown molding, herringbone mahogany wood flooring throughout, and a wrought iron spiral staircase that separated the two floors. On the main floor to the left was a bistro-style kitchen with a skylight, breakfast nook, a butler's pantry, and upscale stainless-steel appliances. There were two walk-in pocket door closets, a laundry room, and a powder room to the right. Then straight ahead was a two-stair, step-down sunken living room with a working wood-burning fireplace. The fireplace had its original stone-carved mantel and columns intact, exposing a brick accent wall. A black baby grand piano left behind by the previous owners was displayed in the center, and two large bay windows facing the east and west side of the building gave them a bird's eye picturesque view of Central Park.

Upstairs in the master bedroom was an identical wood-burning fireplace, a wide French door, and a window that opened to a Juliet balcony with the most majestic view of the Hudson River. Two larger dual pane windows faced the north and south of the building, providing an abundance of sunlight, and a walk-in closet with two built-in bookshelves adjacent to it. The en-suite bathroom had a two-basin vanity sink under a medium-sized stained-glass window with a re-glazed clawfoot bathtub next to the stand alone shower that all sat upon the porcelain mosaic black and white floor tiles. The brand-new commode with the bidet was partially partitioned in the corner. The second bedroom has dental crown molding around the ceiling with a decorative ceiling medallion encasing the antique-style pendant chandelier—also left behind by the previous owners—with a walk-in closet and a half-bath. The hallway was long with a railroad style—three additional closets and a full-size bathroom lining the walls.

Lark's birthday is on Christmas day. I'll surprise her with the apartment as her birthday and Christmas gift plus the other gifts I already have for her. Lark is going to lose her fucking mind, Lovely thought to herself, jingling the apartment keys in her hands.

She decided to leave the major decorating to Lark, but she would take on the responsibility of picking out the bedroom furniture, picking up the Christmas tree, and decorating it. She wanted to buy a real tree but was scared it would catch fire because of the fireplace. So, she bought some pine-scented air fresheners and placed them around the house instead. She couldn't decide on a color scheme for the tree but wanted the scene to be picture perfect when she brought Lark home. So, she purchased five packs of white lights to drape around the seven-foot tree.

Lovely went present shopping and purchased high-end designer gold bangles for them both, a three-quarter red fox swing jacket from Lincoln Furs in Queens, a diamond tennis bracelet with the matching tennis necklace from another high-end designer, a black designer purse with a bottle of that desingers perfume placed inside. And lastly, two open First Class plane tickets to Paris for them to use whenever Lark wanted to go.

Three weeks before Christmas, Lovely, Stanley, and Marcus received some bad news from the nurse.

"Guys," the nurse said, "your father's health is failing. He developed septic rheumatoid arthritis, and it is resistant to the prescribed antibiotics I've been giving him. His inability to tolerate any food has made him very weak, I'm afraid. I can no longer take him out of bed to sit him up in the chair without him screaming out in pain. I'm not sure how much time he has left."

The nurse explained all of this with an expression of sadness on her face.

"Whoa! Wait a minute now. What the hell is septic rheumatoid arthritis?" Lovely asked, raising her hand to halt the nurse's speech.

"I understand this is a lot to digest with the holidays and all, but it's a bacterial blood infection," the nurse said delicately.

"Well, how did he catch it? He doesn't go outside of this house," Lovely said, her hands now resting on her hips.

"Yeah, how did he catch it? Is it contagious?" Stanley asked.

"Yeah, is it contagious? Can we get it, too?" Marcus chimed in.

"A person with rheumatoid arthritis is susceptible to this type of infection. It's something that can just happen, and it can be fatal if the person can't be treated. No, it's not contagious. I'm so sorry," the nurse added.

Lovely's daddy died one week later, and she nor her brothers took it well at all. Lovely took it the hardest, though. She went into a state of depression, and during this time, Lark didn't hear from her and began to get very worried. Lovely had no choice but to bury her daddy, so she had to pull herself together quickly.

Lovely drove over to Lark's apartment to tell her about her dad's passing, but she wasn't able to talk about it without crying. Lark's family welcomed her into their home with open arms and offered her their condolences during her mourning. Lovely told Lark that she was returning her daddy's body to Chicago to bury him next to Madame.

"Baby, I'm so sorry," Lark said, reaching out to hug her. "Do you want me to come with you?"

"Nah, baby," Lovely said, blowing her nose. "I'll call you when I get back. Gimme kiss. My plane leaves in three hours, so I gotta get going."

Lark could see Lovely was trying so hard to hold back her tears.

"Okay, baby," Lark said. "Let me walk you to the door."

She had never seen Lovely's eyes so sad before. It was almost as if the lights went out in them, and that made her want to cry, as well.

"I'll call you when I get back," Lovely said, sniffing as she walked out the door and headed down the hallway.

"I LOVE YOU!" Lark shouted out as Lovely made it down the hallway.

Lovely stopped dead in her tracks and turned around, stuffing her snot rag in her pocket as she walked swiftly back towards Lark. Lovely began kissing and hugging on Lark so tight that she raised her off the floor while sobbing for what seemed like an hour.

"I'm so sorry you're in so much pain, baby. I wish I could take your pain away," Lark whispered in Lovely's ear, letting the tears fall from her eyes and onto Lovely's shoulders.

"I love you, too, baby. I love you, too," Lovely whispered back in between sobs.

Lovely managed to pull herself together.

"I'll be back sooner than you know it, baby but I really have to go now," Lovely said, winking and allowing that last tear to fall.

They gave each other another kiss, then Lark watched Lovely walk away until she was out of sight.

Lovely wore her father's favorite thick gold Cuban link chain with the diamond-encrusted Jesus medallion around her neck on top of her black ribbed turtleneck dress with her black mink coat covering her. A black floppy hat covered her hair pulled back tightly in a ponytail, and a pair of dark sunglasses hid her eyes during the burial.

Lovely and her brothers returned to New York a few days later. The streets were hot when they returned, too, and Stanley and Marcus were being reckless as hell. They kept calling her "sis" outside and saying shit like, "Daddy loved you more than he loved us anyway."

"What the fuck is going on?" Lovely would ask them, raising her voice.

They never gave her any response and just walked away from her. This was very strange to her, but she chalked it up to their daddy's passing. So, she let it slide.

As usual, it was pick-up time, and Lovely went to the crew to collect.

"Yo, I'm tired of answering to you. Who put you in charge anyway, Hazel Blue?" a crew member named Craig asked in a sarcastic tone.

Lovely took a step back, recognizing his aggression.

"Since when you had a problem with me, Craig? I'm confused," Lovely said, raising her brow.

"Since today, you pretty-eyed bitch. Since today! Get the fuck outta here. I ain't giving you shit. Now what?"

"Your ass betta stand down, muthafucka. Stand the fuck down 'cause I promise you, you don't want none," Lovely warned in the calm voice she was known for.

"Or what, bitch?!" Craig said, walking toward her.

Lovely pushed him in the chest, making him swing on her, but Lovely ducked. He swung again, but this time, she grabbed his hand and put his arm behind his back in a cross-arm bar, causing it to break. Craig screamed out in pain while the rest of the crew just stood there in astonishment out of respect for Lovely's skills. A dude they called Black wasn't impressed, though. He helped Craig up after he fell to the ground.

While he walked Craig to the car, Black shouted out, "I know you a dyke, too. My sister is a dyke, and y'all move the same way. All quiet and shit, and I never see y'all asses with no man. I know it, I know it! You better watch your fucking back, you dyke bitch!"

Lovely laughed and shouted back, "I'll be that! You just keep walking, muthafucka. Keep walking, or you gonna wind up getting a bone broke ya damn self!"

Lovely shook her head in disbelief as she walked backwards towards the crew. Lovely wasn't used to this type of chaos or being disrespected. Having to kick somebody's ass to keep them in check was giving her a bad feeling in the pit of her stomach, but she wasn't too worried because her training kept her alert, calm, and aware.

When she got back to where the rest of the crew was standing, she collected her money.

"Those niggas are crazy!" one of the other guys said.

Lovely responded with a "Keep up the good work" and gave them a wink before leaving the scene. She thought it would be useless to tell Stanley or Marcus about the incident because they were being reckless their damn selves. Her emotions were all over the fucking place, which was unfamiliar to her. So, she decided to think about all the money she managed to stack up instead. It was about four million dollars in total—more than enough to take care of her and Lark for a long time to come. It was unnecessary for her to continue hustling every day, or at all for that matter. So, she decided just to collect until their supply ran dry.

Maybe I'll go back to practicing law, she thought. *Yeah, let me leave these streets the fuck alone and make a life for me and my lady. But what you gonna do with the brownstone?*

She wasn't sure if she would keep the brownstone or sell it since she wouldn't be living in it anymore, and her daddy was gone.

My brothers better get their shit together because I'm not letting them stay there. No more free rides, boys Aht aht, that shit is over! I hope they were smart enough to save some of their money.

"Man, I'll think about all that shit some other time because today is the big day!" Lovely said out loud as she drove to the apartment to figure out what she wanted to tackle first.

The bedroom furniture she ordered came last week, and she paid the deliveryman to set it up, but she hadn't put any sheets on the bed yet. Lovely took the white 2,500 thread count sheet set with red satin trim and the red down comforter with matching shams upstairs. Lovely finished cooking the Christmas/birthday dinner for them, and she scattered the wrapped presents throughout the house. Lovely wanted Lark to find a surprise in more than one area so she could tour the apartment at the same time.

"Damn! My baby is going to be so hyped!" Lovely said out loud, grinning from ear to ear.

Everything is better with music, so lemme play some to keep me going while I'm getting all this stuff together. Shit, I never did this for anybody before, she thought, a feeling of unrequited love coming over her.

She sorted through her music collection and chose a song by the Whispers called "In The Mood."

Yeah, this song will never go out of style, Lovely thought, snapping her fingers and singing along.

The dinner menu consisted of lamb chops, twice-baked potatoes—with Italian parsley chives and parmesan cheese—a side of garlic spinach, and a nice bottle of expensive champagne to wash it down. She placed the two crystal champagne glasses she picked up from the boutique on 5th Avenue last week in the fridge next to the champagne to keep them cold. Lark had a bad experience as a child with her birthday cake. Apparently, on Lark's 10th birthday, her friends and family sang the happy birthday song, and when it came time to blow out the candles, the ribbons at the end of her pigtails caught fire, causing second-degree burns to her neck. Lark was in the hospital for a few days. So, instead of a birthday cake, Lovely stopped at Georgie's Bakery on 125th Street on her way home and bought a sweet potato pie with fresh whipped cream to put on top.

Alright, alright, let me see. Lovely rubbed her hands together while thinking. *Okay, I'ma put the big red box with her fur coat and the plane tickets under the tree, and the purse with the perfume inside the gift bag on top of the counter in the kitchen. Then the box with the gold bangles will be on top of the fireplace in the living room, and these boxes with the diamonds will go on top of the piano next to the vase of long-stemmed red roses I put there yesterday.*

Lovely looked out the living room window and noticed snow flurries just when Lark called.

"Hey, baby!"

"Merry Christmas," Lark yelled out cheerfully.

"Merry Christmas, my baby. You finished hanging out

with your family? You ready for me to come and get you, mama?"

"Yes, please! Hurry up! I can't wait to see you!"

"I'm on my way, baby. Mwah," Lovely stated as she checked the stove to make sure she had turned it off.

Lovely grabbed her silver fox coat and then put on her black leather riding boots and black leather fedora before heading out the door.

Thank goodness I drove the Jeep today because if this snow gets any heavier, at least I won't be slipping and sliding all over the damn place like I would if I drove the sedan, Lovely thought.

Lovely called Lark when she was downstairs and asked her if she could come up because she wanted to give her family a little something.

"You know what's so funny, baby?" Lark said in an excited tone.

"No, baby. What's so funny?"

"My mother asked me if you were coming up."

"Stop lying," Lovely responded with a slight laugh. "Let me park, and I'll be right up, baby."

Lovely knocked on the door, and Lark yanked it open so fast it startled her. Lark ran out and gave Lovely the biggest hug and kiss she could, and it almost knocked Lovely down, with the door slamming shut behind her.

"Wow, baby! You missed me or something?" Lovely giggled, gently putting her forehead on Lark's. "Merry Christmas and happy birthday, Lil' Mama."

Lovely gave Lark a quick soft kiss on the lips.

"Thank you, baby," Lark said, a look of love in her eyes as she took Lovely's hand. "Let's go inside now so you can say hello to my family before we leave." "

Okay, come on. Merry Christmas, everybody," Lovely shouted as she walked through the door.

"Merry Christmas," they all shouted back.

"Hey, Karen. Hey, Stacey, Mrs. Taylor, and Mr. Taylor. I wanted to buy you guys something, but I didn't know what you liked, so..." Lovely extended her hand to give Mrs. Taylor an envelope.

"Why, thank you, Lovely. You didn't have to do that, darling."

"Yeah, you didn't have to do that," her husband mimicked.

"I know, but I wanted to."

"Open it!" Lark and Karen shouted out.

Mrs. Taylor opened the envelope with her husband right by her side to find a thousand dollars in cash inside.

"Wow," Mrs. Taylor said softly. "Thank you so much."

Mrs. Taylor looked at Lovely with admiration while her husband couldn't seem to close his mouth.

"Yeah," Mr. Taylor said, clearing his throat, "thank you very much. We sure could use it."

"You're welcome. My pleasure," Lovely said, chuckling softly because of his expression.

Lark couldn't be any more impressed or in love with Lovely at that moment.

"Let's go, baby," Lovely said.

"Okay, let me get my coat," Lark said, skipping down the hall and returning to Lovely's side seconds later. "Alright, I'm ready. Bye, y'all! See you later!'

"Goodnight, Lark and Lovely," the family added as both women walked out the door and down to the Jeep.

"Ooh, it's snowing a lot now, baby! I love it when it

snows!" Lark said, holding out her tongue to catch the snowflakes.

"You're so amazing," Lovely told her. "Let's go, baby. I have a surprise for you."

"Yay! I can't wait for my surprise. You give the best presents. You're so good to me, baby," Lark said, looking over at her with a look of gratitude in her eyes.

"Nothing but the best for my lady. Nothing but the best," Lovely said while looking out her side-view mirror and pulling off.

*****

After parking in a space across the street from the building, Lovely got out of the car and waited for Lark to come around. She grabbed Lark's hand and ran against the light, dodging cars to the other side of the street.

"You're crazy!" Lark yelled playfully while they ran.

Lark punched Lovely in the arm once they were safely on the sidewalk.

"Ouch!" Lovely said, laughing and rubbing her arm as they walked to the building. "Wow! This courtyard is beautiful! Is this where you live, baby?" Lark asked, turning around to look at Lovely.

"Maybe, maybe not, sweetheart," Lovely replied as the doorman opened the door and welcomed them inside.

"A doorman and everything! Well, excuuuuse me! Damn, it's gorgeous in here!" Lark said, taking it all in. "Whoever lives here is living large, that's for damn sure."

Lark continued to look around in awe.

"Indeed they are," Lovely said, chuckling softly.

They got on the elevator, got off on the 3rd floor, and walked down the beige travertine tiled hallway hand in hand until they reached apartment 3B. Lovely took out the keys and began opening the door.

"Oh! So, you DO live here, baby," Lark said, smirking.

Lovely opened the door.

"No, Lil' Mama. WE live here. Happy Birthday and Merry Christmas, baby!"

Lark gasped and turned around to run for the door, but Lovely was in the way.

"Where in the world are you trying to go?" Lovely asked, laughing and grabbing her by the coat.

"Lovely…baby, are you for real? WE live here?" Lark asked, swirling her finger around the apartment with tears of joy in her eyes.

"Yes, baby…WE live here. I take it you like my surprise," Lovely asked, smiling.

"Yes, baby. This is some surprise," Lark said softly, her eyes looking everywhere.

"Lark," Lovey called out, looking into her eyes, "I want to sleep in the bed next to you every night from this day forward. I don't want to be dropping you off at your mother's place where you gotta share a room with your sister anymore," she said, raising Lark's hand to her lips and kissing it. "Come on. Let me show you around OUR place."

Lovely escorted Lark down the two steps into the living room.

"Ooh, baby…the tree is so pretty! You decorated it?"

"Yup. It's just lights, but look, baby, that big red box under there is yours. Go get it and open it."

Lark ran over, ripped off the box top, and pulled out the fur coat.

"OH, MY GOD, BABY! I love it!" Lark shouted, putting it on and twirling around while crossing her arms and rubbing up and down on it. "It's so soft, baby. I love it."

Lark looked down when her foot slipped on something.

"What's this?"

"Pick it up and read it, baby."

"What!" Lark screamed, jumping up and down. "TWO FIRST-CLASS PLANE TICKETS TO PARIS! OH, MY GOD!"

Lark held her head.

"I gotta stop screaming. I'm getting a headache," she laughed.

Lovely thought her face was going to crack. She was smiling so hard at Lark's reactions.

"Come here, baby. You got more over here. Open that red box over there," Lovely told her, pointing to the fireplace mantel.

"Ooh, baby," Lark said as she opened the box. "Gold bangles! They're so pretty and shiny! Wait. Are these what I think they are?"

"Sure is," Lovely said, chuckling. "Gimme. Let me screw yours on. There you go. Now you screw mine on."

"There you go," Lark said, kissing her quickly.

"Thank you, Lil' Mama. I'm glad you like it," Lovely said, holding their wrist up together, admiring them.

"This bracelet is everything, baby," Lark said, running her fingers across the screws. "Gimme another kiss."

"With pleasure."

"Mwah!"

"You have a few more presents. Look over there on the piano, sweetheart."

"Red roses! Those are my favorite." Lark picked one of the roses from the vase and inhaled it.

"Is that all you see, baby? Look down," Lovely told her.

Lark looked down.

"No way! These are blue boxes!"

"They are. Open them, baby."

"Diamonds! You got to be kidding me," Lark said, her hands shaking. "This can't be happening."

"Oh yeah, baby, it's happening. Come here. Let me put those on for you."

Lovely helped Lark put on her tennis bracelet, then put the tennis necklace around her neck. The sun was down now, so Lark could see the sparkle from the diamonds bouncing off the window glass.

"Damn, baby," Lark said, shaking her head slowly while looking down towards the floor.

"What? What's the matter, Lil' Mama?" Lovely asked in a concerned tone.

"I couldn't afford to buy you anything for Christmas," she said, sniffing.

"Baby…baby. Look at me, sweetheart. Lark, look at me."

Lark looked up and looked Lovely in her eyes that were sparkling just as bright as her diamonds.

"You are…the BEST gift…I EVER had. Understand me? And please, baby, don't ever forget that. Okay?" Lovely said as she leaned in for a kiss repeatedly while the tears rolled freely down both of their faces. "We better stop this, or we're gonna miss dinner."

Lovely gently wiped away Lark's tears.

"You ready for some more gifts, Lil' Mama?"

"Yes! What's that smell, by the way? I meant to ask earlier, but I got sidetracked. It smells delicious, though. What is that, baby?"

"Oh, just a little something I whipped us up for dinner. After you open all your presents, we can eat. Deal?"

"Deal!"

"Okay, last one," Lovely said as she walked Lark over to the kitchen's entryway. "Look on the counter, baby."

"No way! How did you know I always wanted this kind of bag?! It makes me feel so sophisticated and bougie," Lark said, flexing her newly encrusted diamond wrist and putting the bag on her shoulder.

"Oh yeah?" Lovely said, laughing. "Look inside the bag, too, baby."

"And the perfume! Now that's clever, baby. Real clever."

Lark ran and jumped into Lovely's arms, and they kissed again. Lark then took off running and laughing to the powder room to wash her hands before dinner. Lovely was directly behind her. Afterwards, they went into the kitchen to plate the dinner.

"Hey, baby," Lovely called out.

"Yeah?"

"Grab that champagne and those glasses out the fridge for me, would you, please?"

"But of course! Ooh, the good stuff! Damn, girl, you think of everything, don't you?" Lark said, laughing as she walked the glasses and champagne over to Lovely.

"Yeah, I guess I learned that from my daddy. He treated

me VERY well," Lovely said, her voice cracking as she tried not to cry.

Lark noticed the mist in her eyes but let her have her moment without interruption.

They sat down at the table and ate. They laughed some and drank half the bottle of champagne.

"That was delicious, baby. Thank you for EVERYTHING!" Lark said, her hand resting on her tennis necklace.

"Aww, you're welcome, baby. I love making you happy."

They were both too full to eat any pie but decided to take the whipped cream with them upstairs to enjoy later.

"Hey, baby, the snow is coming down heavier now," Lark said as she walked over to the window.

"Oh yeah, it is," Lovely said as she walked over to the fireplace and lit it.

While looking in her music collection for the perfect song, Lovely glanced over at Lark, who was still standing at the window with her hand on the necklace. *I got it!* Lovely thought as she put on the "Christmas Song" by Nat King Cole before slowly walking over to Lark *humming the lyrics,* Lark chiming in.

"I love this song, baby," Lovely said as she stood behind Lark, wrapping her arms around her waist and planting tender kisses on her neck.

"Mmm," Lark moaned as they swayed to the music.

They continued to look out the window and watch the snowflakes fall onto the bare tree branches in and around the park as they glistened from the light of the lamp posts nearby. It was so beautiful and so romantic.

"Did I make you happy today, baby?" Lovely whispered.

"I'm the happiest and luckiest woman in the whole wide world," Lark replied softly while interlocking her fingers in Lovely's.

Lark then picked up Lovely's hand and held it against her cheek before kissing it. They stood there in silence, listening to the music and admiring the winter's beauty. When the music stopped, Lark turned around.

"I wanna make love to you, baby. Can we go upstairs now?"

Lovely leaned over and kissed her softly on the lips, then took her hand and started walking towards the staircase.

"Wait a minute, baby. Don't forget that whipped cream. We gonna need that," Lark said seductively.

"Aww shit now," Lovely said as she hurried to the refrigerator to get it, returning to take Lark's hand and lead her upstairs.

As soon as they stepped inside the bedroom door, Lovely walked over to the fireplace and lit it.

"This is spectacular!" Lark said as she sat the whipped cream on the dresser and looked around.

Lovely started unbuckling the belt on her jeans.

"Aht aht," Lark said. "It's my turn to take the lead. Can I take the lead on this one, baby?"

Lovely was impressed with Lark's assertiveness because she had never seen this side of Lark before.

"Do your thing, baby. Do your thing," Lovely said, looking at her lustfully.

I finally met my match, Lovely thought.

Lark began taking off her clothes slowly and ordered Lovely not to move until she was done. Lovely's heart skipped a beat, and she licked her lips as a lustful moan left her lips. Lark removed her panties and looked in the center of them.

"Ooh, look…it's wet and sticky, baby. Can I taste it?" Lovely asked her.

"No," Lark said softly as she threw them on the floor and slowly walked over to Lovely.

Lark began unbuttoning Lovely's blouse before suddenly yanking it open. Her actions made Lovely gasp.

"Wow, baby. I love your peach-laced bra, and I had no idea your breasts were so big and juicy either," Lark said, raising her eyebrows. "Mmm, what a pleasant surprise."

Lark gave Lovely's breast a firm yet gentle squeeze before pinching her nipples ever so slightly. Lovely let out a little squeal, and her eyes rolled slightly up into her head because her nipples were the most sensitive part of her body.

"Oh…I see you like that, huh?" Lark said, biting her bottom lip. "I'll take your bra off last then."

Lark took the whipped cream off the dresser and told Lovely to hold it as she proceeded to unbuckle her belt and unzip her jeans. Lark pulled Lovely's jeans down to her ankles quickly.

"Step out, baby," Lark ordered, looking up at her.

Lovely did as told.

"Ooh la la. Your body is perfect, baby, and you're wearing matching panties. Aww shit. I FUCKING love that," Lark said softly through clenched teeth as she ran her nails up and down Lovely's thighs before squatting to the level of her crotch and planting her face in it.

Lovely's head fell back slightly with pleasure because her love was coming down. Lark took a long, deep breath in.

"Ahh, you smell like pineapples, baby. I love me some pineapples," Lark said, sniffing and nibbling on Lovely's vagina through her panties, causing Lovely to almost lose it!

Lovely wasn't used to being submissive to anyone, and it was blowing her mind because she was also in love for the first time. She reached out her hand to touch Lark's head, but Lark moved back, swaying her pointer finger, gesturing no. She then pulled down Lovely's panties in one swift motion.

"Pass me that whipped cream, baby," Lark said as she stood up slowly.

She took the whipped cream from Lovely and dug two fingers into it before placing it on the floor.

Lark pushed Lovely gently up against the wall and spread her legs open with her right leg before wiping the whipped cream between Lovely's lips with an emphasis on rubbing her clit. Lark breathed heavily into Lovely's mouth, teasing her by not kissing her. Lovely closed her eyes in absolute ecstasy and was shocked to taste Lark's fingers. Lark put them in her mouth while she slid down to suck and lick on Lovely's clit like it was the last supper! Lark removed her fingers from Lovely's mouth and ran them slowly down her belly so that both hands could spread her lips apart wider.

"I want every drop of this whipped cream mixed with your juices, baby," Lark said, looking up at her.

Lovely moaned louder and lifted her leg to assist Lark in her quest.

"Fuck, girl… This shit is unreal, and it feels so fucking good, too, baby," she whispered, holding Lark's head while moving her body in slow motion with her cheeks pressed up against the wall.

"De-fucking-licous," Lark said, standing up slowly and unhooking Lovely's bra, admiring the heavy rise and fall of her breasts. "Am I making you happy?"

"Yes, baby…yes, indeed," Lovely responded as she leaned in for a kiss.

"Aht aht, not yet, baby."

Lark picked up the whipped cream and dipped Lovely's nipples into it one at a time. Lovely bit her bottom lip, breathing deeply with anticipation. Lark cupped both of Lovely's breasts tight and looked her in the eyes. Then she lowered her head and sucked each one of her nipples hard while Lovely gasped with pleasure, squirming and grabbing Lark's back uncontrollably.

"This. Feels. Good. Baby."

Lark teased as she nibbled Lovely's nipple and sucked off the last bit of cream.

"Yes," Lovely moaned, panting rapidly.

"Good. Now you can kiss me."

Lovely kicked her panties off completely and grabbed Lark's face gently—sucking and licking her lips in between while sticking her tongue in and out of her mouth with the most passion she'd ever had. Lark returned the passion while holding onto her tightly.

"Damn, baby," Lovely said when she came up for air.

Lark's face was still in her hand. Lark gently removed

her hand and slowly led her to the bed.

"Lay down, baby. I want my mouth all over your body, and I don't want you doing anything but laying back and enjoying me," Lark told her.

Climbing on top of Lovely and interlocking their fingers, Lark kissed, licked, and nibbled on Lovely's neck. She worked her way down to Lovely's breasts, where she sucked them aggressively then gently before being aggressive again. The subtle difference had Lovely running her fingers through Lark's hair and becoming totally out of control. She squirmed so much that the comforter and top sheet fell to the floor. Lark softly chuckled as her wet tongue glided down Lovely's belly, causing her to arch her back while Lark rolled her nipples between her fingers. The light from the fireplace cast Lovely's silhouette on the wall by the balcony's door.

"You're so fucking hot," Lark whispered as Lovely let out soft moanful cries.

Lark's head was now between Lovely's legs, where she feasted on Lovely's clit slow and steady until she climaxed. Lovely's climax moans were a series of soft sighs that sounded like a sensual whimper, making Lark climax and afterwards resting her head on Lovely's belly. Once Lovely regained her strength and put her hair up in a topsy tail ponytail, she gently flipped Lark over, quickly spread her legs open with her hands, and reached down to palm her vagina.

"Damn, Lil' Mama, your pussy fat," Lovely whispered, breathing heavily into Lark's parted mouth while kissing her and spreading her vagina open further to rub her clit nice and slow. "Aww yeah, baby. This is just the way I want you to be—slippery."

Lovely sighed while placing sloppy kisses on Lark's mouth. Lark's moans were becoming deeper with every stroke of Lovely's fingers and every kiss of her lips.

"Yes, baby, let it out. Don't hold back," Lovely said softly. "Umm-hmmm. You can talk to me, baby. Come on…talk to me."

Lovely nibbled on Lark's ear while rubbing her clit faster before sliding two fingers deep inside her.

"Yass," Lark cried.

"Oh…my…god, baby. It's so fucking warm in here," Lovely whispered, taking one of Lark's nipples into her mouth and finger-popping her the only way she knew how—fast and hard.

Lark thrashed her body around the bed, crying out in pleasure, causing Lovely to hold her tight.

"Don't run from me, baby," Lovely said, sweat running down her face, as her hand moved even faster, causing Lark to climax repeatedly. "That's right, baby. Give it to me. I want it. I want it all."

Lovely slowed down as Lark's walls got tighter around her fingers. Lovely withdrew slowly and pulled Lark to the middle of the bed, bending over to kiss her softly and lifting her damp ponytail up before she fell back onto the bed.

"Damn, baby. You were certainly worth the wait. I didn't know you had it in you," Lovely said, turning her head to face Lark. "You're amazing, baby. Simply amazing."

Lovely put her arms over her head, and her breathing began to slow down.

"You're amazing, too, baby," Lark sighed as she reached over to give Lovely a quick kiss on the cheek.

They both lay there for a while before Lark jumped out of bed and ran to the bathroom.

"Ooh, baby, this bathroom is nice!" she shouted as she admired her tennis necklace sparkling in the mirror.

"Why you close the door?" Lovely shouted back.

"Because I gotta pee! What, you wanna hear me pee or something?"

"That's exactly why I asked you. Yup, I wanna hear you pee."

"Next time, baby. I got you next time," Lark said, laughing.

Lovely picked up the linen from the floor and put it back on the bed, then went downstairs to retrieve the glasses and the remainder of the champagne. When she returned, Lark was already in the bed under the covers.

"Hey, beautiful, let's finish this champagne before it goes flat," she said, plopping down on the bed.

"Good idea, baby," Lark said, sitting up.

Lovely gave Lark her glass and poured both of them some champagne before raising her glass.

"To us," she said.

"To us!" Lark said as she continued to admire her diamonds sparkling by the fire's light. "You're so good to me, Lovely."

Lark laid her head on Lovely's shoulder.

"You're good to me, too, baby," Lovely said and kissed Lark's forehead.

After finishing the champagne, they snuggled up together under the comforter and watched the embers in the fireplace float off the logs until they both fell asleep in each other's arms.

The next morning, Lovely was awakened by the soft scratches Lark was running up and down her back.

"Well, you're up early," Lovely said, stretching and rolling over. "Damn! We get a lot of sunlight in this room, that's for sure!"

Lovely tossed her arm across her eyes.

"Sorry, baby. Good morning."

"Good morning."

"Gimme kiss," Lark said.

"Nah! Stop playing. Let me brush my teeth first, girl!" Lovely shouted playfully, getting up and going into the bathroom.

"Why you close the door?"

"Ahh, you funny."

"What are we doing today, baby?" Lark asked, chuckling.

"Well," Lovely said, coming out of the bathroom as she squeezed toothpaste on her toothbrush, "I was thinking I would take you to your mother's house so you can get your stuff. Then I was thinking about going to that gourmet market on Staten Island for some lobster tails, and they sell regular foods, too, because we gotta put some real food in this house. Unless you have other plans, baby."

"Goodie! I was hoping you'd say that! But, baby, I'm scheduled to work today," Lark said, looking disappointed.

"Nah, no, you don't. Call and tell them you quit. Go to school or something," Lovely said as she began brushing her teeth and walking back into the bathroom.

Lark was so elated she started jumping up and down on the bed like a little kid. Lovely rinsed out her mouth and peeked out the bathroom door.

"Oh, for real? That's how I got you feeling right now?"

"You're amazing. I love it."

They took a quick shower together, got dressed, and went downstairs.

"Ooh, look, baby. This snow hasn't been stepped on over here yet!" Lark said, bending down to pick up a handful to throw it at Lovely.

"Oh! You wanna throw snow, Lil' Mama!? You didn't know I was crowned the snowball throwing champ three years in a row, girl. It's on!"

They threw snowballs at each other and ran around the bird fountain, laughing but falling most of the time because the snow was shin-deep.

"Come on, baby. Maintenance is coming out with the snow blowers now, and we gotta go," Lovely told her, dusting the snow off the top half of their matching black puffer coats before grabbing Lark's free hand to prevent each other from falling while hiking to the Jeep.

"Oowee! Let me put the heat on in here!" Lovely said as she started the ignition.

"Yeah, because I don't know whose bright idea it was to play in the snow anyways," Lark said, smirking playfully.

"Oh really?!" Lovely said, looking over at Lark, her eyes wide and grinning.

Due to traffic moving at a snail's pace because of the weather conditions, it took them almost two hours to drive to Lark's parents' house, which would normally have been a forty-five-minute drive. To make matters worse, Lovely had to double-park. Therefore, she couldn't go with Lark upstairs to retrieve her things.

While she waited, she turned on the radio, and James Brown's "Santa Claus Go Straight to the Ghetto" was playing. While singing along, Lovely looked in her rearview mirror and noticed the navy-blue four-door van that had been parked by their place this morning was directly behind her. It stood out to her because of the large crack in the windshield.

Am I being followed? she thought.

She squinted her eyes to see if she recognized anyone but was quickly distracted when she heard Lark knock on the passenger side window. Lovely unlocked the door, and just before she got out to help Lark put her things in the vehicle, the navy-blue van drove off.

"What's up with the plastic bags, baby? You don't own luggage?" Lovely asked her.

"No. My mother does, though, but she has stuff in them."

"That's alright, Lil' Mama. We can pick some up today after we go food shopping. You're gonna need some luggage when we go to Paris."

"Ooh! Oui oui," Lark said playfully.

"By the way, sweetheart, when DO you want to go to Paris?" Lovely asked, slamming down the hatchback.

"Well, I heard Paris was pretty in the springtime, so I say we go then, baby," Lark said, getting into the car. "Oh yeah, we gotta wear berets every day, too!"

"Hell yeah, we do!" Lovely said, humoring her. "We gotta have the total French experience. So, most definitely,

Lil' Mama. Most definitely," Lovely said, pulling off slowly.

An hour later, they arrived at the gourmet market in Staten Island, but the merchant had run out of lobster tails. So, Lovely settled for their colossal lumped crab meat instead. On their way home, they stopped at the designer luggage store in midtown to purchase Lark some luggage.

"There's that van again. What the fuck?" Lovely said out loud as she placed the luggage in the Jeep.

"What's that, baby? I didn't hear you. What did you say?" Lark asked her while walking around to the passenger side.

"I was talking to myself, baby. It's nothing, Lil' Mama. Get in."

Lovely drove off, stopping at the red light, and that van drove off, as well. However, when the light turned green, it made a left at the corner.

*****

Spring finally arrived! Over the following several weeks, Lovely and Lark managed to decorate the entire apartment and have Lark's family over a few times for dinner and games.

"Baby, when am I going to meet your brothers? I would like to have them over for dinner and games so they can meet my family, too," Lark asked, playing with Lovely's hair as they sat on the loveseat.

"That's sweet, baby. They're always so busy, but I'll ask them just for you. Okay?" Lovely said, smiling and holding Lark's chin tenderly.

"Okay, baby, whatever you say," Lark replied as she got up to join her mother and Karen in a game of Twister.

On March 26th, they boarded a flight leaving JFK Airport to arrive at the Lyon-Saint Exupéry Airport in Paris, France! After landing, they checked into their five-star hotel and ordered room service, eating it on the balcony.

"Baby, I feel like I'm in a dream! It looks like a scene from a movie out here with all the lights and everything. It even smells different. Look! Over there!" Lark said, pointing to the right. "It's the Eiffel Tower! All those lights. It's so beautiful, baby, right?"

"It sure is breathtaking, baby," Lovely said, smiling with her.

Lark looked around in awe while holding the sides of her face, then looked at Lovely with her eyes full of wonder.

"We gotta take a picture under it, if nothing else," Lark said, her voice the epitome of excitement.

"Let's go sightseeing in the morning. Okay, Lil' Mama? I'm a little tired tonight," Lovely told her.

Lark walked over to her side of the table and sat on Lovely's lap.

"That's perfect, baby. Let's get some rest. We'll go sightseeing in the morning."

"You're amazing. Let's go take a bath now," Lovely said, taking her hand and walking to the center of the room where the copper tub was sitting.

They took turns washing each other. Afterwards, they got in the bed and spooned. Lark positioned herself to see the Eiffel Tower from the open balcony door.

"Hey, baby," Lark said softly.

"Yes, Lil' Mama." Lovely's voice was just above a whisper.

"Umm, you feel like a quickie?" she asked while making soft finger circles on Lovely's hand.

"I always feel like a quickie with you, girl," Lovely said, softly kissing Lark's back. "Come here and turn around, baby."

They made love slowly and passionately on their first night in Paris, then fell asleep spooning with Lovely's face buried in Lark's back.

The next morning, they were called down by their tour guide, Jean, who Lovely hired to show them the most famous spots.

"Wait, baby. We almost forgot our berets!" Lark shouted before they walked out the door. "Here you go."

Lark handed Lovely hers, and they took off.

First, Jean took them for breakfast at Pierre's Table, where they feasted on chocolate croissants, seasonal fruits with cream, and hot chocolate while Jean gave them the restaurant's history. Once outside, Lark ran off, having Lovely chase after her. They wound up standing directly underneath the Eiffel Tower, where they embraced and French kissed, with their tour guide posing as the photographer.

The next stop on their tour was a visit to one of the most iconic museums, where they had pictures taken cheesing next to the Mona Lisa. In the afternoon, Jean persuaded them to rent bikes, and they enjoyed a delicious lunch at the Café Lemonet, where they tried a spiced poached egg dish cooked in tomatoes, olive oil, peppers, and onions, with French bread that they both couldn't get enough of.

Afterwards, they visited the Notre Dame Cathedral.

They continued to enjoy Paris for an additional eight days without their tour guide and had sex to mark every place they visited—once at the pear tree orchid at Luxembourg, once in the restroom while having dinner in the Hotel Plaza, once at the vineyard, and once during a tour of a palace. When they weren't having sex outdoors, they were making love on the balcony in their room—with one night being so breathtakingly sensual that Lovely asked Lark if she would have a baby for them.

"Yes. I would love to have our baby," Lark replied softly, her hand on Lovely's cheek.

Lovely's eyes got misty as she reintroduced her fingers inside Lark's vagina while they kissed. They made love slowly and tenderly, with Lovely on top as if she could impregnate Lark herself. As they were both climaxing, passersby looked up to see where the moaning was coming from.

On their last day, they visited Champs-Élysées and the famous Lock Bridge, where they wrote their names on a padlock and locked it on the bridge. Leaving the lock behind represented Lovely and Lark's love for each other. Afterwards, they threw the lock's key into the water, signifying their love was locked away for all eternity. They kissed and walked over the bridge arm in arm until they arrived back at the hotel.

Once in their room, they bathed and had lustful sex, role-playing like it was a one-night stand. Then they quickly fell asleep, exhausted from the day's activities. Thank God they packed for their morning flight beforehand.

They arrived back in America the next evening completely jet-lagged. They caught a taxi from the airport, went home, and got into the bed fully clothed—not waking up until the next morning. Lovely was the first to wake up, but she didn't bother to wake Lark.

"My baby is so beautiful," Lovely said, kissing Lark's cheek before tiptoeing downstairs to use the bathroom and fix herself a cup of coffee.

Damn! This creamer is spoiled, she thought, sucking her teeth and pouring it down the drain. *I don't feel like going to the store, but Lark might want a cup when she wakes up. Shit!*

Lovely put on her red and white leather baseball jacket with matching fitted baseball cap and left out to go to the corner store to buy some.

"Good morning. How was your vacation?" the doorman asked, smiling while holding the door open for her.

"Good morning, Jeffrey. It was magical and romantic," Lovely replied with a friendly smile as she walked out the door and through the courtyard.

Once she turned the corner, she noticed that same navy-blue van out of the corner of her eye moving at the same rate of speed she was walking.

Who the fuck is this?

Stopping, she turned around to face the car. The car stopped, and Craig jumped out of the driver's side.

"Remember me, bitch?" he said with his hand low down by his side.

"Yeah! Remember us?" another guy yelled out as he came around from the passenger side.

Lovely recognized the other guy—Black. She adjusted

the brim of her cap and shook her head while biting a piece of skin on her lower lip and chuckling softly.

"Oh, you think I forgot how you dissed me in front of the crew and broke my fucking arm, bitch? Huh?" Craig growled, his tone low. "Your ass might know martial arts, but your ass can't stop no bullets, though!"

Bang! Bang!

Two shots to the chest, and Lovely went down. While on the ground and holding her chest, she noticed the back window rolling down slowly. It was her brothers, Stanley and Marcus.

You gotta be fucking kidding me, she thought to herself as her vision faded to black.

Because there is no honor amongst thieves, Craig shot Stanley and Marcus in the face—killing them instantly.

"These dirty muthafuckas set they own sister up! They really thought we was gonna let they asses live?!" Black said while laughing demonically.

"Word up!" Craig replied as they were getting out of the car to dump the bodies, but Craig stopped when he saw a few people running in their direction.

"Oh shit! They heard the shots! Come on, man! Let's get the fuck outta here!"

Both men jumped back in the car and burned rubber.

"Oh my god! She's been shot! SOMEBODY CALL 911!" a woman yelled while trying to decide if she should touch Lovely or not.

The doorman from Lovely's building heard the shots, as well, and ran out and walked briskly towards the crowd.

"Oh, my word! It's the woman from 3B! Hello, 911. We need an ambulance right away at 850 Riverside Drive. A woman has just been shot! Hurry!" he said, then kneeled beside Lovely and applied pressure to her chest until the ambulance arrived.

Meanwhile, at the apartment, Lark woke up stretching and calling out for Lovely after she didn't see her in the bed. As she went to the bathroom, she called out Lovely's name again, only louder this time. Then she walked down to the kitchen. No Lovely.

Why is my stomach flipping like this? she asked herself while rubbing on it. *Where in the world did my baby go? Well, she didn't leave a note or anything, so she couldn't have gone that far. Hmmm,* she said, scratching her scalp. *She probably went to the store or something.*

Lark drank a glass of apple juice before going back upstairs to lie down. She fell asleep again and woke up three hours later to find Lovely still out. That's when she got dressed and went downstairs to see if she could find her, but she had no idea where to look. When Lark reached the front door, the doorman stopped her.

"Good afternoon, young lady," he said, clearing his throat before continuing. "I'm afraid I have some bad news."

Lark turned and looked at him quizzically. *What kind of bad news could this man possibly have to tell me?* she thought.

"Excuse my expression, but are you talking to me?" she asked him, her eyebrow raised.

"Yes, ma'am, I'm afraid I am."

"Okay," she said, still looking confused. "Well, what do you have to tell me?"

He swallowed hard before speaking. "Your lady friend was shot this afternoon and was taken to the nearest hospital."

"WHAT!" Lark said, shaking and holding her stomach.

"I'm sorry, Miss. She didn't…"

"She didn't WHAT? Spit it the FUCK out!" Lark yelled.

"Your lady friend…she didn't make it."

Lark's legs buckled, causing her to lean up against the door. Her heart raced as she looked around wildly.

"I heard the EMT say so when they put her in the ambulance. I'm so sorry, miss," he said, his lips trembling and tears forming in his eyes as he walked over to her side.

Lark let out a deafening scream before passing out. The doorman caught her before she could hit the floor.

At the hospital, Lovely opened her eyes, focusing them on the bright bluish-white light in front of her—the silhouette of a person standing directly in the center of it. Suddenly, she was able to make out the person.

"Madame!" Lovely yelled out, running into her arms. "What are you doing here? Wait!"

Lovely took a step back.

"What are you doing here, Madame?" she said, looking around, trying to find anything familiar. "I don't recognize this place. Where are we, Ma… Daddy?!"

Lovely began to run again.

"Wait. What's going on here?" Lovely asked in a frightened voice, but Madame and her daddy just stood there smiling while reaching out for her hand. "Where am I?"

Lovely started to cry and began backing away.

"Baby," Madame said in a soft, calming voice while walking toward her, "don't be frightened. Nobody is going to hurt you here, but I want to ask you something, alright?"

"Yes, Madame," Lovely responded in a childlike voice as she continued to look around.

"Do you remember when I told you the fast life wasn't the life for a person like you, baby?"

"Yeah," Lovely said, still nervously looking around.

"Well…come closer, baby. I want to introduce you to somebody."

"Who?" Lovely asked her, confused.

"You never met her before. Come on, baby. Don't be afraid," Madame said, leaving her hand extended.

Lovely took Madame's hand, and a sense of absolute tranquility came over her, allowing her to follow Madame without one ounce of fear. An unfamiliar yet angelic woman appeared, and although Lovely felt connected to her, she couldn't quite figure out where she knew her from.

"Hello, Lovely Eva James," the woman said with the brightest smile Lovely had ever seen. "I've been watching over you your entire life, sweetheart."

"Who are you?" Lovely asked her softly, tilting her head to one side as if doing so would jog her memory somehow.

The longer she stared at the woman, the more it felt like looking into a mirror.

"Hello, Lovely. My name is Eva. I am your mother," the woman said.

The sound of angels singing resounded in the air as she opened her arms to embrace Lovely.

"Mommy!" Lovely screamed, running towards her. "Mommy?! Am I…?"

TO BE CONTINUED…

Summer Intern

There she was in all her splendor, making love to me through the single lens of a movie camera. It didn't matter what she was doing or who she was doing it with—I connected with her instantly! The graceful movements of her perfectly shaped body and her sassy attitude have my undivided attention. Her blemish-free skin is reminiscent of the finest confections and has a permanent golden glow due to her basking daily in the California sun. I imagine her tasting so sweet and creamy in my mouth and feeling like the softest cashmere in my hands. Her kind of confection can only be found in the finest confectionery shops, like those in Switzerland or Milan. Her lips look as soft as clouds, stained with the slightest pink hue as if she is having an ongoing love affair with a pink teacup rose. Ahh. She embodies the aura of African royalty and had me under her spell at hello. Who is she? Ivy Matthews—the newest breakout star of the late-night television series, The Ivy Chronicles, a police story by S.R. Cooper

Productions. The crew is filming its third season.

"QUIET ON THE SET!" the director belted out, interrupting Robin's daydream.

Robin Stevens, the only child of a former child star, was a productions assistant intern from the Los Angeles Film School on Sunset Boulevard. She decided to go to film school after watching one of the most iconic movies of all time— *Pulp Fiction*. Robin couldn't believe someone else had the same thought process as her! Quentin Tarantino convinced her through his work that her way of thinking wasn't weird and that she had what it took to be the next biggest filmmaker! Robin had been interning as a production assistant at the movie studios in West Hollywood for the past six months. Although production assistants were only supposed to assist directors and producers on movie sets, she was given the rare opportunity of working exclusively with Ivy Matthews. Not because of her unwavering request to do so, but because of her mother's "special" relationship with the series' producer.

Ivy was known to be an unpredictably moody woman with diva tendencies, which most people found hard to deal with. Robin, on the other hand, had an innate ability to critically think and persuade people to act accordingly. People said she was rather charming, and Robin agreed with them, but she was also confident in her abilities, especially since she was intellectually stimulating. In her experiences, most people found these traits appealing, especially those of the same sex. Therefore, it was a no-brainer for the producer to grant her mother's request.

Robin was thirty-three and lived in her mother's

guesthouse on Ashland Avenue in Santa Barbara, with no intention of moving out soon. Her mother insisted that Robin stay under her watchful eye until she learned all the nuances of film production and directing to ensure she became the next great filmmaker. Robin's father was a landscape developer since the 1950s but passed away about ten years ago, leaving Robin and her mother very well off. They not only had the Santa Barbara estate but a beachfront bungalow in Malibu. There were also the two co-op buildings on Washington Boulevard in Culver City that Robin and her mother managed.

"Excuse me, excuse me. What's your name again?" Ivy called out while snapping the fingers of her left hand and holding her Pomeranian dog in her right.

"My name is Robin, Ms. Matthews. How can I assist you?" Robin asked, withdrawing a pen from behind her ear to jot down notes.

"Please call me Ivy, Robin. Ms. Matthews makes me sound so old, and I'm only thirty-five, honey," she said.

"I've always called you Ms. Matthews, but no problem. How can I assist you…Ivy?" Robin replied with a soft chuckle, seemingly confused.

"Well," Ivy said, looking Robin up and down while petting her dog, "I need help carrying some of my items to my dressing room. Then I'll need a glass of my cold peppermint tea that's over there in the icebox, and I also need you to put some water in Sweetie's bowl. Lastly, I'll need you to help me carry some of my things out to my car."

"Absolutely! Let me get those," Robin said as she reached for and gathered the items.

"Wow! You look like you've been working out. How often do you work out?" Ivy asked, feeling on Robin's bicep.

Robin smirked at Ivy's indirect compliment.

"Thanks. I work out sometimes, but I don't actually 'work out work out'. I've just always had an athletic build," Robin informed her as she began walking towards Ivy's dressing room while blushing like crazy.

"This is so freakin' cute!"

"What?" Ivy asked, walking directly alongside her.

"The border. I never noticed the paw print border around your name before. Was this always here?"

"No. My co-star Daniel just did that. He thought it was cute, so he put it there, but I don't mind because it's for my Sweetie!" Ivy said, smiling and rubbing noses with her dog.

"Aww. You have a beautiful smile, by the way," Robin told her, clearing her throat. "Umm, where would you like me to put these things?"

"Why, thank you. That was a nice thing to say. You can put them over there on the sofa. Let me get changed, and I'll meet you in the parking lot," Ivy said, smiling softly.

"Sure, but didn't you want me to bring you the peppermint tea and help you put something in your car?"

"Oh yeah! I forgot about that. Bring the tea out to the parking lot with you in about fifteen minutes, okay?"

"Okay," Robin said, shrugging her shoulders and exiting the dressing room.

Ivy locked the door behind her, put Sweetie down in her doggie bed, and began to undress. Ivy enjoyed undressing behind her vintage silkscreen to throw on her nylon stockings and undergarments. It created a nostalgic effect that made her feel like Dorothy Dandridge or Eartha Kitt in an old black and white Hollywood movie.

Several minutes later in the parking lot…

"Hey, Ivy!" Robin yelled but not too loudly, waving and walking towards her. "Here's your tea."

"Thank you, honey," Ivy said while placing Sweetie in the vehicle.

"You're welcome. Now, what do you need me to put in the car for you?" Robin asked, excited to be helping her with anything.

"Oh, nothing. I changed my mind."

After sliding into the driver's seat, Ivy put the tea in the cup holder, started the ignition, and lit a cigarette before winking and driving off the lot in her white sports car.

Alrighty then, Robin said to herself before walking to her silver convertible and driving off the lot herself.

*****

When Robin arrived at the set the following day, she overheard Ivy yelling at the cameraman like she had lost her mind. Robin had to interject.

"Cut! Take five," the director yelled while removing his cap in frustration.

Robin asked Ivy if they could speak in private. Ivy looked at Robin before walking off the set in a huff and storming through the door of her dressing room. Robin followed behind her, catching the door before it slammed in her face.

"Okay, Ivy, I'm gonna need you to calm down and tell me what's going on so I can help you, alright?"

Ivy turned around quickly to face her.

"Do you see my face?!" she yelled, pointing to it.

"Well, yeah, I see your face, Ivy. Is there something you want me to notice, 'cause your face looks fine to me?" Robin said sarcastically while blinking her eyes quickly.

"My makeup is all fucked up! I don't understand why you can't see that!" she continued to shout, still pointing at her face.

"I'm not sure what's wrong with your makeup, Ivy," Robin said, looking confused. "Did you eat? Yeah, that's it. Let me bring you something to eat."

"OH, MY GOD!" Ivy yelled as she stomped her foot on the carpeted dressing room floor. "This is useless."

Ivy closed her eyes, took a deep breath in, and ran her fingers through her hair.

"I need some air," she said, opening her eyes and heading for the door.

Robin gently grabbed her arm, pulling her back inside.

"Alright, hold on a minute, sweetheart. Let me try and figure something out so I can help you feel better, okay?"

Ivy didn't resist.

"Come…sit down. Uhm, so you're not hungry. Okay then," Robin said, tapping her temple and trying to come up with something. "I think I got it! I'll have your makeup artist do your makeup over for you. How does that sound?"

Ivy stood up and responded through clenched teeth, her arms held stiffly against her sides.

"MY makeup artist ISN'T here today, AND nobody

told me that she WASN'T coming! They know I ONLY use her because she's the only one who knows EXACTLY how I want my makeup done."

"Oh! I see," Robin said, raising her eyebrow. "So…"

Before Robin could finish her sentence, Ivy interrupted her.

"And another thing! That stupid-ass cameraman kept shooting me from my right side when he knows DAMN well my left side is my best side," she continued to rant while pacing back and forth. "Oh yeah, and one more thing! Let me tell you about the new guy they have me working with today. This guy smells like he's been up all night fucking and sucking out somebody's ass! And they have the nerve to expect ME—Ivy Matthews—to do a kissing love scene with that muthafucka! Well, they can kiss my ass is what they can do. Gotdamn it. I'm not in the mood for this shit today. Where's my damn cigarettes?"

"Wowzers," Robin said, softly picking at her cuticles and trying to think of what NOT to say next. "I think filming can be halted for today and resumed tomorrow. I'll go and tell the director your stomach is upset or that you have to take Sweetie to the vet or something. Then I'll walk you out to your car. Okay?"

"Fine, I guess," Ivy said, shrugging her shoulders. She appeared to be less agitated now as she looked for her cigarette lighter. "Hey! While you're at it, tell them to have ole boy take a shower and brush his fucking teeth before trying to do a scene with me. Otherwise, my stomach will be upset tomorrow, too!"

"Alright, will do. You get changed, and I'll be back to walk you to your car," Robin said, chuckling on her way out the door.

Ivy exited the building to the parking lot wearing a pair of turquoise and rhinestone-encrusted cat-eye sunglasses with matching thong sandals, a white bikini top, and a turquoise sarong loosely tied around her white bikini bottoms.

Damn, she's beautiful…so sweet and so petite. I could scoop her fine ass up right now and put her in my back pocket! Robin thought to herself.

"Looks like you're going to the beach today. I like your outfit, Ivy," Robin said while escorting Ivy to her reserved parking space.

"Thank you, honey. Yeah, I'm going to the beach. I need to be by the water right now so I can relax. You wanna come?" Ivy asked, lifting her sunglasses off the bridge of her nose and turning her head to look directly at Robin.

"I would love to come with you, sweetheart, but I have some editing to do on my film today. Can I get a rain check, though?" Robin asked, holding her hands above her brow to block the sun's rays.

"Well, the beach is open every day to everybody," Ivy said, pushing up her shades and opening her car door. "But no problem. Some other time maybe. I'll see you tomorrow, and good luck with your editing."

"Thanks. I'll see you tomorrow then."

Damn. She's so fine, but she gets aggravated so quick!

Robin shook her head as she walked towards her parking space.

Later that evening, Robin went over to her mother's house to gossip about what happened on the set between Ivy and the cameraman.

"Ma! Where are you?" Robin yelled, walking towards the kitchen.

"I'm in the kitchen, baby!"

"Hey, Ma," Robin said.

The two kissed each other on the cheek before she started telling her mother about the day's events.

"Well, you know Ivy and that cameraman had an affair since she's been shooting the series, right? He just broke it off with her a week ago, and they said he was married the entire time," her mother informed her.

"For real?! I didn't know that! Now that explains why she was so angry with him," Robin said, folding her arms in front of her and leaning up against the fridge. "She's probably pissed off that she still has to work with this guy then, huh?"

"Probably," her mother said, wiping down her kitchen counter.

"Well, I'm still crazy about her, so that doesn't bother me," Robin said, grinning.

"Well, be prepared to have your hands full dealing with that woman. You know what they say about her at the studio, baby. Don't let that woman cause you to lose focus on your goals. Besides, is she even into women?" her mother asked as she dried her hands with a paper towel.

"She's not difficult or a diva, Ma. She's just misunderstood, that's all."

"Okay, baby, if you say so," her mother said, chuckling.

"ANYWAY…I have a feeling she's into women. But if she's not, then she will be if I have anything to do with it. All she needs is a little bit of 'act right', and she'll be just fine," Robin said, chuckling.

"Act right?" Her mother frowned.

"Ahh, never mind that," Robin said, fanning her hand. "But, yeah, I hear you, Ma. I think I can handle her. All she needs is love, and I'm willing to give her all the loving she needs. She'll forget all about Mr. Cameraman in no time."

Robin thought, *I'll turn that tigress into my sweet little pussy cat.*

"Alright then. You better work you're magic on her fast, though, because your internship will be over soon. And take that pen from behind your ear! You're not on the set anymore. Ooh, I gotta go! Judge Judy is on!" her mother said after looking at the wall clock, then took off, speed walking to the living room with her silk kimono flying in the wind.

"I know, I know," Robin said, scratching her head with the pen top. "Isn't tonight Mexican food night?"

Robin looked around the kitchen for food.

"Did Daisy cook something good for us today?"

"Yes! There're some green chicken enchiladas on the stove. Help yourself, baby."

"Thanks, Ma," Robin said. After grabbing two of the enchiladas, she walked to the back door. "I'll be at my place if you need me!"

Next morning on the set…

"Five, four, three, two, one, and ACTION!"

"The violence in this neighborhood has gotten worse over the last few years, which is why they assigned *us* to this precinct, Daniel! We get the job done," Ivy's character said, pointing at her co-star passionately and raising her voice. "You shouldn't be here if you're gonna turn a blind eye. I need help cleaning the crime off these streets, and I can't do it alone. So, if you're no longer interested in helping these folks, I'll ask for another partner who will!"

Ivy's character picked up her badge and gun off the desk and walked away.

"CUT! That's a wrap. Good job today, guys."

The entire cast applauded as they left the set.

"Hey, Ivy," Robin said, jogging to keep up with her. "Good show today. Are you feeling better?"

"Hey, Robin! I'm so much better, honey. Thanks. Be a doll and get my tea for me."

"Absolutely! I'll be right back," Robin said, hurrying off. "Here you go," she said, returning to Ivy.

"Mmm. Thanks, honey," Ivy said, dabbing the sweat off her chest with a cotton and lace handkerchief. "This is so refreshing. You should try some."

Ivy held out the mug for her to take a sip.

"Hold on. Lemme get a straw," Robin said, looking around for one.

"I don't have cooties. Just drink from the other side if you're that worried," Ivy told her with a slight attitude.

"I'm not worried about me. I was only thinking about you."

"Oh, so you have cooties then?" Ivy asked, raising her brow.

Robin shook her head. *This woman,* she thought as she took a big gulp of the tea.

"Wow! That IS refreshing."

"See? I told you. Now give it back," Ivy said as she sat down at her vanity table to remove her makeup.

"Where do you buy this tea from?" Robin asked,

chuckling as she placed the mug down. "I would like to buy some for myself."

"Well, I don't trust anyone else to make it right. So, I make a pitcher of this every night before I go to bed and bring it with me to the studio. What are you doing this afternoon?" Ivy asked.

"Just a little more editing. Why?"

"I was thinking you can come with me to my house, and I'll make you your very own pitcher. I only use the finest ingredients," Ivy said, smiling slightly.

"Oh yeah? Like what?"

"Well, I use organic peppermint leaves that I grow in my terrace garden, thirteen times purified water, and monk fruit to sweeten it."

"Oh wow! Not the thirteen times purified water!" Robin said jokingly. "Hmmm, no wonder it tastes so good!"

"Ha, ha, ha! Don't you worry…I'll use some tap water for yours," Ivy said playfully and stuck out her tongue.

"I'll come with you to your house so you can make me some," Robin said, grinning. "I'll meet you in the parking lot in twenty minutes. Okay?"

"Okay, twenty minutes," Ivy said, winking and rubbing cold cream on her cheeks.

In the parking lot…

"Okay, let's go. Are you riding with me or following me in your car?" Ivy asked.

"I'll follow you. I don't want you to have to drive me back here for my car. How far do you live from here anyway?"

"Yeah, you're right. That makes perfect sense. I live in the Carol Apartments in Santa Monica. It's about thirty minutes from here, depending on the traffic."

"Okay, cool."

"Alright, come on then. Let's go!" Ivy said, walking quickly to her car.

"I'm right behind you," Robin said as she got into her car and followed Ivy down the Pacific Coast Highway to Exit 1-A.

Once they arrived at Ivy's apartment complex, they parked in the underground garage and went upstairs to Apartment #406.

"Your apartment is beautiful, Ivy. I gotta say, you have nice taste. Wow! And you have so much space for Sweetie to run around!"

"Why, thank you, honey. I lucked up getting this place. It had just gone on the market when I got it. Make yourself at home, honey."

"Alright, thanks. Hey, where *is* Sweetie?" Robin asked, looking around for her.

"It's time for her walk now, so the sitter has her out. Come on, let me show you around. Over here, as you can see, is my kitchen."

"Ooh, nice quartz countertops," Robin commented as she glided her hands across them. "This is a gigantic refrigerator for one person, though, ain't it?"

"No, it's a necessary convenience is what it is. For one, I make a week's supply of homemade dog food for Sweetie, and two, I don't have to go shopping that often because I can stock up. I hate going to the supermarket, honestly. But enough of that. Let me show you the terrace where I grow my peppermint. Watch your step, honey," Ivy warned as she pointed to the small step. "I don't need you suing me because you fell." She laughed and added, "I eat out here most of the time when I'm at home."

"I don't blame you. Look at these gorgeous mountain views! They're nothing short of spectacular. I had no idea your apartment would be facing the mountains, Ivy. Shoot, I'd eat out here ALL the time!" Robin said, obviously impressed. "And what's that sweet perfume smell?"

Robin sniffed the air, trying to pinpoint the location.

"Oh! That's my little Magnolia tree over there," Ivy said, proudly pointing to the corner. "And Venice Beach is about fifteen minutes to your left. I usually drive my car down there, but sometimes I'll ride my bike so the wind can have its way with me."

Ivy sighed and outstretched her arms for dramatic effect while smiling.

"Maybe I can join you one of these days," Robin said without taking her eyes off the mountains and resting her elbows on the terrace's railing.

"I would like that," Ivy said, smiling. "Okay now. Pick your peppermint, and I'll start heating up my thirteen times purified water to pour over them!"

Ivy laughed, leaving Robin on the terrace, and walked into the kitchen to turn on the teapot. Afterwards, she went to her bedroom to take off her clothes and put on the grey silk robe she had hanging up behind her bedroom door. She tied the robe loosely around her waist before walking out to rejoin Robin on the terrace.

"Oh, there you are. I was wondering where you went," Robin said, holding a handful of the peppermint leaves.

"Girl, I had to take those clothes off! I prefer to walk around naked, but I didn't want to offend you."

Robin remained silent because she almost told Ivy putting the robe ON was offensive!

Shit, this woman turns me on with her clothes on! So, I can only imagine how I would feel seeing her naked.

"Here's the leaves I picked," Robin said, handing them to Ivy.

"You can place them in that glass bowl I put over there on the island for now."

"Alright, no problem. Can I use your bathroom? I need to wash this peppermint off my hands before I make a mistake and rub my eyes for some reason."

"Sure. It's the door right before you get to my bedroom. The door is open. You can't miss it. It's the room with the white toilet bowl in it," Ivy said, smirking. "Hey…would you like to listen to some music?" Ivy shouted out.

"I sure would. What you got?" Robin shouted back from the bathroom.

"I listen to all types of music, so let's see… I have some jazz, neo-soul, soft rock, R&B, alternative, and country."

Robin unconsciously interrupted Ivy by turning on the faucet to wash her hands after flushing the toilet.

"Hey…do you have any paper towels? I need to dry my hands," Robin asked, walking out of the bathroom, holding up her hands so the water didn't drip on the floor.

"You could've used the towel in the bathroom, honey, but there are some paper towels over there on the counter," Ivy said, waving nonchalantly. "So, tell me…what do you wanna hear, Robin?"

"I think I heard you say you have some neo-soul,

right?"

"I'm surprised you heard me since you turned on the water while I was talking," Ivy said sarcastically. "But yeah, I did say that."

This girl, Robin thought to herself and chuckled out loud.

"I'm sorry about that, but okay… I would like to hear some Erykah Badu if you have it."

The teapot's whistle began to blow.

"Ooh, turn that pot off for me, please, Robin. I don't want the water to be too hot 'cause it will burn the leaves and make the tea bitter."

"Sure, no problem. By the way, I like that LED light strip around your bathroom mirror," Robin said while walking briskly to the kitchen. "It's so…Hollywood."

"Yeah, I know. I love that feature," Ivy crooned. "The mirror was made that way. I had nothing to do with it, I swear!" she said, laughing. "Alright, I found it! Erykah Badu's 'Didn't Cha Know' coming right up for your listening pleasure."

Both sang the smooth lyrics in unison.

"Robin! I didn't know you could sing like that! You betta sing that song, girl!" Ivy teased, grinning from ear to ear.

You didn't know Robin sang playfully, walking back into the living room and winking at Ivy.

"Let me start making your tea," Ivy told her, then winked back before walking to the kitchen.

Ivy's robe slowly fell off her left shoulder, but her subtle perspiration kept it up halfway. Ivy looked over that shoulder as she poured the warm water over the peppermint leaves.

"Would you like to partake in a snack with me while we wait for the tea to develop, honey?"

"Sure, that sounds good. What you got?" Robin said, walking over to her.

"I can make us a couple of Greek yogurt parfaits, and we can eat them out on the terrace."

"Mmmm, sounds yummy. What's in it?"

"First things first," Ivy said. "In the cabinet next to the stove, on the second shelf, are two scalloped edge glass dessert cups. Put them on the island, please, while I get the ingredients out of the refrigerator, honey."

"Of course!" Robin said, going into the cabinet.

"Alright, put them right here," Ivy said, patting the countertop. "Okay, now…I'm gonna use two cups of organic vanilla Greek yogurt. I would only use one cup if I were making this just for me. One half-cup each of macerated organic strawberries, blueberries, sliced seedless green grapes, and raspberries that I soaked overnight in violet honey. That way, the fruit is extra sweet when I want to mix it with the yogurt. I can't stand fruit that isn't sweet. Yuck!"

"I hear you. Me either," Robin said, faking a frown.

"A sprinkle of wheat germ and an extra little drizzle of the violet honey on top, and VIOLA! Greek yogurt parfaits, honey!" Ivy said cheerfully.

"These look better than the gourmet ones I've seen in the store! I love it! This is impressive, Ivy. Wow."

"Thank you, honey. One day, I'll cook you some of my famous stuffed peppers. But right now, let's go on that terrace you like so much," Ivy said, winking.

They both smiled and walked out to the terrace. Erykah's "I Guess I See You Next Lifetime" belted out from the speakers.

"Does this woman make any bad music?" Robin said through a mouth full of her parfait.

"I can't say she does. Oops! I almost forgot!"

"What?" Robin asked.

"The dessert wine," Ivy said as she jumped up, almost losing her robe completely.

Ivy placed her parfait down on the patio table and jogged into the kitchen. She returned with two wine glasses and a bottle of dessert wine from her wine fridge. The belt to her robe was below her waist now, and had it not been for her small perky breasts, the robe would've exposed her naked body fully.

The sun enhances this woman's natural beauty tenfold. Damn! Robin said to herself, shaking her head slowly.

"Here you go, honey," Ivy said as she handed Robin a wine glass before sitting down next to her.

"I can only have one glass of this stuff," Robin told her.

"Why?" Ivy asked while filling Robin's glass.

"Alcohol goes straight to my head, and I can't be held responsible for anything I might do under the influence of it," she said, laughing.

"Well, we'll just have to see about that," Ivy said seductively while unconsciously placing her tongue at the corner of her top teeth.

Woman, you have no idea how much I want to devour your pretty little ass right now. Don't tempt me, Robin thought as she looked Ivy up and down, wishing her robe would just fall off her and drop onto the terrace floor. Robin pushed her chair back a little so she could get out of her head.

"I never heard of this wine before," Robin said, reading the label. "Tell me a little bit about it, if you don't mind."

"Oh, that's not surprising, honey. Not many people have. Wait…you at least know it's a dessert wine, right?" Ivy asked, placing her hand on Robin's thigh.

"I figured as much," Robin answered, trying to maintain her composure with Ivy's hand still resting on her thigh.

"Okay, so these grapes were dried for like five months and aged in oak barrels for at least five years before being sold to the public," Ivy said, holding up the bottle. "I like this particular brand because when it's paired with fruit like the ones we're eating, it brings out the honeyed nuts and sappy prune notes in it."

"Well now… Honeyed nuts and sappy prunes, huh?" Robin said jokingly, raising her eyebrow and looking down at the glass.

"Are you making fun of me, Robin?" Ivy asked in a serious tone, squinting her eyes.

"No!" Robin said, holding up her hands in a gesture of peace. "I was just joking, sweetheart. It sounds delicious. I just never heard anyone describe wine in such detail before, that's all. Let me give it a taste."

"Hmmm…alright."

Ivy smacked her lips together lightly before picking up the bottle, pretending to read it again.

"It's sweet but not overly sweet, and it kinda breaks down the thickness of the yogurt on your tongue, too. I really like this, Ivy. Good choice," Robin said, sounding genuine.

Ivy smiled and took a spoonful of her parfait.

"Well, I can go into detail like I do because I used to date a sommelier a few years back. He taught me a few things about alcohol that I wouldn't know otherwise. Unfortunately, that's all we had in common. Anyways, how did your editing go the other night?"

"Oh, not bad. Thanks for asking. I pulled an all-nighter and woke up on my projector desk in the morning," Robin told Ivy, laughing.

"Oh wow. So, are you almost done?" Ivy asked, leaning back in her chair and crossing her legs while holding her wine glass in both hands.

Her robe fell open, exposing her golden thighs, but their conversation was interrupted by Ivy's phone ringing.

Ring, ring...

"Hold on a sec, honey," Ivy told her, getting up and going into the living room to answer it, wine glass still in hand.

Where the hell is my phone? Ivy asked herself while looking around frantically. *Oh! Here it is,* she said, turning it over and looking at the number before answering it. *Oh, hell no! I don't know why he's calling me anyway,* she said to herself in an annoyed tone and quickly threw the phone down on the sofa before returning to the terrace.

"Continue, honey."

Ivy sat down and took a big swallow of her wine.

"Oh no...that was it," Robin said. "I'm just gonna do a little more editing once I get home this evening."

"You do realize you're almost a two-hour drive away from your place in Santa Barbara, right?" Ivy said with raised eyebrows.

"Yeah, I know, but I'm going to my place out in Malibu tonight. It's like a thirty-minute drive from here. I do most of my editing out there for obvious reasons," Robin said, softly chuckling.

"Oh! I didn't know you had a place in Malibu, hun," Ivy said in a surprised tone.

"Yeah, I'm out there a lot because of the commute, but I have editing equipment in both places, though. Malibu makes life easier for me," Robin said, smiling. "I'll invite you out sometime."

"You're so modest," Ivy said, looking at Robin dreamy-eyed. "I always wanted to hang out in Malibu. Now I have a reason to!"

"Would you happen to surf?" Robin asked, but Ivy's phone began ringing again before she could answer. "Somebody wants your attention bad."

Robin chuckled and sipped her wine.

"Well, you're here right now, and I'm not interested in talking to anybody else," Ivy replied, pouring herself another glass of wine. "I'm really digging our conversations, too. And to answer your question, no, I don't know how to surf, but I know how to roller skate. Do you know how to roller skate, Robin?"

"I don't know how to roller skate, so how about this? I teach you how to surf, and you teach me how to roller skate. Deal?" Robin said, holding out her pinky, encouraging Ivy to grab it with hers.

"Deal!" Ivy said.

Robin grinned and ate the last spoonful of the parfait before pouring a little more wine into her glass.

"Here's to good friends! Thanks for spending the

evening with me," Ivy said, raising her glass.

"Ditto, sweetheart! Here's to good friends! It sure has been a good evening," Robin said before taking a sip.

They both sat in silence for a while, taking in the scene and getting lost in their own thoughts. Robin looked over at Ivy and noticed the top half of her robe was now entirely down, exposing her small tantalizing breasts that were glistening with tiny beads of sweat. From the corner of her eye, Ivy noticed Robin looking at them.

"You don't mind, do you?" Ivy asked in her most seductive voice, turning her head slowly in Robin's direction.

Robin licked her lips, indicating she was pleased.

"Not at all, sweetheart. Actually, I better get going. It's getting late, and I don't like the editing process interfering with my sleep," Robin said as she stood up and started walking off the terrace.

"Hold on a minute, Robin. You don't—"

Ding dong…ding dong.

Ivy was interrupted by the doorbell.

"Hold up," Ivy said while walking towards the door. As she adjusted her robe by pulling the belt tighter, she intermittently looked back at Robin. "It must be Ingrid, my dog sitter, because I'm not expecting anybody else."

Ivy opened the door, and it was indeed Ingrid.

"Hey, Ingrid. HI, SWEETIE! Hi, my baby," Ivy said gleefully, using a baby voice as she picked Sweetie up.

Sweetie wagged her tail and licked Ivy's cheek in absolute excitement.

"You missed your mama? Yes, you missed your mama!" Ivy said, scratching Sweetie's coat. "That was a long walk you took my baby on today. Where did you take her?"

Ivy noticed Ingrid looking at Robin.

"Hey, Robin. This is my dog sitter, Ingrid. Ingrid, this is Robin. Robin's the PA at the studio."

"Oh, that's nice," Ingrid said. "Nice to meet you, Robin. You're very pretty."

"Why, thank you. Nice to meet you, as well, Ingrid," Robin replied, smiling as Ivy cleared her throat.

Ivy seemed agitated by Ingrid's comment regarding Robin's beauty.

"I had to stop and pick up my children from school. Sorry I took so long."

"Oh, you know that's not a problem, Ingrid," Ivy remarked, gesturing with her hand. "I know my baby is in good hands with you. Besides, my friend Robin over there kept me company."

"Would you like me to stay with Sweetie again tomorrow, or will she be going with you to the studio?"

"Let me think about it. I'll call you later this evening before I go to bed and let you know. Alright?"

"Sure, no problem, but remember, I go to bed by eleven o'clock, and I turn my phone off."

"Yes, Ingrid. I remember, honey."

"Alright, goodnight. Nice to meet you again, Robin," Ingrid softly shouted to her.

"Likewise! Goodnight," Robin replied, leaning on the countertop.

"Alright, goodnight, Ingrid," Ivy said, practically pushing her out the door.

"Let me use your bathroom one more time before I hit

the road," Robin said, pretending not to remember that Ivy was in the middle of telling her something before the doorbell rang. She hoped Ivy forgot, too.

Lord, please don't let this woman ask me to stay with her tonight, Robin silently prayed once in the bathroom, then made the sign of the cross. *'Cause, Lord, if she does, you can't hold me responsible for what I might do to her,* she added, looking towards the ceiling.

When Robin came out of the bathroom, she found Ivy sitting on the sofa smoking a blunt with Sweetie in her lap. Ivy looked over at her, then extended her hand.

"You want some?" Ivy offered.

"No, thank you. That stuff makes me horny and sleepy, so I better get going," Robin said, chuckling.

"Suit yourself," Ivy said, shrugging her shoulders as she took another pull of the blunt while starring seductively at Robin before blowing the smoke in her direction.

When the smoke cleared, Ivy slowly turned away.

"Alright then, honey. Do what you gotta do. I'll see you at the studio tomorrow."

"Alrighty then. Tomorrow it is," Robin said, expecting Ivy to get up and see her out.

Ivy stood up but not to walk her to the door. Instead, she put Sweetie down, walked over to the terrace door, and leaned on the frame to stare out at the mountain views while puffing her blunt. Confused, Robin let herself out.

During her drive home, a barrage of sexual thoughts about what she wanted to do to Ivy ran through her mind.

Damn! I can't wait to put my hands, tongue, and body all over hers! But I can't lose focus. I HAVE to get this editing done, she said out loud as she pressed down on the accelerator.

*****

Thank God it's Friday! Robin thought as she walked into the studio the following day. She was moments away from knocking on Ivy's dressing room door to say good morning but paused when she heard her speaking to someone on the telephone. Her curiosity got the best of her, causing her to stand closer to the door so she could make out what Ivy was saying.

"Elliot, why do you keep calling my phone? I thought you said it was over between us?"

Robin realized Ivy was talking to her ex, the cameraman. So, she put her ear even closer, pretty much on the door. She didn't want to miss a word.

"Well, you're full of shit! ... Why?! Stop playing fucking games, Elliot! You know damn well why. Because your ass has been lying to me this whole time, that's why! ... About what?! About your wife, ASSHOLE! Remember her?! Listen, I'm not doing this shit with you. Get off my phone and don't call me anymore. I'm serious! … Hell no, you can't come over! What the fuck is wrong with you?! ... Don't worry about who was at my house last night. That's none of your gotdamn business, Elliot. Wait! Hold up! You're following me now? … Oh, you're laughing? This shit is funny to you? You think this shit is funny?! Go fuck yourself, Elliot, because you won't be fucking ME anymore, that's for damn sure! … Oh, really?! You think so, huh? Go fuck yourself! Fuck you! STOP CALLING MY FUCKING PHONE!" Ivy yelled and threw her phone against the wall.

Startled, Robin almost fell into the door, but her reflexes were on point. So, she was able to jump back immediately. She could hear Ivy crying and trying to ignite her cigarette lighter. Robin decided to walk away so Ivy could pull herself together in private. She didn't want to embarrass her. A few moments later, Ivy walked out of her dressing room looking fresh as a daisy!

Well, damn! She cleans up well. I'm impressed, Robin said to herself, nodding her head.

"Hey! Good morning, Robin," Ivy said, winking at her before walking onto the set.

"Good morning, Ivy. Looking beautiful as always," Robin responded cheerfully.

Ivy looked back at her and just smiled.

"Take one!" the director yelled out.

The introduction music for the series played as the announcer introduced "tonight's episode," titled Living in Confusion. Everyone was quiet on the set, waiting for their cue.

"And ACTION!"

"I believed in you. I thought I was the only one, Daniel," Ivy's character said, looking discouraged.

"You are the only one," Daniel replied.

"So… Wait. What? You think I'm desperate? No. Don't answer that. You think I'm just a fool, huh, Daniel? I should've known it was a bad idea to sleep with my partner," Ivy's character said before dramatically turning away from him.

"Listen to me, baby," Daniel said, walking over to her and grabbing her shoulders gently, causing her to spin around. "I just got carried away, that's all. She came over, we had a few drinks, and one thing led to another. I was a victim of circumstance, baby. Can't you see that?"

Ivy stood silent before covering her face with her hands, pretending to weep.

"Damn. Maybe..." he said, walking away slowly with his hands in his pockets and shaking his head.

"Maybe what, Daniel?"

"Maybe we should cool it for a while, huh?" he asked her sincerely, his eyebrows slightly raised.

"Yeah, Daniel. Good idea," Ivy's character said, clearing her throat. "That's the best thing you said all evening, and just so you know, I already asked the captain for a new partner."

Ivy's character's eyes welled up with more tears.

"Come on now. Why'd you go and do a thing like that? We work well together! Don't throw that all away over some girl. Come on," he pleaded.

"Daniel, are you listening to yourself? You told me that you loved me, then you cheated on me after a few lousy drinks! How do you expect us to work together after something like that? Huh? You really think I trust you to have my back?" she said with a scowled expression. "It'll never be the same. You made sure of that. Just go away, Daniel. I don't want to look at you right now!"

"Now hold on. Wait a minute," he said, walking over to her. "Let's get one thing straight now. I never told you I loved you."

Ivy turned around, wiping her tears away angrily as Robin watched from the sidelines, the clipboard held tight against her chest. Robin knew there was nothing fake about

Ivy's tears because of what she just went through with that jerk Elliot over the phone. Daniel tried to soften the blow by hugging her, but Ivy slapped his hands away and ran out of the room, enraged.

"And SCENE!" the director shouted.

Ivy walked around to the front of the set.

"This might be some of your best work yet, Ivy! Good job!" the director said, kissing her on the cheek. "Good job, Daniel. Well done, guys! Okay, that's it for today, folks. I'll see some of you tomorrow. Same time, same station."

"Whew! Art imitating my life, huh?" Ivy said as she winked and reached out to hug and kiss Daniel on the cheek, which he reciprocated before they exited the stage.

Robin went right away to get Ivy's tea to bring back to her dressing room.

"Right on time, Robin," Ivy said as she reached for the tea. "Thanks, honey. Did you get a lot of editing done last night?"

Ivy took a sip of tea while pulling off her false eyelashes.

"I did! And in just a few more days, I'll be completely done," Robin said happily.

"That's good news, honey! Are you editing today?"

"No, I'm gonna take a break today."

"Oh, so would you like to come over and have dinner with me tonight? I'm making my famous stuffed peppers that I told you about," Ivy said, looking through her vanity mirror at Robin's reaction.

"Only if we get to eat them on the terrace," Robin responded, grinning.

"Wonderful! I just gotta go to Dons on Wilshire Boulevard to pick up some red and yellow peppers because I only have the green ones at the house. Although, I could use those," Ivy said, contemplating the idea while tapping her nails on the vanity table. "Nah, the flavor of the green peppers is too strong. I have everything else I need, though. Oh, wait…do you like jasmine rice?"

"Never had it, but I'm willing to give it a try."

"I like you," Ivy told her while wiping the cold cream off her face.

"I like you, too, Ivy. Now hurry up so we can get out of here," Robin said before jogging to the door.

"Alright, honey. I'll be right out."

"See you in the parking lot," Robin said softly as she left the dressing room, pulling the door closed behind her.

Robin sat and waited in her car until Ivy came out.

"Hey, honey! Follow me," Ivy said, smiling as she walked swiftly to her car.

"I'm right behind you, baby," Robin whispered as she pulled out and tailgated Ivy down the Pacific Coast Highway.

Once inside Dons, Ivy went to the produce section, and Robin went to look for a bottle of wine but noticed the area of fresh flowers first. She picked out a floral arrangement with a variety of colored blooms surrounded by soft green leaves and baby's breath.

These are as beautiful as she is. I hope she likes them, Robin said to herself, deciding to leave the wine buying up to Ivy as she made a beeline to the register to pay for the flowers.

After going outside to hide the flowers in her car, Robin returned to the supermarket without Ivy even knowing she ever left. When they arrived at Ivy's apartment, Ingrid and Sweetie were already inside.

"Oh, hey, Ivy! Hi, Robin! I was just about to leave," Ingrid chirped.

Sweetie dashed to them, excitedly running in and out of Ivy's, Robin's, and Ingrid's legs, indicating she wanted to play.

"Hi, Mama's baby!" Ivy said, again using her baby voice. "Wait, Sweetie! Wait, baby…you're gonna make your mama fall. Let me put the groceries down, and I'll pick you up. Hold on! Hold on!"

Ivy continued putting the bags on the counter.

"Sweetie went to the bathroom three times. She should be good until the morning," Ingrid told them before hanging up Sweetie's leash at the front door. "You ladies have a good weekend! Call me if you need me, Ivy!"

"Goodnight!" they both shouted back in unison.

Ingrid waved, closing the door behind her.

"Robin, would you mind taking the groceries out of the bags while I jump in the shower?"

"Of course not! Do you mind if I put on some music?" Robin asked.

"Not at all, honey. Play something good. I need to decompress," Ivy said as she lit a cigarette on her way inside the bathroom.

Oh shit! I forgot about the flowers! Damn it! Robin thought, snapping her fingers but then decided to wait until Ivy got out of the shower. She would use the excuse of needing to get something out of her car.

Looking through Ivy's music collection, she chose Toni Braxton's "It's Just Another Sad Love Song" and put it on repeat.

Ten minutes later…

"This is my jam!" Ivy said, drying her hair with a towel as she walked out of the bathroom.

Robin could see Ivy's nipples through her white satin robe, and it instantly turned her on. Clearing her throat, she told Ivy that she had left something in her car and would be right back.

"Okay, honey. I'll start chopping up the onions and garlic and cleaning out the peppers," Ivy told Robin with her back turned.

As Robin walked briskly to the door, Ivy could hear Sweetie running behind her.

"Come back here, Sweetie!" Ivy yelled, stopping Sweetie in her tracks.

"It's okay. I'll take her with me," Robin said, chuckling as she bent down to pick Sweetie up. "We'll be right back."

Robin winked and scratched Sweetie's coat. When Robin got to the door, she noticed Ivy's keys resting inside a silver leaf dish on the console table.

"Ivy!" she yelled out. "I'ma take your keys. Okay? I don't want to leave the door open."

"Of course, honey," Ivy responded, smiling while turning her towel into a turban before peeling and cleaning the vegetables.

Moments later, Robin returned to the apartment with the aroma of onions and garlic filling the air.

"You got it smelling good in here!" Robin told her as she walked into the kitchen with one arm behind her back.

"Thank you, honey. Did you get what you needed out of the car?" Ivy asked, glancing over her shoulder while sautéing the vegetables.

"Yes, I did," Robin replied, smiling.

"Okay, that's good. What's with your arm behind your back?" Ivy asked suspiciously.

"Oh. These?" Robin said as she slowly revealed the bouquet to Ivy. "I bought these for you today. I hope you like them."

"Oh, my goodness! They're beautiful!" Ivy said, then placed the wooden spatula on the spoon rest on the stove and reached out to take the flowers. "When did you have time to buy these, Robin?"

"When we went to Dons. I was hoping they would cheer you up because I didn't like hearing you cry today."

"Well, they do, honey. They're beautiful," Ivy told her, looking at them with genuine happiness and gratitude just before realizing what Robin had said. "Wait a minute. What do you mean you didn't like hearing me cry?"

"Well…on my way into the studio this morning, I came to knock on your door to say good morning, but I stopped when I heard you arguing with Elliot on the phone. Then I heard you crying after you threw your phone at the wall."

Ivy just stood there looking down, not in an embarrassing way but in a "wish you didn't" kind of way.

"I wanted to come in and hug you, but I wasn't sure how you would react to me doing that. So, I just waited for you by the set."

"I appreciate that, honey," Ivy sincerely said while reaching out to squeeze Robin's hand. "Hey! Do you wanna help me cook?"

"Sure. Let me wash my hands first."

"While you're doing that, I'm gonna find a vase for these beauties," Ivy said, continuing to admire the bouquet.

Robin felt good about her decision to get the flowers as she walked into the bathroom with Sweetie on her heels.

"I see my baby likes you. I guess she takes after her mama."

"That's a beautiful thing!" Robin said, smiling as she dried her hands with the hand towel before coming out of the bathroom. When she stepped into the kitchen, she noticed the flowers on the island. "Ooh, that vase is pretty, Ivy. It really complements the flowers."

"I know it does," she said, glancing over at them. "But listen, I gotta take this robe off, honey. I need to be free! I'll put on a bra and panties if that's alright with you."

"Of course, it's alright, sweetheart. It IS your house. Besides, there's not much that offends me," Robin told her, grinning.

"Okay. I'll be right back," Ivy said, then jogged off to her bedroom.

"What do you need me to do in the meantime?" Robin yelled out.

Ivy didn't answer since she was walking back into the kitchen, lighting a blunt. Her curly hair hung freely, and she wore a sheer black bra with a matching thong. Robin could see her nipples and hairless vagina through the material, and the sight made her mouth water.

"That's a pretty set, Ivy. Whew! Did it just get hot in here, or is it me?" Robin asked, fanning herself.

"Well, the oven is on, so maybe it's the oven getting you hot," Ivy said, holding her blunt on the side of her mouth as she adjusted her bra straps.

"Oh right. I forgot about that," Robin replied,

chuckling.

"Well, do you mind if I take my shirt off?"

"Mi casa es tu casa, honey," Ivy said while walking over to the stove to turn down the burner under the jasmine rice.

Ivy put her blunt in the ashtray on the counter, then pulled out her glass bakeware from the lower cabinet to arrange the peppers in.

"Let's put on some different music while we cook," Robin said, walking to the living room.

"Good idea, but put on something mellow, honey," Ivy told her while she finished coring the peppers.

"I got it!" Robin shouted. "Oh yeah!"

"Which artist did you pick?"

"Frankie Beverly and Maze's greatest hits."

"Good choice," Ivy replied as she began swaying her hips to the melody of "Joy and Pain".

They both sang the lyrics as Robin removed her shirt, throwing it over the sofa and dancing into the kitchen to assist Ivy.

"What you need me to do, sweetheart?" Robin asked, snapping her fingers.

The white lace pushup bra and low rider jeans she was wearing showed off her six-pack.

"Well, damn!" Ivy blurted out, dropping the paring knife she was using to clean out the peppers. "Your stomach is banging, girl! What does the rest of your body look like? Shit!"

Robin blushed at Ivy's compliment.

"Thank you, sweetheart. Maybe if you're a good girl, I'll let you see what the rest of me looks like one day," Robin said, winking. "Now, what can I help you do, sweetheart?"

"Mmmph!" Ivy said, turning away briefly. "Okay, you can add that ground turkey over there to the pan with the onions and garlic in it. Just stir it around until it looks kind of grayish, and then I'll add the rice."

"You know what?" Robin asked her.

"What, honey?"

"I was going to buy some wine when we were at the market, but I didn't think you would like grocery store wine. So, I hope you have some wine to go with this."

"Of course, I do, baby."'

Baby? Wow! She never called me baby before, Robin thought to herself. *I like it.*

"I have a nice bottle of Sauvignon Blanc that will pair very well with the peppers," Ivy said, pointing to the wine fridge.

"Ivy, sweetheart…I think Sweetie needs water. She's panting a lot, and her bowl is empty."

"Look at you noticing," Ivy said, tapping Robin's arm playfully and grinning. "Mama's sorry, baby."

Ivy put some water in Sweetie's bowl and then returned to the kitchen to show Robin how she liked her stuffed peppers prepared.

"Alright, baby, you did good with the turkey. Now let me mix in the rice."

The next record on the album called "Lady of Magic" began to play.

"Oh wow! I haven't heard this song in a while. It brings back some good memories," Ivy said softly, continuing to sway her hips while she mixed up the stuffing.

"Yeah, I like this song, too. It's slow but not too slow,"

Robin concurred, arranging the peppers in the baking dish.

They both began singing the lyrics together.

"This song is making me feel some kinda way," Ivy said, glancing at Robin as she walked over to the island with the stuffing and temporarily closed her eyes. "Okay, let's stuff these babies."

"How long do they take in the oven?" Robin asked her.

"Not long. It's practically cooked. We're just waiting for the peppers to soften up, that's all."

As they stuffed the peppers together, they continued to sing. Ivy was standing so close to Robin that her nipples touched Robin's arm each time she reached over for more stuffing. Robin knew she was doing it on purpose but allowed it.

Once the peppers were stuffed, Ivy set the stove's timer for twenty minutes before exaggeratedly bending over directly in front of Robin to put the peppers inside. Robin's heart skipped a beat as she noticed the glow running down the curvature of Ivy's back. She found herself getting even more turned on.

She's flirting hard, Robin thought before clearing her throat and asking, "Where's your corkscrew, sweetheart? I want to open the wine."

Ivy pointed to the island's drawer as she relit her blunt using the eye of the stove. She then took a puff before sashaying her way over to the cabinet to retrieve two wine glasses and meet Robin at the island. Robin popped the cork and poured them both a glass of wine.

"Cheers," they said in unison, looking at one another before taking a sip.

Without warning, Robin moved the flowers from the

island to the counter by the sink and took another sip of her wine. She watched Ivy with lustful eyes. Ivy recognized that passionate look and returned the favor before turning around to place her glass on the counter. No sooner than she did that, Robin walked towards her, picked her up by her ass cheeks, and sat her down on the island. Ivy gasped but didn't resist.

"This is what you wanted, right? Walking around here practically naked in this sexy-ass underwear," Robin said while pulling on Ivy's bra strap as she stared at her nipples and licked her lips.

Ivy sat still and just watched her.

"Then you bent over in front of me like that and thought I wasn't going to do nothing?" Robin continued, her hands resting on Ivy's thighs.

Robin's voice was soft as she leaned in and kissed Ivy softly on her neck, causing Ivy to repeatedly moan as her palms rested on the granite behind her. Ivy tried to speak, but Robin gently placed two fingers across her lips.

"Shhh…be quiet."

"Your lips are so fucking soft, though," Ivy moaned and seductively licked her lips.

Robin caressed the back of Ivy's neck, pulling her close and looking her in her eyes before they kissed each other as passionately as one would a lover returning home from war. In the heat of the moment, Robin grabbed one of Ivy's legs and pulled her forward—a look of great sexual hunger in her eyes. Ivy's heart palpitated as her moist hairless vagina kissed Robin's six-pack abs, causing her to inhale deeply while slowly wrapping her legs around Robin's waist. The stove's timer sounded, interrupting their groove. They both laughed and softly kissed once more before Robin helped her off the island.

"The wine tastes good, by the way, but it tastes even better sucked off your lips, sweetheart," Robin said, smiling from ear to ear at Ivy.

"Thanks, baby. You're not so bad yourself," Ivy replied with a wink before removing the peppers from the oven. "Shit!" Ivy shouted while placing the bakeware on top of the trivet.

"What? What happened, sweetheart?" Robin asked in a startled voice.

"I almost forgot the cheese! I want to sprinkle some on the peppers while they're still hot."

Robin chuckled and slapped Ivy's ass as she hurried past her to get the cheese from the fridge. Ivy looked back, blushing.

Would you look at that! Robin said to herself. *I'm turning her into a pussy cat already. Me-fuckin-ow.*

Ivy sprinkled the cheese on the peppers and then walked over to the cabinet to retrieve the dinner plates. Robin couldn't take her eyes off of her—hypnotized by Ivy's every move.

"Are you ready to eat, honey?" Ivy asked, smiling and walking over to the terrace with the food.

"Oh, we're back to 'honey' now?" Robin asked playfully, her eyebrows raised. "Okay, okay."

"No! I'm sorry…I meant, baby," Ivy said in her baby voice that she usually used when talking to Sweetie. "Calling people 'honey' is a habit of mine, but I'ma call you 'baby' from now on, HONEY."

"That's better," Robin teased, chuckling as she took the

plates from Ivy's hands and walked them out to the terrace.

Ivy picked up their wine glasses and the bottle of wine to follow Robin to the table on the terrace, where they sat down to eat.

"Would you like a refill?" Ivy asked as she poured herself another glass of wine.

Robin waved her hand, gesturing no while chewing on her food.

"This is delicious! You outdid yourself for real, babe."

"Thank you, baby, but you helped," Ivy said, blushing. "Why don't you want another glass of wine, though?"

"I had like one and a half glasses already, sweetheart, so I think I've had enough. Don't you?" Robin asked, cutting another piece of her pepper. "Besides, I gotta drive home. You forgot?"

Robin slowly licked a grain of rice off the side of her mouth.

"You're so fucking sexy. Damn, girl!" Ivy commented, her fork pausing at her lips. "And no, I DON'T think you had enough."

Ivy put down her fork and poured the remainder of the wine into Robin's glass.

"Who said you had to drive home tonight anyway?" she seductively said while gently clinching the fork between her teeth.

"Alright, don't say I didn't warn you," Robin said, picking up her glass and leaning back in her chair, resting her free arm on the back of it before taking another sip of the wine. "Cheers, sweetheart."

With a devilish look in her eye, Robin raised the glass to her lips.

"Cheers, baby," Ivy said, raising her glass as well and winking. "Robin…what would you say if I invited you to my bedroom tonight?"

Ivy leaned on her elbows while twirling her wine glass between her fingers.

"I would say…I'm not sleepy yet."

Ivy playfully rolled her eyes.

"Do you find me attractive, Robin?" Ivy asked, sitting back in her chair and picking up her last forkful of food.

"You can't be seriously asking me that, baby. Right?" Robin asked, her eyebrow raised.

Ivy gave no response.

"Okay…I'll tell you what. I'll show you better than I can tell you when we go to your bedroom," Robin said, then winked as she placed the last forkful of her food in her mouth and gulped the last of her wine.

"Good girl!" Ivy said jokingly while clapping. "You ate all your food! I'm proud of you, baby!"

"That's not all I'm eating tonight." Robin chuckled in a serious yet sexy tone. "I left room for dessert, so take it in your room for me. I'll eat it when I get out of the shower. Okay?"

Robin stood up, rubbing her abs slowly and sucking on her bottom lip. Robin's words turned Ivy on so much that her heart skipped a beat, and her inner thighs moistened from the extra juices her pussy was creating.

"I got just the thing for you to taste, and I can't wait for you to tell me how you like it," Ivy responded, batting her eyes slowly. "Let me put the dishes in the dishwasher while you go take that shower."

Ivy got up from the table and walked towards the

kitchen.

"Oh!" Ivy said, turning her head around without missing a step. "There are some clean towels in the closet behind the bathroom door. I'll meet you in the bedroom when you're done."

Ivy placed her tongue at the corner of her top teeth before bending over to load the dishwasher.

A few minutes later, Robin finished taking her shower and walked into Ivy's bedroom, anxiously waiting for "dessert" with her towel wrapped around her waist. Robin glanced at the bed and noticed Ivy's beautiful petite body lying across the bed. Robin untied her towel and let it drop to the floor with the quickness. The sight of Ivy's naked body made her drool at the mouth. Climbing onto the bed, she picked up one of Ivy's feet and started licking it slowly.

"This little piggy went to market," Robin said softly as she placed Ivy's big toe in her mouth.

Looking at Robin through barely open eyes, Ivy cried out from the pleasurable sensation.

Robin liked being watched whenever she was having intimate relations with someone. So, she continued to suck on Ivy's toes while Ivy continued to open and close her eyes in insurmountable ecstasy. Their interactions were deliberately slow and sexy.

"This little piggy stayed home," Robin continued, placing another one of Ivy's toes in her mouth, licking in between them.

"Oh my God, baby," Ivy cried. "You're making me so…"

"So what?" Robin asked softly as she slowly opened her eyes and stared directly at Ivy while continuing to suck on her toes.

"Weak, baby. You're making me weak," Ivy said, planting her face in the pillow.

Robin picked up Ivy's other foot.

"This one is getting jealous," Robin whispered to Ivy as she began licking and sucking the toes on that foot with more passion than the first foot.

"I never had anybody make love to my feet before, baby. You're the fucking best," Ivy whispered in between her constant moaning.

Robin brushed the nipples of her firm breasts across Ivy's calves while licking and kissing them on her way up to Ivy's thighs.

"Yes, baby," Ivy moaned. "Yes, gotdamn it."

Robin licked on Ivy's thighs as if they were her favorite ice cream flavor until her tongue wanted to get a taste of her ass cheeks. Then she moved to licking and nibbling on Ivy's cheeks, making her squirm even more when she licked in between them.

"Turn around, baby," Robin commanded softly. "I wanna see the expression on your face when I make you cum."

Her words practically took Ivy's breath away. Nobody had ever been this forward yet gentle with her in bed before now.

"Look at your body, though. Damn," Ivy said, her voice just above a whisper.

As she admired Robins' body, she ran her hands across her breasts and down her arms, squeezing her biceps before finally rubbing them across her six-pack abs. "I admire how you take care of yourself, and you look so feminine doing it, baby."

"Thank you, baby. I'm glad you like it," Robin said, kissing Ivy's lips tenderly before putting her mouth around Ivy's small perky nipples, teasing them by slurping and nibbling them.

Gripping Robin's back, Ivy pressed her nails into it.

"Oh, FUCK yes!" Robin belted out. "I like that shit, baby."

Robin continued to suck on Ivy's breast while she reached between her legs to play with HER pussy. Her forearm rubbed up against Ivy's box in the process.

"Fuck! Are you playing with your pussy, baby? Huh?" Ivy whined.

"Mmm-hmmm," Robin moaned in response. "This is so sexy! Shit!"

Ivy grinded harder on Robin's forearm.

"My pussy is soaking wet now, baby," Ivy told her.

"Oh yeah?" Robin responded after taking Ivy's nipple out of her mouth to look up at her.

"Yeah, it is. So, what are you gonna do about it?" Ivy whispered.

"Let me show you."

Robin took a quick nibble for the road and then worked her way down to Ivy's moist hairless pussy.

"Open wide."

Ivy let her legs fall open to the side.

"Flexible, too, I see," Robin seductively said as she began slurping on Ivy's pussy like it was a Sunday dinner straight after church and directly from the oven. "Your pussy tastes so…fucking…good."

"Oh, my God, baby! You're. Trying. To. Make. Me.

Cum. Already. Aren't you?"

Ivy gyrated her pussy on Robin's face while holding her head firmly in place. Robin placed her hand back in between her legs, and they began moaning together softly.

"Damn, baby. The more I suck on your pussy, the wetter I get! I fucking love this!" Robin gasped, continuing to slurp. "I don't want you to cum now. I wanna scissor you, baby. Assume the position, sweetheart."

"Yes, baby," Ivy replied while dabbing away the perspiration on her face with the top sheet.

Robin straddled Ivy. Their grind was slow, steady, wet, and very noisy.

"Fuck! Even your legs have muscles, baby. Shit! This feels so fucking good!" Ivy shouted.

Ivy held onto Robin's thigh as their clits French kissed. Both women picked up the tempo, screaming and gripping one another as they climaxed hard together.

"Fuuuuuuuck!" Robin squealed before falling backwards on the bed.

Ivy's right leg wouldn't stop shaking, so Robin held it gently for her as she continued to release residual cum. As Ivy calmed down, Robin crawled up to cuddle and rock her until her shaking stopped completely.

"You enjoy yourself, baby?" Robin whispered in her ear.

"Very much," Ivy replied, taking Robin's hand to hold in hers. "Thank you for staying with me tonight. I didn't want to be alone."

Ivy looked over her shoulder, stroking the side of Robin's face with her free hand.

"I do what I can," Robin said jokingly, then nibbled on

Ivy's earlobe.

"Hey," Ivy said softly and turned completely around so they could be face to face. "You don't think I'm just using you because of what happened between Elliot and me today, do you?"

"Listen, beautiful; I don't trip over stuff like that. You're not with him anymore, and we're consenting adults, right? But...in the words of Bill Withers, ``If it feels this good" Robin sang while smiling, then kissed Ivy's forehead.

"You see!" Ivy said, sitting up and pointing her finger. "This is why I fucks with you!"

Ivy gave Robin a long, sweet smooch on the lips before jumping out of bed and running to the living room to retrieve her blunt. She returned to the bedroom, lighting her blunt and taking two pulls before extending her hand to Robin.

"Nah, sweetheart. I'ma pass."

"You don't smoke, do you?" Ivy asked while picking the fallen weed off the tip of her tongue.

"Sometimes I do, but not tonight, baby."

Ivy shrugged her shoulders and took another puff before putting it out in the ashtray and playfully jumping back into the bed and under the covers. They exchanged tickles and kissed once more before Ivy snuggled up under Robin's left armpit until they both fell asleep.

*****

The next morning when they awoke, Ivy was still under Robin's arm, while Sweetie and her favorite chew toy were at the foot of the bed. Ivy took a big sniff of Robin's underarm before reaching over, gently squeezing her right breast, and sucked on her left nipple until Robin woke up.

"Ooh…good morning, sweetheart," Robin crooned, smiling and looking down at Ivy.

"Good morning to you, beautiful," Ivy said, removing her mouth from Robin's nipple as she started rubbing Robin's abs.

"Are you staying for breakfast?" Ivy asked, resting her face on Robin's chest.

"I could go for some bacon and eggs if you have any," Robin said while stretching.

"As a matter of fact, I do!" Ivy responded cheerfully, then kissed the tip of Robin's nose before jumping out of bed.

Sweetie barked as she jumped off the bed to follow Ivy into the bathroom.

"Is Mama's baby hungry?" Ivy said to Sweetie in her baby voice, and Sweetie wagged her tail in excitement. "Come on, Mama's baby."

After flushing the toilet, Ivy bent down to pick up Sweetie. She rubbed her nose against Sweetie's as she carried her into the kitchen to retrieve her food to fill up her bowl.

"There you go, my baby."

Ivy put Sweetie down in front of her bowls before walking into the kitchen to fix her and Robin's breakfast.

Robin couldn't stop smiling as she listened to Ivy's interaction with her fur baby. She pulled the sheet up and over her head and lay back down to wait for Ivy to call her when breakfast was ready. However, before Robin could drift back off to sleep, her phone rang. She blindly reached to grab it off the nightstand and looked at the illuminated screen while remaining under the sheet.

Hmmm. Who is this?

"Hello? … Yes, this is Robin. Who am I speaking with, please? … Hello, Jerry Myles," she replied with a raised eyebrow. "Have I met you somewhere before? You'll have to forgive me if I have because I don't recall meeting anyone named Jerry recently."

Robin listened intently to Jerry's response, which caused her to remove the sheet from her head and sit up in the bed—excitement written all over her face.

"Are you serious?!" she yelled in delight, then covered her mouth with her hand. "Sure! Yes! I can meet you in… Wait, what time is it now? Alright, it's ten o'clock. I can be there in the next two hours. … Alright, see you then, Jerry, and thanks a million!"

Robin hung up the phone, threw back the sheet, and jumped out of bed, running to the kitchen to share her news with Ivy.

"Baby! Baby! Guess what?" Robin shouted.

"Hey, baby. Where's the fire?" Ivy asked, grinning while cracking eggs in a bowl.

"You'll never believe this!" Robin said ecstatically, hopping from foot to foot while trying to calm herself.

Pausing from what she was doing, she gave Robin her full attention. "What has you so excited, baby? Tell me. I'm listening."

Robin smiled broadly.

"My mom contacted a movie producer in Hollywood named Jerry Myles. She told him what I wanted to do in the industry, and he wants to meet with me. He might want to produce my first film, baby! Isn't that shit awesome?!" Robin said, jumping in place.

"Hell yeah, that shit is awesome, baby! I heard of Jerry Myles! He produced that blockbuster vampire movie last summer. Umm..." Ivy snapped her fingers, trying to remember. "Oh yeah! It was called *Blue Valentine*!"

"Oh wow! I didn't know that! I saw that movie, too! Now I'm extra hyped!" Robin said, bumping her fist together.

"Oh my God, baby! Congratulations! We have to celebrate this!"

"Hold on now, sweetheart. He didn't say he would do anything yet," Robin told her, laughing.

"But he will, babe. I can feel it!" Ivy shouted.

"Thank you for that," Robin said sentimentally, her hands crossing her chest to express gratitude.

"Oh shit! Let me turn this pan down before we just have eggs for breakfast," Ivy said, chuckling. "Hand me that splatter cover over there, please, honey."

Ivy pointed to the location and turned down the heat under the bacon.

"No problem. Here you go," Robin said, walking slowly up behind her and putting the lid on the pan herself while kissing Ivy softly on her neck.

"I really like you, Robin. You need to know that," Ivy expressed as she slowly turned around and gently pushed Robin away from the stove.

"Aww, baby. I like you, too," Robin said as the two women stood face to face.

She placed her arms around Ivy's waist and bent to kiss Ivy softly on the lips.

"Mmm," Ivy crooned. "What time do you have to meet up with him?"

"I told him I'll meet him in two hours. So, I'ma jump in the shower right quick," Robin said as she ran off to the bathroom. "Hey," she called out, "I wanna take you out to my place in Malibu when I'm done. That's if you don't have any plans today, sweetheart."

Before Ivy could formulate her words, she heard Robin turn on the shower, so she decided to wait until Robin came out to give her an answer.

Ivy was walking over to the table with their breakfast plates when Robin walked out of the bathroom with a towel wrapped only around her waist.

"This looks delicious, baby," Robin said, rubbing her palms together as she sat down.

"Girl, this ain't nothing but some plain ole bacon and eggs. Stop it," Ivy said with a smile and walked back into the kitchen for the orange juice.

Shrugging her shoulders, Robin took a forkful of the eggs and put them in her mouth.

"I cut up some strawberries, babe, and poured us some orange juice," Ivy softly shouted from the kitchen.

"Yummy!" Robin said, folding a strip of bacon into her mouth.

"Here you go, honey…I mean, baby," Ivy said, smiling.

"No biggie, sweetheart. I'll answer to honey or baby if you're the one calling me it," Robin told her, blowing air kisses at Ivy and playing footsie with her under the table.

"Hey, sweetheart, I can pick you up later and take you out to Malibu with me. Sound good?"

"Of course, babe," Ivy said after taking a sip of her

orange juice. "I have a few errands to run today, but I'll make sure to be finished before you come to pick me up."

"Cool," Robin said as she finished her breakfast.

Robin then got up to get dressed and head out to meet Jerry.

"Alright, sweetheart. I'm estimating I'll be back to get you and Sweetie around four o'clock," Robin said as she leaned in for a kiss.

"Aww, baby," Ivy said, blushing and returning her kiss. "We're taking Sweetie with us? That's so nice, baby."

"Why wouldn't I? She's your baby girl, right?" Robin asked, grinning.

"Yes, she is," Ivy replied softly while still blushing. "We can't wait!"

Robin smiled, then lightly jogged to the door before pausing halfway and turning around.

"Oh, would you happen to have a helmet by any chance?"

"A helmet? A helmet for what, babe," Ivy asked with a puzzled look.

Robin chuckled. "Well, your response already let me know you don't have one. Don't worry about it, sweetheart. I'll see you later."

They blew each other air kisses until Robin was on the other side of the door.

*****

Four hours later, Ivy's phone rang. It was Robin telling her to come downstairs. When Ivy went outside, she stood in front of her complex looking around anxiously for Robin while holding Sweetie in her arms.

Where is she? Ivy said to herself, scratching Sweetie's fur while continuing to look around for Robin's car. *I hate waiting for people,* she said to herself, not in an angry way, but more like frustrated.

Suddenly, Ivy heard Robin's voice calling out her name. She turned to her left and saw Robin standing in front of a custom, burnt orange, top-of-the-line motorcycle with tallboy seating. She held a helmet in each of her hands.

"What the fuck, baby?! I didn't know you were a motorcycle rider!" Ivy screamed, swiftly walking over to her. "This shit is the bomb, girl! I fucking love this shit! Sweetie is happy to see you, too, I see. She never tried to jump out of my arms to go to anybody else before. You're a pretty special person when my baby likes you, too!"

Ivy winked while smiling from ear to ear.

"I'm glad you're both excited to see me just as I am excited to see you two," Robin said, smiling big herself. "Here you go, baby. Put this helmet on, and I'll help you two get on."

Robin helped Ivy onto the bike and waited until she put the helmet on properly before she put hers back on. Once she checked on Ivy and Sweetie to ensure they were safely in the seat, she took off for the Pacific Coast Highway en route to her place in Malibu.

"Whoo-hoo!" Ivy screamed out with one arm up in the air and the other holding Sweetie tightly.

Robin exited Highway 1 directly onto her property at 17100 Sea Vista Drive. She parked her motorcycle in the two-car garage and removed her helmet before helping Ivy out of her seat.

"Wow! It's gorgeous up here! And totally off the beaten path. My goodness," Ivy said, her voice trailing off into a whisper of awe as she took in the scene with Sweetie in the crux of her arm.

"Thanks, sweetheart. I enjoy my solitude out here. I get to edit my film, swim, and surf without being bothered. The hustle and bustle of Hollywood can be overwhelming sometimes. Not to mention the studio is closer from here than Santa Barbara."

Ivy remained silent as her eyes took in everything.

"Come on, baby. Let me show you around," Robin said, smiling as she took Ivy's hand.

The home's décor was navy-blue and white with an open concept design. The expansive windows on the main level provided a view of the ocean from every room. The chef's kitchen included top-of-the-line appliances, with the pièce de résistance being a restored vintage cobalt blue stove adorned with brass-trimmed knobs, which looked like no one had ever cooked on it.

The indoors met with the outdoors on every level of the home's aesthetic as both patios extended from the living room and the master suite. The patios were dressed in white with pergolas and fire pits in their center. There was an infinity pool extended from the master suite's patio that overlooked the Pacific Ocean. It was breathtakingly beautiful.

"I want you to fuck me…right now," Ivy told Robin seductively while taking off her clothes at the top of the staircase, staring at Robin with extreme lust in her eyes.

"You ain't said nothing but a word, baby," Robin told her, stepping out of her khaki linen pants and pulling her white t-shirt aggressively over her head.

She rushed over to Ivy, swept her off her feet, and carried her to the bedroom—tongue kissing her all the way there. Robin threw Ivy on her floating king-size bed and stared at her as the ocean breeze gently blew the sheer white curtains hanging from the patio doors in and out of the room. Robin finally crawled up on the bed, laying half of her body on top of Ivy's and throwing one of her legs over hers as they passionately kissed. Ivy held on to the back of Robin's head, her fingers gently grabbing her hair, while the nails of her other hand softly scratched Robin's back.

"I wanna eat your pussy while you're eating mine," Ivy told her in between kisses before she slid down to give Robin some legroom at the top. "Come. Sit on my face."

Robin crawled over Ivy's head and straddled her face. Ivy slapped her ass while she licked and sucked on Robin's clit, making Robin moan as she bent over to plant her face between Ivy's legs. Robin opened her vaginal lips with her tongue. Ivy spread Robin's thighs further apart so she could turn her mouth into a suction cup over Robin's entire clit while Robin continued to lick and suck on her.

"You taste so fucking good, girl," Ivy moaned as they grinded on each other's face slowly.

"This shit is so good…we need our own fucking theme music, baby," Robin crooned when she came up for air.

Both women griped each other's thighs, and Ivy's eyes rolled back with each orgasm that caused her left leg to shake violently with pleasure. Robin's last orgasm made her body contort so much that she fell off Ivy's face, landing sideways on the bed, her body sticky from sweat and cum.

She moved the wet hair from her face, then looked over affectionately at Ivy with pure satisfaction in her eyes.

"Damn, baby," Ivy whispered, her head slowly moving from side to side as the shaking in her leg calmed.

"I know, baby. It can only get better from here," Robin said as she leaned over and kissed Ivy's forehead.

Robin plopped on her back while Ivy cuddled in her arms, with both of them waking up thirty minutes later.

"You be nutting me out!" Robin said jokingly, looking down at Ivy when she awakened.

"For real! I didn't even realize I fell asleep," Ivy said while stretching and grinning.

"Would you like to go to dinner, or do you want me to cook something for us?" Robin asked.

"Can we go out tomorrow night?" Ivy asked in a shy voice.

"Of course, we can, baby! Besides, I was hoping that would be your answer, because I bought us some lobster tails. I wanted to cook for YOU this time," Robin said, pointing at Ivy and smiling. "Come on. Let's go downstairs."

As Robin picked up her panties and t-shirt to put back on, Sweetie ran in and out of the room.

"I'ma go fire up the grill."

"You have any wine, baby?" Ivy asked, scooting off the bed and skipping up behind Robin, clasping her hands around her waist.

"I sure do! I bought some Chardonnay."

"That goes perfect with lobster, baby. Good job!" Ivy said, her head now resting in the middle of Robin's back.

"I asked the guy in the liquor store," Robin admitted

with a chuckle.

"Whatever works, baby," Ivy said, loosening her hands to hold on to the banister. "I gotta use the bathroom, but I don't remember where it is, honey."

"Make a left down the hall. You can't miss it, sweetheart," Robin said, then started walking briskly to the kitchen to retrieve the 10 oz. lobster tails, garlic butter, and corn on the cob from the fridge.

Robin placed all the items on a stoneware tray sitting on the countertop and went to the outdoor kitchen to heat the grill.

Ivy was impressed with the design of the bathroom. Navy and white marble tile flowed seamlessly from the floor up the walls. A frameless hinged shower door in satin navy—with navy matte hardware—and a free-standing, rolled-rim, glossy white slipper tub—also with navy matte metal hardware—gleamed brilliantly with the crystal chandelier hanging above. The toilet, located in a nook, had a free-standing tank and gold chain pulls.

As Ivy sat on the toilet, she was taken aback by the lush green landscape she observed out of the large picture window in front of her.

This is stunning! she whispered to herself. *Absolutely stunning!*

After taking a quick shower, Ivy walked back into the kitchen looking for Robin but was met with Sweetie sleeping in a doggie bed next to the cabinet. A bag of fresh gourmet dog food sat next to it.

She never said anything to me about having a dog, Ivy said to herself, scratching her head and looking puzzled.

"Hey, Robin! Where are you, honey?" Ivy called out.

"I'm out here, baby! I'm prepping the grill! Can you bring out the tails and the corn for me? I left them on the counter."

"No problem. These suckers are huge!" Ivy said as she walked them out to her.

"Yeah, baby," Robin said, taking the tray from Ivy's hands.

"I never knew you had a dog."

"I don't," Robin replied while putting the lobster tails on the grill.

"So why do you have a doggie bed and dog food?" Ivy asked, still confused.

"I went to the pet store after my meeting with Jerry this afternoon—which went well, by the way," she said, winking. "And I picked up that stuff for Sweetie."

"I cannot believe I didn't figure that out," Ivy said, tapping her head. "You're so thoughtful, baby.

Ivy looked at Robin with admiration.

"Why are you single? For real," Ivy asked with her hands on her naked hips.

"Who said I was single?" Robin said, raising one of her eyebrows.

Her response caused a look of surprise from Ivy.

"I'm just playing with you. I'm picky, baby."

Robin reached for the corn to put on the grill next.

"The bathroom is gorgeous. And that view!" Ivy said, her eyes wide and mouth open.

"Thanks, babe," Robin said, closing the grill's lid. "I recently renovated the bathroom. You're the first person to see it. My mother hasn't even seen it yet."

"Ooh, I feel so special," Ivy said, smiling coyly.

"After dinner, let's say we get in the pool, do a few laps, and then watch the sun go down?" Robin asked.

"I'm down for that!" Ivy responded, smiling, "Hey, Robin…thank you for making me feel so special, baby."

Ivy walked over to hold Robin's hand.

"Aww. Just so you know, I'll do almost anything for you, girl," Robin told her. "Now gimme a kiss."

They quickly kissed before Robin ran over to the grill to remove the food.

"I don't wanna overcook these tails 'cause then you'll think I'm a lousy cook," Robin said, laughing as she took the food off the grill and placed it on the table next to the fire pit. "Shoot!"

"What, baby?" Ivy asked, shucking her corn.

"I forgot the Chardonnay. I'll be right back."

"This looks wonderful, baby. Let me find out you're an undercover chef!" Ivy teased, admiring the grill marks on the lobster and corn.

"Hmmm," Robin said, walking out with the wine and placing it in the center of the table. "You think that's something? Watch this!"

Robin slowly poured the herbaceous garlic butter over the lobster tails and corn.

"You betta pour that butter, girl!" Ivy joked, making them both erupt in laughter. "This lobster tail is so tender. You did that, baby!"

Ivy took another piece and placed it in her mouth.

"I'm glad you like it," Robin said, wiping the butter from the corn off her chin.

"May I?" Ivy asked, reaching for Robin's wine glass.

"Yes, please. Thank you, sweetheart."

Ivy poured their glasses, then raised hers to toast. Robin picked up her glass after sucking the butter from her fingers.

"What should we toast to?"

"To many more nights like this one," Ivy responded.

"I'll toast to that!" Robin said, touching her glass to Ivy's.

They continued to eat, drink, laugh, and have small talk.

"That was delicious, baby," Ivy told her once they finished eating. Then she stood, walked around the table, and leaned over Robin's chair to kiss her. "Let me help you take the dishes inside," she offered while walking back to her side of the table.

"I got it, baby. Relax," Robin told her as she gathered the plates.

"Alright, I need a cigarette anyway. Hold tight!" Ivy said, smacking Robin's ass on her way inside the house.

Robin chuckled like always.

When Ivy returned smoking her cigarette, she asked Robin if she had any playing cards.

"I do," Robin responded. "What, you trying to play spades or something?"

"Yes! Thank God you know how to play spades!" Ivy said, relieved. "But, I'm warning you. I'm the best at it, baby."

"Oh really?" Robin asked, smiling.

"I sure am. Let me tell you HOW good," Ivy said, clearing her throat. "I'm so good that my grandmother used to get me out of my bed to come downstairs and play folks for money when I was a little girl."

"Oh shit! I'm in trouble then!" Robin teased, pulling out a small drawer under the counter to retrieve the cards.

They played four rounds of spades, and Ivy won every single time.

"This is unfair," Robin blurted out while laughing.

"Don't be a sore loser," Ivy teased as she put the cards back in the box.

"Hey, sweetheart, the sun will be going down soon. We can watch it set in the pool if you still wanna go for a swim," Robin told her.

"Of course, I do, baby. Grab that bottle, and let's go!" Ivy said, running up the floating staircase towards the master suite.

They jumped in the pool and started splashing water on each other like two little schoolgirls. Then they raced two laps around the pool before getting on the swan floats. They held hands and watched sections of the sky turn yellow, red, and purple while sipping wine as the sun set.

"This is so beautiful and romantic," Ivy said, sipping on the remainder of her wine.

"It sure is, baby," Robin agreed, looking over at her. "But not as beautiful as you."

Ivy blushed.

"Not as beautiful as you, either."

They stayed there until the moon cast its soft white glow on the still waters of the infinity pool and the ocean below.

"You wanna listen to some music, baby?" Robin asked, swallowing her last bit of wine.

"I do. What you got?" Ivy asked in an excited tone.

"You remember mixed tapes, right?"

"I do. What about them?"

"My mom made me a playlist with some 80s music on it 'cause she knows I like that kind of music. You wanna listen to it?"

"Sure, why not!"

When they got out of the pool, Sweetie was waiting right there for them, happily wagging her tail. Robin picked Sweetie up this time, and she and Ivy started walking down the stairs towards the living space. Ivy suddenly stopped and turned around.

"I'll be right back, baby," she said, jogging back up the stairs.

"Where are you going?" Robin asked, putting Sweetie down and continuing to walk towards the living room.

"To get my blunt!" Ivy yelled from upstairs.

Ivy returned in time to see Robin singing and dancing to Carl Carlton's "She's A Bad Mama Jama." Ivy joined in and sang along.

"Yass!" Ivy sang, pointing at Robin and snapping her fingers while puffing on her blunt as she danced her way over to her.

They continued to dance and sing along until the song ended.

"Whew!" Ivy said, drawing another puff and passing it to Robin.

This time, Robin took it and drew two puffs before passing it back to Ivy.

The next song to play was Evelyn "Champagne" King's "Love Come Down."

"This song couldn't be more perfect," Robin said, then grabbed Ivy gently around her waist and pulled her closer so they could dance together.

Robin sang the lyrics softly in Ivy's ear.

"You ready for round two?" Robin asked, grinning hard because she was buzzed.

"Hell yeah," Ivy said, seductively biting her bottom lip. "But can I ask you something first, baby?"

"Of course! What's up?" Robin said while walking away to get some crushed ice from the fridge. "Damn, my mouth is dry."

"I'm not the first woman you've been with like this, right?" Ivy asked her.

"Well, damn!" Robin said, her eyebrows raised. "I'm THAT bad in bed?"

"No! No, baby, that's not what I'm trying to say at all!" Ivy said with her right hand raised. "I guess what I want to know is...do I have to worry about some woman coming up to me and trying to kick my ass over you?"

Robin nearly choked on her ice.

"Hell nah!" she said, clearing her throat. "I don't get down like that, baby. Trust me, you don't have anything to worry about. I'm greedy but only for one woman at a time. I don't cheat, sweetheart."

"That's good to know because..." Ivy paused and stared out the patio.

"Because what, baby?" Robin asked with concern in her voice as she walked over to Ivy.

"Well..." Ivy turned around to face her. "...you know I just went through something similar with Elliot, and I don't think I can go through no shit like that again."

"Nah, you good, baby. Come here," Robin said, playfully grabbing Ivy and nibbling on her neck with her ice-cold lips.

Ivy yelped, then broke away and ran up the solar-lit floating staircase with Robin dead on her heels.

"Oh, you in trouble now, girl!" Robin shouted.

Ivy screamed like a schoolgirl in anticipation of Robin catching her. Robin caught her and tackled her to the bed, where they wrestled until Robin pinned Ivy's arms down so she couldn't move. Ivy kicked wildly as Robin pretended to bite her neck.

"You're gonna make me pee on myself!" Ivy repeated, practically drooling until Robin finally stopped.

Robin and Ivy continued to laugh until Robin got serious and looked deeply into Ivy's eyes.

"Listen," Robin started, "I'll always be here for you unless you tell me different. I'm not like anyone you've ever dated before or anybody you'll ever date again. If we're honest with each other, I don't see why this wouldn't work."

"You're very sure of yourself, huh?" Ivy asked, rolling over to her side. "So you want us to date exclusively?"

"Yes, I do," Robin responded without any hesitation.

"Can I ask you why?" Ivy said, playing with the sheet.

"Well…why not?" Robin asked, raising her eyebrow and running her finger down the bridge of Ivy's nose before tapping the tip of it.

Ivy inched her way over closer to Robin and pressed her head up against her chest, indicating she wanted to lay on it. Robin laid back and wrapped her arm around Ivy. They both got lost in their thoughts for a few moments before Robin got up and stood at the foot of the bed. Grabbing Ivy by her ankles, she pulled her down to the edge and placed her feet flat on her stomach.

"Ooh!" Ivy said, her tongue at the corner of her top teeth.

Robin smiled at her as she bent to kiss her feet. Then she slightly opened Ivy's legs and placed them on her shoulders. Next, she kneeled and started planting tender kisses on Ivy's hairless box.

"Hold on, baby," Robin whispered before standing up.

Holding Ivy's ass in the palms of her hands, she slurped on Ivy's clit slowly. Ivy was in awe of how Robin was handling her. She moaned and interlocked her fingers tightly around the back of Robin's head to prevent herself from falling, even though Robin had a firm grip on her. Ivy wasn't going anywhere.

Robin continued to please Ivy until the sun rose the next morning.

*****

The sweet sounds of the birds singing woke them up.

"Good morning, beautiful," Robin said as she looked over to Ivy, who was just opening her eyes.

"Good morning yourself," she replied, smiling as she threw one of her legs out from under the sheet. "I don't think I had these many orgasms in my life!" Ivy said, getting out of the bed to use the bathroom.

Robin smiled, licked her thumb, and placed it on an imaginary board in the air.

"Let's go out for breakfast," Robin said while getting out of bed and going into the bathroom, too.

"Sure. Where do you wanna go?" Ivy asked.

"Do you like rancheros?" Robin asked, turning on the

shower.

"I do," Ivy replied.

"Good! Because I love the rancheros at the Farm Café. It's at the end of the pier, not too far from here. So, we can walk there in no time, and they're pet-friendly!" Robin said with a smile before stepping into the shower.

"Can I get in with you, baby?" Ivy asked in her childlike voice while standing outside the shower door.

"Of course. You don't have to ask me that," Robin said as she pushed open the door to let her in.

When they finished showering, they got dressed, and Ivy took a few drags from her blunt before they left for the café. While en route, Ivy asked Robin about her meeting with Jerry. Ivy expressed oohs and aahs, and the two exchanged plenty of flirty banter before they reached the restaurant. After breakfast, they walked on the beach and rented a couple of bikes to ride along the bike trail adjacent to it. Afterwards, Ivy got to watch Robin do her thing out in the ocean on her surfboard.

"Is there anything you CAN'T do?" Ivy asked, grinning as she handed Robin a towel she got from the surf stand.

When Robin returned to shore, she was smiling in her orange bikini top and Hawaiian swim shorts. Robin appeared so Zen as she put her arm around Ivy's neck to walk on the pier back to the house.

Once home, they took another shower together and had a glass of wine out on the living room patio, where they stretched out on the reclining lounge chairs and fell fast asleep.

The following afternoon, Robin drove Ivy home in her car instead of on the motorcycle. They chilled for a couple of hours at Ivy's house, both expressing how wonderful the weekend had been while they had a bowl of ice cream and watched a movie on the sofa. Robin left shortly after the movie ended, kissing Ivy goodbye and telling her she would see her at the studio in the morning. Ivy would've preferred Robin to stay, but she still walked her to the door and watched until she was out of sight.

Four weeks later…

Ivy finished her last episode of the season, and it was also Robin's last day as an intern.

"Well, beauty, since production will be on hiatus for the summer and you're no longer my assistant, what are your plans, honey?" Ivy asked, reaching for Robin's hand as they stood in the dressing room.

"I'm glad you asked," Robin said, smiling and leaning in for a kiss. "Jerry has decided to produce my film, baby."

Ivy quickly let go of Robin's hand and took a step back in shock before throwing her arms around Robin's neck with excitement.

"Congratulations, baby!" she yelled while hugging her tightly.

"Thank you, sweetheart," Robin responded with her arms wrapped around Ivy's back, spinning a half turn. "I'm so excited to finally have my work on the big screen. I waited a long time for this."

Robin loosened her embrace.

"I wrote this film before I enrolled in film school, but I didn't shop it around until I knew more about the business. I still can't believe it's real," Robin said, her voice calm.

All Ivy could do was hold her hand over her mouth and

look in astonishment at Robin.

"Are you alright, sweetheart?" Robin chuckled.

"Of course, baby. It's just… I'm so FUCKING happy for you!" Her voice raised in excitement. "Besides, I never dated a big-time filmmaker before."

"I'm glad you could be a part of it," Robin said, smiling seductively before gently grabbing Ivy's chin and lifting it to kiss her lips. "No more dating cameramen. You're in the big leagues now, baby."

"I have no clue what you're talking about," Ivy said, smiling from ear to ear.

"I love you, Ivy," Robin said, looking deeply into her eyes.

Ivy bashfully looked away.

"Hey," Robin said softly, "I didn't say I love you for you to say it back. I said it because I needed you to know that."

Ivy looked up at Robin with such innocence in her eyes it pulled at Robin's heartstrings, causing her to lean in and kiss Ivy tenderly once again.

"I gotta meet up with Jerry, baby. I'll call you later. Okay?" Robin told her, preparing to leave.

"Aww, man!" Ivy said, lightly stomping her foot and playing with the buttons on Robin's blouse. "I wanted to celebrate the good news with you tonight."

"I know, sweetheart, but we gotta face some agony if we want the ecstasy later, right?" Robin said, raising her eyebrow seriously yet playfully. "Don't worry, baby. We have a lifetime of celebrations waiting for us."

Robin kissed Ivy's semi-pouted lips and winked at her on the way out of the dressing room.

"Talk to you later, baby," Ivy said, blowing Robin air

kisses before walking over and taking a seat at her vanity table, where she began taking off her makeup.

"I love you, too, Robin," she whispered and smiled at her reflection in the mirror.

*****

A month later, the prescreening of Robin's debut film *You Can Come Out Now* was all the rage as per Hollywood's most recognizable film execs. Robin was so excited she could barely contain herself. The coming attraction had the general public buzzing and anxiously awaiting opening night.

"Oh my god, baby! What are we going to wear to the premiere?" Robin asked Ivy, both nervous and excited as she paced the floor.

"Aww, baby! You're taking me with you to your movie premiere?" Ivy asked, misty-eyed.

"Of course, I am!" Robin replied, taking her thinking finger out of her mouth. "Who did you think I was taking, baby?"

"Oh, I don't know. Your mom?" Ivy said, her voice timid while she looked down at her fingernails.

"She's going, too, but didn't I tell you I love you, Ivy?" Robin asked, her facial expression soft.

"Yes," Ivy responded while looking up at Robin with childlike eyes.

"Alright then. I'ma need you to listen to me, baby."

Robin pulled Ivy close in her arms.

"I'll never have you second-guessing your position in my life. Okay, sweetheart?"

Robin kissed Ivy on the forehead.

"Okay, baby. I won't," Ivy responded, smiling softly.

"Good! Now…" Robin stepped back and rubbed her palms together. "Do you mind if our clothes match a little?

"I wouldn't want to dress any other way," Ivy said, jumping on her and planting playful kisses all over Robin's face.

Premier night…

Robin, Ivy, and Robin's mother arrived at the premiere in a chauffeured black luxury car. Robin wore a tailor-made woman's soft grey and white pinstriped tuxedo jacket cut low on a bias in the front with matching tuxedo pants and a white gold and diamond-encrusted pinky ring. Ivy wore a form-fitting, light grey, silk evening gown with a low-cut cowl on the back and a long thin white gold necklace with a teardrop diamond at the end adorning the curvature of her spine with two dainty diamond and ruby tennis bracelets. Robin's mother wore an off-the-shoulder white brocade evening gown with a sheer shawl that hugged her curves and a ton of Gordy diamond jewelry.

As they were escorted into the theater, a few attendees recognized Ivy, which created a domino effect of people screaming "Hello." Ivy waved and thanked everyone for being there and for being a fan. She was about to introduce Robin as the filmmaker, but Robin firmly gripped her hand, gesturing for her not to do it. So, she didn't. Before the crowd got unruly with their requests for autographs, the three women were quickly ushered into the theater and taken to the VIP section to be seated.

Although Robin observed her mother and Ivy's reaction to her film, she was most concerned with the crowd's reaction. There was laughter, crying, and awe-inspiring dialogue heard between the audience members. Some even applauded at the end. It was so much more than Robin expected, and she gave God all the glory.

Once outside, Ivy signed a few autographs before bodyguards escorted the three to the awaiting car. Ivy and Robin's mother congratulated her on a job well done, and each mentioned their favorite part of the film.

"Thank you, ladies. That means so much to me," Robin said as she blushed.

Ivy leaned over to kiss her while Robin's mother popped the cork on the champagne bottle and poured each of them a glass. Robin raised her glass to toast.

"This is only the beginning."

"CHEERS!" they shouted in unison.

"Cheers!" Robin said once again, looking lovingly at Ivy. "Ivy, baby?"

"Yes?" Ivy replied, raising her champagne glass to her lips.

"I want to ask you something, sweetheart," Robin said, resting her arm on the car's door rest.

Robin's mother hung on her daughter's every word while sipping her champagne.

"Sure, baby," Ivy said nervously, then took a gulp of her champagne as she looked at Robin's mother and back at Robin.

"Umm," Robin said before glancing over at her mother and clearing her throat. "Baby, what would you say if I asked you to...?"

TO BE CONTINUED...

Lightning Source UK Ltd.
Milton Keynes UK
UKHW020753040522
402470UK00010B/2101